A THING OF BEAUTY

By Gale Owen Holt

Sweet Annie Tales Press

Gale Owen Holt

COPYRIGHT

A Thing of Beauty by Gale Owen Holt. Published by Sweet Annie Tales Press, 5480 Winchester Avenue, Martinsburg, West Virginia 25405

www.sweetannietales.com

© 2009 and 2019 Gale Owen Holt

All rights reserved. This book or parts thereof may not be reproduced in any form, stored in any retrieval system, or transmitted in any form by any means—electronic, mechanical, photocopy, recording, or otherwise—without prior written permission of the publisher, except as provided by United States of America copyright law. For permission requests, write to the publisher, at "Attention: Permissions Co

ordinator," at the address below.

Sweet Annie Tales, 5408 Winchester Avenue, Martinsburg, West Virginia

This is a work of fiction. Names, characters, places, and incidents either are the products of the author's imagination or are used fictitiously. Any resemblance to actual persons, living or dead, businesses, companies, events, or locales is entirely coincidental.

Edited by Tracy Burns-Wilson
Cover by Jenny Zemanek

eBook ISBN: 978-0-578-46026-0
Paperback ISBN: 978-0-578-45976-9

DEDICATION

For my mother, Iris Erwin Owen

For my friend and mentor, Peggy Jean Edwards Butts

CONTENTS

COPYRIGHT
Dedication
PROLOGUE — 1
CHAPTER ONE — 12
CHAPTER TWO — 20
CHAPTER THREE — 29
CHAPTER FOUR — 36
CHAPTER FIVE — 41
CHAPTER SIX — 46
CHAPTER SEVEN — 51
CHAPTER EIGHT — 56
CHAPTER NINE — 61
CHAPTER TEN — 67
CHAPTER ELEVEN — 71
CHAPTER TWELVE — 76
CHAPTER THIRTEEN — 80
CHAPTER FOURTEEN — 86
CHAPTER FIFTEEN — 91
CHAPTER SIXTEEN — 96
CHAPTER SEVENTEEN — 101

CHAPTER EIGHTEEN	110
CHAPTER NINETEEN	114
CHAPTER TWENTY	122
CHAPTER TWENTY-ONE	129
CHAPTER TWENTY-TWO	134
CHAPTER TWENTY-THREE	140
CHAPTER TWENTY-FOUR	143
CHAPTER TWENTY-FIVE	149
CHAPTER TWENTY-SIX	157
CHAPTER TWENTY-SEVEN	164
CHAPTER TWENTY-EIGHT	170
CHAPTER TWENTY-NINE	176
CHAPTER THIRTY	185
CHAPTER THIRTY-ONE	191
CHAPTER THIRTY-TWO	197
CHAPTER THIRTY-THREE	203
CHAPTER THIRTY-FOUR	207
CHAPTER THIRTY-FIVE	212
CHAPTER THIRTY-SIX	217
CHAPTER THIRTY-SEVEN	223
CHAPTER THIRTY-EIGHT	228
CHAPTER THIRTY-NINE	233
CHAPTER FORTY	237
CHAPTER FORTY-ONE	242
CHAPTER FORTY-TWO	247
CHAPTER FORTY-THREE	252
CHAPTER FORTY-FOUR	260
CHAPTER FORTY-FIVE	267

CHAPTER FORTY-SIX   269
CHAPTER FORTY-SEVEN   276
ACKNOWLEDGMENTS   282

PROLOGUE

March seventeenth may look fun, all shamrocks and rainbows, but since last year's argument it means a whole bucket load of craziness in my family. And I'm feeling leery about this year.

See, my grandfather and great-uncle Clayton got into some sort of uproar over a school reunion, and it looked like Granddaddy was about ready to fight his little brother over it. Uncle Clayton's the lanky, silent type and not one to fight, but he will dig in his heels on his opinion. He'll stand his ground, even if Granddaddy is twice his size and calls him Shrimp.

My dad's a high school counselor, and even he couldn't smooth things over, and he said (when he thought we girls couldn't hear) that there was no point because Granddaddy was on his annual binge and there was no reasoning with him. Great-aunt Louise tried to persuade Ma-maw to go to the reunion—like anybody could ever budge Ma-maw from a decision once she made it. They both cried and carried on. Who pitches a fit over a school reunion? Just buy a new dress and go already.

"What's the big hairy deal?" I said to my mother.

"It's always been that way, and this year is just more of the same," said Mama, but she wouldn't go into it.

Dad was put out. "I have just about reached my limit. I could pack up and leave right now."

My sister and I looked at our mom in a panic and she

whispered, "He doesn't mean it." Looked to me like he did. The stubborn set of his square Ramey jaw said so. Knowing the same mess could happen again this year just sits on my shoulder like a big old fat temperamental leprechaun.

And now, I just want to get through this school day with peace and quiet and without my family going hog-wild nuts, if I can swing it. Trouble is, Saint Patrick's Day is an unpredictable holiday. On the good side, you don't have to worry about presents or valentines. Who gets one, who doesn't? What if someone gets you one when you didn't buy one for them? No day off from school though. Just have to live with that because it won't be long until Easter and then summer break.

Also, important to know: Do you need a jacket? East Texas March weather is uncertain, and a jacket might hide your green and then you have to fight off the pinching. I hate pinching. Another thing. You never know whether teachers are going to celebrate or not. Some teachers are like their own visual aids, and you can count on them wearing a holiday shirt or doodad every time or even passing out green candy. Some teachers want nothing to do with pinches or green or shamrocks and let you know there will be no fooling around or rude limericks before you even walk in the door. Saint Patrick's Day is testy and uncertain, but this year the school part passes without too much trouble. I get by with answering only one question in class, and I sit out the rest of the day all nice and quiet and to myself.

We'll see how it goes back home.

"Score! We'll get our seat!" I whisper to my cousin Tabby on our way to the school bus.

"Yes!" says Tabby.

We are first in line and way ahead of the boys who like to be a pain and get our seat. When it's already a weird day, you don't want a bunch of aggravation piling up on you. You just want to sit there and rest and prepare yourself for whatever is waiting and then get to the horses as fast as you can.

Today, I wear a green plaid shirt with pink stripes, and even though I am a quiet girl, the boys know I will pinch back or slug hard. I don't talk—I act. Tabby wears a pink plaid shirt with little green stripes and she'll pinch too. We try to dress twinsies when we can, but this was the best we could do on Saint Patrick's Day. Sometimes folks think we are twins, but Tabby's hair is straight dishwater blond with light streaks and mine is crazy-curly dark. My sister, Jessica, is two grades older and she is dressed from head to toe in green. She flirts and picks at people and practically invites pinching, and squeals and carries on when boys try. She waltzes down the aisle, swinging her blond ponytail like she's the Queen on the Tyler Rose Parade float. She can have the pinches and attention.

Just when we are about to seat ourselves, here comes the New York kid rushing past us and plopping down on our seat. "Get up, Elliot. That is our seat. We always sit in our seat," Tabby demands.

"Excuuuuse me!" he says and then plops down behind us. "Is that a pink blouse, I see?"

I turn around and glare at him. "Somebody better keep his fingers to himself," I mutter, mainly for Tabby's benefit.

"There are green stripes in this plaid," Tabby warns.

He can't shut up. "Today there would be this huge parade in New York. My dad and I always go—we're Italian, but we can wear green. And then we would go get..."

"The best pizza in New York," we all chorus. "Yeah, you've told us before."

"Hey, it's a tradition. You gotta respect tradition. At least in New York, you've got places to go, things to see. Statue of Liberty, Broadway..."

My sister Jessica stands up, tosses her hair, and starts singing "The Sun'll Come Out Tomorrow."

The whole bus erupts in cheers and claps. "East Texas don't need Broadway, we got Jessica," someone calls out. "Take that Mr. Know-it-all New York." Elliot grows quiet and looks out the window.

Jessica is still bowing and eating up the applause. "Good gravy," I mutter to Tabby. "They don't need to swell her head any bigger than it already is."

Tabby snort-laughed. "My sister just whacked Jessica with her shoulder bag. They'll squabble the rest of the way home."

The boys are all wound up, horsing around, probably due to all that nasty green lime candy, and among the general uproar, Riley calls across the bus aisle, "Hey, Elliot, don't worry about them. They don't mean any harm." Good old Riley, taking up for the outsider. Elliot just shrugs.

And then snotty Ed pipes up—he has this runny nose all the time, and it's worse than ever now that it's spring. He was the shortest kid in our class for the longest time, and then he got his growth spurt. He still thinks he needs to prove something. "Hey, Riley! Jessica needs a Little Orphan Annie wig. See if you can loan her your Afro. Oh, no, sorry. It's the wrong color. It's black."

I glance back at Riley's older brother. Burgess's eyes are hooded, staring straight ahead. The brothers sit side by side, Burgess with his giant Afro and Riley his smaller one. Riley murmurs to Burgess, "I got this." Then louder, he says "Ed, I believe you're the one who needs some hair after that last report card." Ed's eyes narrow. His mama made him cut his hair short. He acts like he's going to get up and start something.

I'm putting a stop to this right now. "You boys are getting on my nerves. Ed, sit down... Don't you even try anything. I will knock you into the middle of next week, and if you don't get those grades up, your mama's going to slap you baldheaded." Then I whisper to Riley, "He doesn't have any sense."

Tabby says, "You better listen, Ed. Becky's quiet, but she'll clobber you and you know it." Folks know how I am, so I don't have to say much. I'm a good Baptist girl, but I don't put up with foolishness. I don't make a regular habit of cutting short nonsense, so the fifth-grade teachers like it and look the other way. You know, send the buttinskis who try to cut in front to the back of the line. When some boy yanks a little girl's hair, I go and yank his hair harder. Like that. And my folks don't know, so it works out okay. More peaceful that way. I walk into PE, and the gym teacher calls out "Becky, the Enforcer." I act like I don't hear it.

Our older cousin—he's a junior on the high school football team—he lumbers up the steps. As Dub goes by, I whisper, "Did my granddaddy come to school today?"

Dub says, "Naw, Coach didn't make it in." Tabby and I glance at each other, eyebrows raised. That can't be good.

"I say we head to my house, grab some cookies, and then head for the horses," I advise.

"Right." Tabby nods. "Dodge as much of that as we can."

Then Ed cries out. "Ow! Dub, you thumped my head with your ring."

"That's right. My class of 1979 senior ring and you just got off easy. I saw you reaching out that hand. You just try pulling Rebecca Ramey's hair. Son, she will tear you up." Dub's got our back. It's the family way.

The bus driver, Miz Lessie Mae, calls out, "That's right, Ed. You done wore out even Becky's patience. Y'all settle down now." That's her final verdict and she puts the bus in gear, and everyone settles back for the ride. Tabby and I squint out the window, seeing if we can spot the very first dogwood blossoms among the pine trees. They could appear almost any time now. Tabby points out some buds about ready to pop, and it feels like good luck. Soon we spot home—Daddy calls it the Ramey compound. Our house, Granddaddy and Ma-maw's place, Great-Aunt Ethel's trailer, and Great-Uncle Clayton's farm are on the family property. You could draw a wobbly parallelogram between the dwellings. Tabby's trailer is just a short piece up the way.

The bus lurches to a stop, and Jessica, Brittany, Tabby and I rush out and across the road to my little old white-frame house. Sure enough, Mama and Aunt Janet are drinking iced tea, going all out in some serious conversation. A plate of St. Patrick's Day cookies leftover from Aunt Janet's home ec class are waiting for us. Brittany and Jessica attack the cookies and Tabby and I just manage to get our share.

Janet plows ahead, telling how she and Ma-maw butted heads for the umpteenth time. "And then I said, 'Mom, you spent good money for my home economics degree. Give me some credit for my informed opinion that a gas stove is without question superior for cooking. If I am ever going to cater, I absolutely had to get rid of that antiquated electric stove—furthermore, I know what gas smells like and I know how to turn off a burner.' And then she said, 'Well, don't come crying to me if that trailer burns down.' You'd think I was three." Aunt Janet looks just like Ma-maw: same frown, same dark eyebrows and lady mustache. They fight all the time.

Jessica butts in, "Mama, did you ask Ma-maw about the blue paint for our bedroom?"

"Yes, and I could have told you what the answer would be. This is Ma-maw and Granddaddy's first place and she's particular about what goes in it."

"And she only wants eggshell white," Jessica concludes.

"Sorry. Right now was probably not the best time to ask."

Janet sighs. "Every year in March, she clamps down. Tries to keep everything nice and safe and the same."

Tabby's sister, Brittany, and my sister latch onto the last two cookies without asking do we want them or do we want to share.

"That's all right. Tabby and I are dropping by Aunt Ethel's. She always has snack cakes for us."

Mama looks up sharply. "Don't you spoil your dinner. And don't be late. Do your chores and practice and come on home." Mama doesn't really much care for Aunt Ethel or for horses. She doesn't trust horses, and she doesn't appreciate Great-Aunt Ethel's trashy gossip one bit.

Tabby and I cross the road to Ma-maw's yard and head for the barbed wire fence. We take turns crawling through and head to the barn. As we enter, our eyes adjust to the dark. Through the little bit of light coming through boards, bits of straw and motes float on the sun beams. We see our chores are done. Uncle Clayton is putting up the pitchfork and such in the utility closet.

"Uncle Clayton, you did our chores. That's our job," says Tabby.

"Aww, I just wanted to spend a little quiet time with the horses." He rubs old Domino's muzzle. "Nothing like a little visit, is there Dom? Besides, it'll give you a little more time to practice."

We take just a moment to say hi to our horses. Tabby strokes her paint's withers, and I give Sugar Bear part of the apple leftover from my lunch. I ask, "What'll we do until we practice with the horses? Missy is just now leaving LeTourneau campus," I say.

"Well, why don't you two go pick some flowers in the pasture and carry them over to your great-aunt and ma-maw. They could use a little pick-me-up today. Take Domino. He can be your Pony Express. He needs the exercise. Don't worry. I'll saddle the horses." The whole plan makes us smile. It's sort of like we could smooth over any hard feelings. Spread peace and goodwill on horseback.

Sneezing, Tabby and I make short work of those bouquets. My eyes are streaming, and my head will be stopped-up tomorrow for sure, and since Tabby is holding the flowers, she must wipe her watery nose on her shoulder. It won't be too long before the two of us are too heavy to ride Domino, but he seems happy to carry us now. We trot on over to Great-Aunt Ethel's trailer. We knock, and it takes longer than usual for Ethel to open the door only a tiny crack. "Hi, Aunt Ethel, we brought you flowers," Tabby says. Ethel slips her flabby arm through the crack and receives the bunch of blooming weeds and is about to just shut the door on us.

I call out, "Aunt Ethel, you were right about our cousin Melissa. She *is* slipping out and seeing that older boy." Aunt Ethel's eyes light up briefly at the thought of fresh gossip, but she just whispers "Thanks, girls," and shuts the door. No snack cakes. No nothing. There's nothing to do, but head for Ma-maw's.

We can't take a horse through the fence, so we take the road and turn into Ma-maw's driveway. We knock, smiling, just sure Ma-maw will think our Pony Express is cute and brag on our flowers. But it's Granddaddy, smelling beery at the door. This one time of year, he drinks. Ma-maw is Baptist, and normally she won't have it, but somehow, he gets a pass for this annual spell. Granddaddy reaches for the flowers and drops them. Embarrassed, our grandmother pulls him away from the door. I pick up the bouquet and whisper, "These are for you."

Ma-maw mouths "Thank you" and "Talk to you later," and disappears to take care of our grandfather.

Just then Missy's Ford truck passes up the road and we know it's time for our work with our horses, and it's a relief. Missy steps down from her pickup and frowns a little when she sees us on Domino. "Aren't you girls saddled up and ready to go?" She won saddles and belt buckles barrel racing before she married and had Dub, and now she takes her coaching seriously.

Luckily, Uncle Clayton comes through the barn door, leading the horses. "I sent the girls on a little sunshine mission while I got the horses ready. Sometimes I just need a little horse time."

Missy laughs and hugs her dad and declares, "Yes, you do!" and she pets his whiskery face with her small strong hands. She turns to us and says, "So Tabby, Becky, how's Elliot? I hope you girls are making him feel welcome. Did you know I work with his dad at the college?" I guess we look guilty, because she says, "Y'all be nice now. I know he's different, but he's not a bad boy and he's homesick." She looks us both in the eyes to make her point. Then she says, "Tabby, you ride Patchwork and loop around the two barrels nice and slow. Becky, I believe my Sugar Bear is used to the barrel enough for you to lead her around just the one barrel in loops. Remember, you are going to start out wide and then spiral in. After that, you girls can just take them up the trail." The loops are tedious, but it's like they drain away this day's aggravation and worry, and when we can be with our horses on the trail, whatever problems are left will disappear on the way.

My mother walks up and speaks to Missy quietly, and I strain to hear. "Is it all right if Becky stays here a little longer?"

Missy nods. "Sure."

"Ask Tabby to go straight home when she's done. It's your Uncle Milton. Clifford is over there, helping his mother now."

My mom looks over at me and jumps when Sugar Bear just nuzzles my shoulder. I reach over and kiss Missy's horse on the muzzle, and Mama sighs and turns away.

Missy gives Mama the "are-you-kidding-me?" look and says, "She's fine, Liz." Missy doesn't get Mama with her snazzy big hair and perfect, long fingernails, and Mama can't see why any grown woman would choose a sensible ponytail and plain short nails. The ponytail makes sense to me. Best way to keep frizzy curls out of my face.

Mama opens her mouth to reply, but then everybody jumps when we hear my granddaddy hollering. Standing in his yard, yelling at the top of his lungs.

"Everybody's just talks about that reunion. Why don't I go to the reunion?" My dad tries to quiet his father and ease him back into the house, and my grandfather slurs, "You were never the football player you could have been. All these advantages. Not every kid got what you got. You don't know what it is to lose everything because you have everything."

My lean, fit father just stands there, floored. He's dressed in his running shorts, but he will not do his daily jog up the road today. He's dealing with this.

Ma-maw is hot now. Daddy's her favorite child. "Milton, you come back in this house this minute!"

Missy quickly directs, "Girls, just head on up the trail for a while. Let's do that now."

The yelling fades away, but Tabby and I just stop at the first clearing and lean over our horses and cry, and then we get down and hold each other and cry some more.

We head back, and all seems quiet. Mama is gone, and Missy is waiting for us. She smiles, but she's troubled too. She nods her head and says to no one in particular, "Only sensible thing a person can do sometimes. Go down the lane. Good run on a horse works out a lot of things." Then she looks at us, "Girls, your horses are almost there. Just a bit more practice. Then we have to get them used to an arena and racket and smells." And then out of the blue, Missy says, "My dad knows what heals. Horses."

"Healed from what?" I want to know.

"Sad stuff. Old people have sad stuff." And then Missy smiles. Her mother is headed our way, carrying a dry cleaner bag with a pink dress. "Did you see your Aunt Lou's dress? She's got herself a reunion dress. That always helps her sadness. My daddy visits horses and my mama shops!"

Aunt Louise just beams, all proud of her new outfit. "I'm putting it aside special for the reunion next year." And then as though she's afraid she might forget something important she says, "What did that grandson of mine wear today?"

Missy hugs her short, plump mom and says, "A Dallas Cowboy shirt and those jeans you ironed with a crease. He had a fit, but he wore them."

And then she whispers, "Have you talked to Aunt Eileen?"

Her mom closes her eyes and shakes her head. "I don't think things are going so good."

"Right." Then Missy says, "Well, you girls head on home now. I think things have settled down. I will take care of the horses—don't get used to it. Next time, business as usual. Go on now." I head for home, but I glance back and see that Missy and Aunt Louise have their heads together talking. I am pretty sure I know the subject.

I go up the road to my house. I avoid looking at Ma-maw and Granddaddy's place. I step up on our porch and I hear my father say, "It's not just this. It's at school. I am a good school counselor and I get stonewalled at every turn. A football player flunks or gets in trouble and there are no consequences. The other kids do not get the same treatment and they know it."

Mama sits at the table, twirling a stray curl and messing up her sprayed-perfect hairdo.

My father sighs and shakes his head. "Dad took it personally when I even suggested that Burgess should only do basketball his freshman year."

I just stand there because I know they will clam up as soon as I walk in the door.

Then Dad says, "Liz, I am just letting you know. I sent in that application and I am going for that interview."

I step in the door, my face flushed. "What interview? Where?"

"Just a school, a bit closer to Dallas. Say, why don't we take a little trip. How about we go house shopping?"

"What's wrong with our house?"

"It's just time to get our own. Time to make some changes."

"Do horses go with those changes?" I swallow hard.

My parents look at each other, and every worry I ever knew comes rushing back.

CHAPTER ONE

"Granddaddy, it's a thing of beauty," I say. "Just watch her."

The announcer calls out "Lexie Howard up, Debbie Bechtal on deck, Ann Butler in the hole."

The sticky heat, the yellow dust of the arena, the greasy concession stand smells all disappear, when the outline of a girl and dancing horse stands in the summer glare of the entrance. The horse is raring to go, and the girl must make him circle and then steady and line him up for the takeoff.

My grandfather chuckles. "A thing of beauty?" That's what he says when some football player makes an outstanding play.

"Just you watch," I say.

"She's good, Granddaddy, real good," my cousin Tabby says.

We're both lanky, long-legged girls dressed just alike in green Western shirts, and we have twin patches of sweat between our shoulder blades. Tabby's braid has blond streaks, but mine is dark and ends in frizzy curls. Our hair is damp at our temples and perspiration traces down our cheeks and our "family" square jaws. We look good if I do say so myself—pink ribbon in our pigtails. Tabby and I even worked green ribbon into our horses' French-braided manes. We planned these getups for weeks.

The girl on the horse has something Tabby and I don't

have yet: a winner's silver belt buckle. No telling how many she's won in barrel racing.

Girl and horse explode from the entrance. The palomino's hooves hardly touch the ground. I draw in my breath as they head straight for the first barrel. Girl and horse slow, his hindquarters sliding around the barrel, while his forelegs churn away in golden East Texas soil. The air I've been holding leaves in a "huh" while Lexie and her mount head to the second barrel.

Tabby grabs my wrist. "Becky, did you see that?"

"Perfect!" I whisper.

How fast *are* they going? I can't tell, but the turns are first-rate. They make the loop around the last barrel and the girl's strawberry blonde hair streams behind her. They fly down the straightaway. Light ripples over the horse's powerful muscles, as girl and gelding burst through the halo of the sunlit doorway.

The announcer declares, "Lexie Howard on Daily Sunshine, 13.5 seconds."

Tabby looks at me with bright eyes. "Far out!"

I turn to my granddaddy and grin. "A thing of beauty!" I would do anything to hear that from him. Could I do "a thing of beauty" at this Play Day? It could change everything.

We would not have to move. My dad is yanking us away, because he doesn't think East Texas is good enough, and he doesn't care one thing how I feel about it. Before, I never thought about the only home I've ever known, like I never thought about air. Once I knew we could be leaving, I could hardly breathe. I'd lift my shoulders high to catch a breath and I still could not draw in enough air. Adults think they can change everything, and kids don't matter. You can't just make a kid move away from everybody, every place, everything that matters. I am determined. If I could do that thing of beauty, then they would all know. We'd have to stay.

I watch my Granddaddy raise his eyebrows and smile kind of crooked. "Uh-*huh*! So now what is the objective of this event?" Granddaddy asks. He flicks donut crumbs from the jacket of his green leisure suit and waits for our reply. He knows.

He's just making us say.

I smooth out my Egg McMuffin wrapper on the bleacher between Granddaddy and me and dump the powder from one of my last grape Pixy Stix on the greasy paper. I spread out the sugary stuff, and I poke dots in it, arranged like the points on a triangle.

"Okay, first you go to the barrel on the right and loop around it..." Tabby begins.

"Without knocking the barrel over..." I say.

Tabby frowns. "Yes, without knocking over the barrel, and then you loop around the second barrel on the left..." My short-nailed finger traces up to and around the top dot and then whisks back to the beginning.

"And you make a clover leaf, except you draw it with the horse's hooves," I finish and dip my finger and lick it.

"Ewww! Nasty," Tabby says.

"God made dirt, dirt don't hurt," I say.

"Well, do you ever do a four-leaf clover? It might be lucky."

"Granddaddy-y," Tabby says.

I feel the jolt of folks stepping up the bleachers, and I look up and brace myself. Daddy's talking to his cousin Missy as they step up. She doesn't look happy, but Missy brightens when she spots us. She knows Daddy and Granddaddy have been barely speaking since March. The sad, edgy, exploding month.

"Woo-ee!" Missy calls out. "Just look at that green suit!" She and Daddy head for the row behind us. Missy tries to keep it light and peaceful. Good luck. I hope it works.

Granddaddy brushes off the shoulders of his gray-green double knit and says, "Just trying to honor the occasion. Eileen says these square pockets make me look like a green Captain Kangaroo."

Missy and Daddy chuckle and she says to Granddaddy, "How are you doing, Coach?" And then to Tabby and me, "Did you all see that?"

"A thing of beauty," Granddaddy says. "That girl has got

some talent. She's going places."

"What did she do right, girls?" Now Missy quizzes us.

"Well, she was cool and calm…" Tabby frowns, thinking.

"The way she made his head go just right on the turns." My hands mimic Lexie's hands—balanced, tugging on the reins.

Missy nods, approving. "Good catch." She looks at my daddy with raised eyebrows and sits down by him.

"Where is everybody, Daddy?" I ask.

Daddy says, "Your sister is at her piano and voice lesson."

Figures. Jessica couldn't show up for a barrel race.

Daddy continues, "And Ma-maw and your mother are starting to pack."

Granddaddy says, "You were sorta late getting here."

Daddy tenses a bit. "Well, I had to wait in line for gas." Then Daddy lowers his voice and says, "But before that—got a phone call. Wes is on suicide watch again. Felt like I better go check in on Aunt Ethel."

Granddaddy sighs and looks down. "Mmm-Mmm."

Tabby looks at me, but I pretend to concentrate on the arena, so they'll say more. Daddy's cousin has been at the state pen for years, but nobody talks about it.

Missy clears her throat. "This sounds like a good move for you, Clifford, but we're sure going to miss you around here."

I look back. Daddy smiles a little. He's probably glad she changes the subject. "It's going to work out. I'll be working with two other guidance counselors. The new house is close enough to the high school. Jessica's new music teacher went to North Texas State. That's where Jessica wants to go."

Missy frowns a little. "Jessica's thirteen? She's a little young to worry about college."

So, this is all about Jessica. Figures.

"Can't start too early." Daddy lowers his voice. "We can tell she's already dwelling on being adopted. Thirteen *and* adopted. It's not easy. We're hoping if she can focus on her music, it won't matter so much."

"What about Becky?"

"Oh, she'll do fine. She's a Ramey. Nothing fazes her. Tough as nails. And really this will be good for Becky too. Get her out of a rut. Make friends with somebody besides family."

I bite the inside of my cheek, and my fingernails dig into the palms of my hands. My run is coming up. This could be my last chance ever. I just want to show Daddy what *I* can do. If he could just see, maybe we won't have to leave. I can hear their whispers behind me.

"She's come awful far to stop racing now," Missy continues. "Did you hear what Rebecca said? She doesn't just watch. She studies good riders. She's more than ready for those racing clinics. I just hope you've thought this through."

Daddy lets out a deep breath. "Nobody's saying Becky has to give up barrel racing forever. We've agreed…"

"He's *decided*," I think.

"…that for just this first year at the new job…at a new school…in a new town, we're going to focus on school and track and basketball. She's only eleven. Besides there's the Mesquite Rodeo, Dallas State Fair, Cowtown in Fort Worth…"

"Clifford, you don't seriously think that watching rodeo every so often is going to be enough…"

I don't dare look back, but I feel Daddy's silence like a blanket. Then he says, "Missy, I'm sorry. Until we can get on our feet, that's the best we can do."

"A high school counselor ought to know there's a lot of creative alternatives, if a family will just look for the opportunities," Missy says. "Of all people, you should know there are college scholarships for barrel racers."

"Not like there aren't opportunities here," Granddaddy mutters. Tabby and I tense like the uproar could just break out again.

I sigh, wipe the drops of sweat weeping from my upper lip, and turn and look at them. "Y'all, I'm going where I can concentrate. We gotta go warm up anyway. Come on Tabby."

"Sorry, girls," Granddaddy says. "Didn't mean to break your concentration…"

barrel. Sugar Bear slows just enough, makes our first turn...and then lets up. "No-o-o-o, Bear, go!" She runs to the second barrel. Oh, no. She leans in. I try to correct her, but she hits the barrel with her shoulder and it rolls away making a hollow, lonely sound. There's one last barrel, and I'm determined to finish the best I can. Bear feels the pressure of my outside leg, and she goes clean and snappy around the third barrel. Now we're dashing back toward the alley, as a tear escapes toward my ear.

The announcer's voice echoes above me, "Rebecca Ramey, 17:05, five-point penalty. 22:05. Better luck next time, Becky."

Next time. I just hope there is a next time someday.

I take my time letting Sugar Bear cool down. "Just a little bit of water, Bear. I'll give you more soon." I stroke her neck as I walk her, knowing each step we take together will be one of the last for a good while. I take off the saddle and tack, so I can hose her down. The water that flows over the sorrel's back looks like warm syrup. I groom Sugar Bear's coat and clean her hooves with just a little more tender care than usual, and I whisper, "You're a good girl, Bear. You'll do better next time."

Then Missy's at my side, "Becky, you did a good job."

"I knocked over a barrel."

She walks me back to the arena. "Yes, *Sugar Bear* knocked over a barrel. She still has a lot to learn." Missy looks at my father sitting in the bleachers. "She's like some people. She just needs to learn to bend around things, instead of knocking them over. That just means we've got to be patient and work with her."

I look off, blinking away tears. "Wish I could help."

Missy reaches around and gives my shoulder a squeeze. "I do too, Becky. Me too."

CHAPTER TWO

"You're going to have to go over there sometime."

"But I don't have to like it," I say to Tabby.

My cousin and I stand by the barbed wire fence at the back of Granddaddy's property and watch the adults annoy each other and argue about Jimmy Carter. They can't decide. First, they like the president because he gets out of his limousine and walks like everyday folks, then they say he just isn't the Baptist they thought he'd be. Carter pardoned the draft dodgers, and Tabby's daddy will never forgive him for that. Uncle Richie lost some buddies in Vietnam—he calls it Nam. He gets up and walks off. Aunt Janet has forbidden him to rant at this family picnic.

Most of the Rameys are under our grandparents' carport sitting in folding lawn chairs or on the picnic table benches, while an electric ice cream maker grinds away, "Wor-worr-ry-worry worrr-ry-worry." Uncle Richie feeds it rock salt and ice and glances up at Daddy now and then. He's losing his best fishing buddy and his mustache looks sad and droopy. Mama says the fishing trips are healing. Just sitting quiet with my Daddy.

Loblolly pines around us sway in the breeze and pinecones thud on the grass. Tabby and I hear my sister Jessica singing "Who's sorry now..."

"Who'll Shut up now?" I bellow back.

Tabby snickers, but somebody claps for Jessica anyway.

Jessica's perfect straight blond hair falls forward as she takes a bow for her carport audience.

"She isn't happy unless she has the whole world's attention," I say.

My parents, my sister and I are moving to Dallas in the morning, but I already feel gone. Our relatives look back at us like they can't believe we could leave East Texas for some suburb. That Daddy could leave his old high school and go work for a rival. Granddaddy flat came out and said Daddy's *abandoning* Rusk County. Anyway, our family's gonna do their duty and have this picnic to tell us 'bye' and make us feel sorry.

"I don't *want* to say goodbye. I don't even want to be around this mess," I sigh. "All the grownups do is squabble."

"They're just sorry you're going, Becky," Tabby says. Like I ought to be grateful for guilt.

I turn away and look across the fence at Great-Uncle Clayton's pasture and Domino; the old overo horse stops cropping and munching grass and looks up at me like he expects something. I'm torn. I'll miss crossing the road to Ma-maw's and Granddaddy, but I'm ready to get this move over with. "Between packing up and Mama making us retouch all the paint in the house..."

"Eggshell white?" Tabby asks. She's smirking. She knows.

"What else? That's all Ma-maw will have." We lived in our grandparents' first house, so Mama and Daddy could save money for our own place. Ma-maw was real particular about what anybody did in her old house and made real strong "suggestions." Made Mama crazy.

"That's one reason y'all are leaving, isn't it, Becky?" Tabby says.

"I guess. One of them."

Tabby points at a pregnant girl sagging in one of the lawn chairs. "There's another."

Our cousin Melissa's ankles are swollen in the July heat and her navy-blue smock strains across her belly. She's barely fourteen and her Mom's only twenty-seven; Daddy says some folks will shame 'em down in a rural area, but they won't do much to help the girls do any different. He says he wants Jessica and me to have opportunities. That means he doesn't want us pregnant.

"Uh-oh," I warn. "Ma-maw and Aunt Janet are fussing over the potato salad again."

"Janet, folks are hungry. We've got to get this food out on the table." Ma-maw's voice reaches clear up here.

"We're going to send them off with food poisoning if you lay that out in this heat too soon!" Aunt Janet says.

Tabby and I look at each other and shake our heads, then I look at my cousin and frown. "Your so-called best friend tells me you two got shirts just alike." That was our special thing. Now Tabby's dressing "twinsies" with some boy-crazy stranger. I look at Tabby and think, *Traitor*. At first, I didn't want to move at all, but now I'm not so sure.

"It was Debbie's idea, Becky." Tabby fools with the end of her streaky blond braid, frowning at split ends. "I didn't want to be rude. She invited me to go with them to Shreveport." Tabby squints, the setting sun in her eyes. "You're not going to be here, remember?"

"Like I have a choice." Our shoulders lift and fall in identical sighs.

Tabby fidgets irritably. "You better tell Domino bye."

"I'll do it tomorrow," I whisper. "Remember riding him when we were little? Missy says we've outgrown him."

"I don't even *want* to ride anymore." Tabby looks away.

"What do you mean? You can't give up riding just because I have to move."

Tabby shrugs and looks down. "It just won't be the same. It won't feel right—waiting for the school bus without you," Tabby whispers.

We've been in the same classes since kindergarten for seven years. I haven't needed any other friends. I swallow hard. "I'll miss you too."

We hear heavy steps behind us. I look back and smile.

"Dub's coming—let's mess up his hair."

"Here they are," our cousin Dub hollers back toward the carport. "I told you they'd be with the horses. You two come on—your ma-maw wants you."

Tabby and I walk by Dub and leap up trying to rumple his styled hair. It falls in little poufs over his ears. We all tease him because Cousin Missy's boy plays varsity football, but he blow-dries and styles his hair with hair spray like a girl. Uncle Clayton always says, "Well, at least it ain't no long strangy hippie 'do.'"

Dub lumbers along and blocks our hands with his bulky arms. "Cut it out."

"We'll quit if you'll shoot baskets with us," Tabby says.

"Ple-e-ease, Dub," I say.

Dub shrugs. "Okay, just a few, Squirt."

I jump up and hold onto his shoulders for a piggyback ride and Dub doesn't shrug me off.

"Glad you folks could join us," Ma-maw calls out. "Come here and give me hug." I give her a quick one and she brushes back my stray curls and fusses. "Going off and leaving your grandmother—Who's going to help me set up my classroom? How will I ever get all my cookies decorated?" I watch my daddy over her shoulder.

Daddy sees me watching him. "Becky, show Ma-maw what you can do."

My cousins and I go to Daddy's old basketball goal at the other side of the driveway. I take aim with the ball, but it falls short.

"Follow through, Becky, follow through." Dub grabs the ball from me and swings his arm and hand into one long graceful arc. The spinning ball goes "whoosh" through the net. "Now you do it."

"Keep throwing after the ball's gone, Becky," Daddy adds.

"I know," I say. Tabby catches the ball and passes it to me. I make my move. "Linebackers can shoot, but they can't guard." I laugh. I maneuver around Dub's massive legs for a layup and it's good. Dub grabs me and puts me in a headlock and rubs my scalp hard with his knuckles. I duck out before he can give me one of his nasty wet willies.

"See what I mean?" Daddy says and chuckles. Cousin Missy just snorts and looks off at the horses in the pasture and frowns.

Granddaddy is flipping burgers at his grill. Uncle Clayton calls out, "Brother, make mine pink in the middle. It's…"

"I know, Shrimp, good for your blood," Granddaddy chimes in.

Mama and Daddy sit frazzled in the double rocker. Mama had most of her boxes labeled and color coded. She wanted to group and pack them according to the room they go in, but Daddy said all the heavy ones had to go to the back of the van.

"Organization obsessed—absolutely obsessed," Aunt Janet says with a grin. Mama frowns. Aunt Janet scolds her, "We told you not to worry about making any food."

"It's just my Watergate salad."

"Let us know if you find any tape in it," Daddy teases. Mama whacks his arm, but she smiles.

Mama calls me over. "Sugar, you're a sweaty mess." She takes down my ponytail and tries to tame the wild curly strands that escape no matter what I do.

I hop up before Mama can fuss anymore. "It's okay, Mama. It's only a picnic." I wrestle my hair back into the elastic and Mama sighs. My ornery curls spring right back out.

My parents and sister and I are here, but we're already cut loose from the family. Our cousin Brittany is making plans that don't involve us right in front of Jessica. "Y'all just rub it in. Going to the Rose Festival without us—Queen's Tea and all!" Jessica's acts like she's kidding, but she's not. We'll be miles away just outside Big D. I feel like I'm stepping off a cliff into who knows what.

Jessica and Brittany start in playing Snake Bite. Rules: say spiteful, personal things and smile while you're doing it. Skilled players do it where adults cannot hear. Objective: making your opponent mad. The madder she gets and the more she shows it, the more she loses. Jessica and Brit are both thirteen. They practice a lot. They oughta just hush.

"So, you still taking those drill team lessons?"

So far Jessica hasn't scored, but Brittany's on her guard—it's just a matter of time before Jessica executes the zinger. Our cousin stands arms crossed with one leg turned to the side, jiggling a bit.

"Well, I'd keep it up. Kilgore Rangerettes don't take anybody with legs like Miss Piggy."

Now that's just mean. Brit's nostrils flare and she turns bright red. Brittany has a snub nose and big eyes; all she needs is a blond wig to look just like Miss Piggy.

Brittany squints at my sister for a split second and then smiles. Good recovery. "Well, Lord only knows who you look like."

Personal foul—very personal. Jessica's adopted. Every bit of color drains from Jessica's face and her freckles stand out like speckles on a broken bird egg.

But wait. Jessica tilts her head, juts out her dimpled chin. "Well, I may just look up my real family, and I'd be willing to bet good money that every member actually has ankles."

Crushing achievement, but I think it's a draw. Jessica's still pale and neither one scores enough aggravation to deliver the ultimate blow: "Just kidding."

"You two stop whatever meanness you're saying to one another and come help Uncle Clayton." Ma-maw's onto them.

All us kids take turns freezing our legs, because Great-Uncle Clayton makes ice cream the old-timey way. He's going to crank away at a freezer, while one of the grandkids sits on it and holds it down. Dub's graduated to cranking when his grandfather gets tired.

"You first, Miss Brittany."

"No-o-o, please, Mom?" Brittany looks at her mother.

Ma-maw scowls at Aunt Janet and she bristles with the same frown. Their dark brown eyebrows look like big check marks colliding over narrowed hazel eyes.

"No, Miss Priss—you take a turn," Aunt Janet says.

Brittany whines, "But the newsprint... I'm wearing white shorts."

Her mother hisses, "That's not all you're going to be wearing on your hiney, if you don't hush."

I need to talk to Uncle Clayton anyway. "I'll go first," I speak up. "I'm wearing my old cutoffs. I don't care."

Brittany makes a sour face at me, so I sit and shove her off the freezer with my hip. Dub winks at me, licks his finger and sticks the slimy tip into Brittany's ear as she passes him.

"Y-y-yuck, Dub!" Brittany swats at Dub's arm and he dodges her, laughing.

"Don't you pester Uncle Clayton about riding that horse now." Daddy has his "Show-your-best-manners-around-family" face.

"I wasn't going to say a word." Not right this minute anyway. Not where Daddy can hear it.

Three layers of newspaper are between the ice and me, but salty ice water runs down my bare legs like chilly tears. I put my arm around Uncle Clayton's sunburned, wrinkled neck, and he leans in a little for a hug. "Heard you did a good job today at the barrel race."

"Sort of. Not really."

Tabby brings us a plate of chips and salsa to share.

"Don't you fill up on chips, now girls," Mama warns.

"You sit for a minute, Tabby. I'll go get us some burgers." I go over to Granddaddy for two meat patties, charred at the edges, and a side hug.

He whispers to me, "Don't you worry, Ranger—we're still going to talk football. I'll call you after every Cowboys' game." Ranger is Granddaddy's special name for me. He's called me Ranger for as long as I can remember.

I nod and swallow hard.

"You jog with your Daddy, girl. Keep up training and keep him from getting fat."

"Yes, Granddaddy."

"I'm not the only person around here who could stand

some jogging," Daddy says and laughs.

"Those track boys are sure gonna miss you, Clifford." Granddaddy shakes his head. "It's hard to get good athletic staff." He scratches his big old football coach belly—seems like all coaches have one.

Daddy's smile fades. "They'll do okay."

"So, all you're gonna do there is counseling. They're gonna keep you hopping in a school that size. Well, you know our address." Granddaddy flips some burgers before they're ready.

"We'll be fine, Pop." Daddy has a hard edge in his voice.

"I'm just saying…"

"That we're sure you're going to do a wonderful job, Cliff, and it's time to give the subject a rest," Ma-maw finishes. And then she begins to cry. Daddy gathers her to himself and hugs her. Her words are muffled against his shoulder. "I just don't want this family to fly apart."

"It'll be all right, Mom. We're not even two hours away."

She nods. "Milt, why don't you tell us why you call Rebecca 'Ranger.'" Everybody knows that story, but it settles us down and brings us together. Stories do that.

"Everybody was looking for her, and I found the little ol' thang toddling over to the horses." Everybody laughs, then he tells a good one on Aunt Janet. "She thought she'd caught an alligator on her line and then when we landed it, she screams, 'It's a horrible gar!'" says my granddaddy in a shrill soprano.

Aunt Janet says, "Dang old fish had the ugliest snout with these na-asty teeth—it might as well have been a gator. Y'all ain't right." She laughs too though.

I go back to Uncle Clayton and take Tabby's place on the freezer. Uncle Clayton's cranking harder now. Pretty soon he'll give it over to Dub and the ice cream will be done. He checks to see no one's looking and says to me between his teeth, "Horse will be ready at six."

"See you first thing."

"Don't make any racket or they'll catch us." Then Uncle

Clayton calls out, "Dub, come take over for your pappy." My scrawny great-uncle stands up, stretches, heads for the grill. "Brother, you got my pink burger ready?"

CHAPTER THREE

I hear the numbers click as they flip over on Ma-maw's alarm clock. I squint and read 5:30. We should sneak out now. Daddy says we're leaving for Dallas at eight. The orange moving truck and our Impala are parked outside packed and ready to go. We'll have just enough time for our goodbyes.

Jessica is already up. She comes to my side of the bed. "Come on, Becky, wake up."

"I'm awake."

"You've got to get dressed."

"Nuh-uh. I warshed up and put on my top last night." I slide out from under the covers and get up. My top is rumpled, but I'm clean and half dressed.

"Warshed? You sound like Aunt Louise."

Ma-maw's striped orange cat is batting my ponytail doodad on the floor. Tigre glares at me when I grab it. I wipe off a dust bunny from one big blue bead and wrestle back my hair.

I pull on my jeans and follow Jessica to Ma-maw's back porch. We'll have to be extra quiet if this is going to work. We step over Granddaddy's boots and sneakers. I'm carrying my boots and Jessica gently eases open the screen door.

"Where you girls going?"

Aw, shoot. Ma-maw's up.

"Shhhh, Ma-maw." Jessica puts her finger to her lips. "We got to go say goodbye to Uncle Clayton and Aunt Lou and Domino, and Miz Ethel said to stop by her trailer."

"Well, you girls better hurry, before your daddy wakes up. I'll hold off on banging around too much in here, but I have to start breakfast soon."

Breakfast could cut into riding time. "Don't go to any trouble Ma-maw," I say.

"We're too excited to eat," Jessie adds.

Ma-maw says, "Your daddy will pitch a fit if he thinks you're going to hold him up."

"Yes, ma'am. Please don't tell. We'll hurry." I step into my boots and hobble into them as fast as I can.

We can hear Granddaddy whispering. "Where are the girls going, Eileen?"

"For one last ride, I expect."

We cut across the back yard. It's cool, yet, but humid. It's going to be a sweaty day, even under the pines once the sun is up. We walk past Granddaddy's vegetable garden, heavy with the aroma of his beefy tomatoes.

We reach the loblolly pines and Jessica strokes a gray-brown trunk as we walk past. Her hand tightens around the wadded-up top of a paper sack.

"Whatcha got in there?"

"Something for Aunt Lou. We better start running."

There's only a barbed wire fence between Granddaddy and Uncle Clayton's place. I stretch apart the middle and the bottom wires, so Jessica can get through without snagging her clothes, and she does the same for me.

"Let's go by Miz Ethel's first."

I nod, and we run across Uncle Clayton's pasture. Miz Ethel is Ma-maw's long-lost sister, and after they found each other, Granddaddy moved her away from a broken-down trailer in a trashy park on the edge of Crockett to the far corner of the family place. Nobody in the family much cared for it, but they weren't about to cross Ma-maw over it. Our mother tells us not to ever eat over there because her kitchen is none too clean, so Jessica and I go over every chance we get. Miz Ethel gives us cheap snack cakes and the icing leaves this greasy coating on the roof of your mouth. She tells us all the family gossip that Mama says isn't fitting for our ears. Jessica and I knew about our cousin's baby before Mama did.

If Ethel finds a new souvenir plate at a yard sale, she'll show it off. She has them from eleven different states already and she hasn't left Texas once. We sneak over, sit at her rickety card table, and eat the greasy cakes and listen to gossip. That would drive Mama crazy. She says those snacks are white trash food with no nutritional value whatsoever.

A broken TV set is in the yard. I jump over an old tire planter. My legs are long enough, so there's no chance I'll land on a petunia. It wouldn't much matter, because the old pink flowers are about played out anyhow. We won't have to knock on her door, because it's already open. She's standing in the open door, holding out a sack from the feed and grain store. I spot a grimy "Best Mom" plate on the wall behind Aunt Ethel, and I wonder about her boy Wes in prison, but it doesn't seem nice to ask about him.

"You two girls come give Aunt Ethel a hug now and run on, so you can get your ride in, Becky. Here are some Little Debbies. I put 'em in a hardware store sack, so maybe your mother won't spot them. The only thing she'd hate worse would be something I baked in my nasty kitchen." She chuckles. "Oven's broke anyway, and it's a good thing in this heat." Aunt Ethel hugs us with her flabby white arms. "Y'all be sure and come by for a visit, next time you're up."

"Yes, ma'am," we say together.

"Run on now. Your daddy's itching to move off, and your mother's wig don't need to get any tighter. I'll watch you ride from here." She tugs at the bra strap that's wandered from under her Kmart housedress.

We're making good time. Got our cakes with time to spare.

Jessica stops and waves. "There's Uncle Clayton. He's already got Domino out and saddled."

Rascal, Uncle Clayton's border collie, trots up to greet us. It's like he's escorting us to the quarter horse. Domino's ears are forward, and he hops up a little. I walk over and stroke his neck and withers.

"Get on. Don't use up your riding time." Uncle Clayton doesn't talk much. He just says what he needs to say. I like that.

Jessica gives her gift to our great-aunt and Lou pulls out a little decoupage box as Domino and I walk by. "See what your sister brought me?" Aunt Lou hugs Jess. They are big craft buddies, always making some kind of pretty little thing.

Domino and I find the path we've walked, and trotted, and jogged, and run since I was big enough to sit in a saddle. A bug buzzes about his right ear and he flicks it to drive the pest away. I lean over and rub his neck and whisper, "You're a good old fellow." We walk through the knee-deep grass and pass the three practice barrels. Uncle Clayton and Missy coached and trained me there, run after run. Tabby and I have taken turns, training and walking the new horses loop after loop around first one and then gradually all three barrels.

Here and there tall dark green stalks topped with white cup-shaped blossoms wave in the breeze. Rascal wanders through the field with his feathery tail swishing like a flag, but sometimes he runs back to walk along and keep us company. His spooky blue eyes look at us like he's telling us, "Come on! Something good is ahead."

"Somebody's gonna have to check him for ticks, Domino." I take a deep breath, and I draw in peace and air.

Rascal woofs and I jump, and Domino tosses his head. I turn and spot Daddy marching through the weeds. I pull the reins and head back to my family.

"Ma-maw said you'd be here." Daddy looks sleepy. His hair's contrary, sticking up, and one seam on his white undershirt is twisted over toward his middle, the shirt tail half stuffed into the top of his jeans.

Jessica and I both scowl. Ma-maw told.

"Do you have everything packed up?" Daddy asks.

A Thing of Beauty

"Since last night. Our bags are by the door. Bed's made too." Jessica crosses her arms.

Daddy looks mad and a little foolish. "Well, I do not want to get on the road any later than eight."

Jessica looks at her watch. "It's quarter till six, Daddy."

"Well, Preacher H.J. is coming by to pray over us and see us off."

Uncle Clayton and Aunt Lou look at each other. Mr. H.J. is Daddy's football buddy from high school. He's black.

"Uncle Clayton and Aunt Louise, I'm sorry they put you out like this."

"It wasn't any trouble at all, Clifford." Aunt Louise hugs Jessica's shoulder.

"Take one more loop around the pasture and then let's go," Daddy says and sighs.

Domino and I head toward the woods in the north corner of the property, and I decide to cut short my ride. Grownups know how to take the joy right out of things sometimes. I turn Domino's head and come on back.

Daddy's still fidgeting. "Okay, girls we need to go now. Ma-maw has gone to the trouble to fix a big breakfast. You two help with the horse and come on and eat."

Uncle Clayton says stiffly, "I can take care of Domino. I'll cool him down, Becky."

Daddy sighs and looks off. "I can't win." He turns and heads back over the pasture.

Our great-uncle calls out to our father's back, "Your daddy is sure going to miss you."

"I know, Uncle Clayton—we'll miss you all too," Daddy calls back. "Jessica, you girls don't keep Ma-maw waiting."

"Ma-maw's not the one with the problem," I mutter as Daddy stomps back through the tall grass. Uncle Clayton and Aunt Lou shoot me the "now-be-nice" look.

Our short, plump aunt hugs my sister. "I love my box, but you won a Four-H ribbon for that. Don't you want to keep it?"

Jessica's smiles and shrugs. "I've got my ribbon. I want you to have the box."

Aunt Louise hugs us again and says, "We'd better get you girls over there."

"Can't I help you, Uncle Clayton?" I put my hand on Domino's saddle.

"Naw, girl. Better go mind your Daddy. I'll be over and hug your neck before you go. Hug, ol' Dom and tell him goodbye. You've been making good progress with your riding. I believe you could set some records."

"You think so?"

That ought to make me happy, but it just makes me want to stay even more. I bury my face into Domino's neck, rub his nose, and whisper, "Bye." I turn away fast now.

"Let me walk you girls over to your Ma-maw's," Aunt Louise urges.

Jessica's mad that we have to leave too early, but she's keeping a poker face. Her jaw is set and that means she's got a plan. She slips me something from the hardware sack.

Ma-maw and Mama are sitting at the dining room table, and Mama looks sort of cornered. Our Ma-maw can make a person feel that way, when she's got something on her mind.

"Liz, I'd be lying to you if I said this move didn't worry me. The schools offer a lot, but urban areas have their dangers." Ma-maw's apple curtains whip and pop in a sudden breeze.

Aunt Louise joins in, "Law, yes. That awful fella in Georgia—why he killed and—you know—a young girl before they caught him in New Orleans last May." Aunt Louise looks appalled, but she likes reading about a gruesome crime better than nearly anything.

"Louise, the girls," Ma-maw cautions.

Aunt Louise's chin trembles. "Well, you be sure to check the girls' clothes before they leave for school."

Mama hugs her tight and whispers, "We will, don't you worry." Mama takes the chance to change the subject. "Girls, let's get you fed." She seats me with a clean plastic apple place mat in front of me. Everything's apple because Ma-maw and

Granddaddy are teachers.

Daddy steps by to check on our progress. He's loaded up with pillows and Mama's overnight bag. It's only ten after six and Daddy's still rushing us along. "Y'all put your dishes in the sink after you finish Ma-maw's good breakfast."

Jessica and I look at each other and nod. Jessica daintily sets a small package on her plate and begins opening it, and I pull out my snack cake as well.

"We already have our breakfast from Miz Ethel."

Ma-maw frowns at the Little Debbie cakes and then at Mama and Daddy, daring them to say anything against her sister. Mama and Daddy open their mouths to speak and then close them.

We got 'em this time.

CHAPTER FOUR

Breakfast was long put away and everything washed up with forty-five minutes to spare. Mama and Daddy made me go shower and put on clean clothes, so I wouldn't smell sweaty and horsy and make a bad impression in Dallas. Brittany and Jessica hug like they're never hateful to each other and chatter like they'll see each other tomorrow. Tabby and I settle in under the carport, so we can see the Preacher H.J. and Daddy show.

Preacher H.J. and his sons roll up in a spotless old Lincoln and Uncle Richie frowns and crosses his arms.

Tabby whispers, "There's another reason y'all are leaving. Our redneck family."

She's right. Daddy says Uncle Richie isn't quite the redneck he was before Vietnam, but he still doesn't approve of Daddy's black friend or his big shiny powder blue car. He's not going argue with Daddy over it. Uncle Richie goes and checks the van's oil.

Daddy's jaw muscle clenches—I would miss it if I weren't looking—and then he smiles at his friend. The preacher leaves his car and he and Daddy hug and pound each other on the back. Preacher H.J. shakes Ma-maw's hand and smiles, but he and Granddaddy look at each other without saying a word.

Preacher nods, breaks the silence and says, "Coach."

Granddaddy nods back. "Harold James."

H.J.'s oldest son, Burgess, stands by his father's car with angry eyes and crossed arms. He doesn't want any part of this. His little brother, Riley, waves at Tabby and me. We played Batman all the time in kindergarten. Somehow, we stopped, but we always say hi.

Ma-maw smiles real big and says, "H.J., can I offer you some coffee? Some juice, fellas?"

"Thank you, thank you, but no." Mr. H.J. pats Riley's shoulder.

I whisper, "Ma-maw likes Mr. H.J. because he was in her English class. She says she's proud because he 'made a preacher.'"

Tabby whispers back, "Why do they say it like that? Sounds like Frankenstein." Tabby looks at me sideways. "He's why Uncle Clifford goes to church."

Granddaddy goes to church Easter and Christmas and Fellowship of Christian Athletes and calls it good. Uncle Richie 'worships' on the lake with a six pack of Lone Star beer. They thought Daddy would get over church, but he didn't. Sometimes Daddy's church deal is okay; sometimes it's inconvenient and a pain. Like today.

"Shhhh. Mr. H.J.'s praying now," I whisper. All the women and Daddy are happy. Granddaddy and Uncle Richie get quiet and study the toes of their shoes.

"And we ask you Lord, to look upon us this day and bless our loved ones in their new home. Just give them traveling mercies..." Preacher H.J. tells us bye and shakes my hand like I'm a grownup and then he's gone.

"Y'all oughta come shop in Dallas with us sometime," Mama offers to Aunt Janet.

"Maybe we could all finally go to Six Flags." Aunt Janet looks hopeful, but I think we all know we'll just get busy. We've made the same plans for years. Hasn't happened yet.

"Now what's the zip code there?" Tabby's double-checking to make sure we have our mailing addresses right.

"And what's your street number?" Funny that I need to ask Tabby's address. I never had to think about it before.

Tabby slips something braided into my hand. "I cut off some hair from Domino's tail. I don't know what you'll do with it, but I thought you might like it."

I look in her teary green eyes, and I realize they look just like mine. I blink back tears and look away. I hear pinecones thump the ground behind me. "Hey, Tabby, quick, help me get some cones for Christmas." Tabby and I gather five big stickery cones. Jessica will paint the tips white and we'll set them out for decoration.

"Girls, we can't take anything else in the car." Daddy's getting antsy. I sneak in one cone when he's not looking.

It's five till eight, and even Jessica and I can't think of any good reason to stay any longer. Our Uncle Richie drives off in the moving van while the four of us pile into the Impala. We're off and the green trees and vines that line the street are farther away on the farm to market road and stand farther still away from the interstate.

Soon we see North Central Texas brown and sky above us like a hard, blue bowl. You know exactly where the rivers run—the trees along the banks are the only green in sight.

I sigh. "This part of Texas is ugly as sin."

"Green grass burnt up this month." Daddy smiles. "Only two seasons here: spring and brown. And the worst pollen count in the nation." Like he's proud of it. "The neighborhoods will be greener."

Scrawny cedar trees dot a field. "Those are poor folks' Christmas trees," Mama explains. "When Granny B. and I were on our own, we couldn't afford a Christmas tree from a lot, so we would cut down a cedar tree."

Cedar trees make me sneeze, and now they make me miss the tall pines back home.

Jessica leans forward. "Daddy, what are the kids like at your new school?"

"Oh, I don't know. They're just kids—like you."

Jessica and I look at each other. I doubt that.

Daddy looks at us in the rearview mirror. "We've got a real

fine choir. Good football too, Becky. Great track for running. Developed sports programs for boys *and* girls."

Jessica relaxes a little. "But what do the girls wear?"

Daddy shrugs and looks helpless at Mama. "I don't know—clothes?"

"What about Four-H?" I want to know, but nobody answers.

"Just wait until you see our rancher." Mama's eyes shine. She and Daddy looked at houses every weekend for weeks. "You girls will have a much larger room, central heat and air, a den."

A ranch house, but how much land I wonder? Maybe I can talk Daddy into a calf or a goat for now?

Suddenly, I think of the kid from New York. "Remember Elliot, that new kid in school. His dad worked for LeTourneau College?"

"Couldn't stand him." Jessica sniffs. "No manners. Know-it-all and cocky."

"I felt sort of sorry for him." Teachers hated him because he didn't say, "Yes, ma'am, No, ma'am" and kids hated him because he thought East Texas was backwoods and ignorant and the girls' clothes were about a century behind. He talked funny too; he said, "Six Flags over Texas" instead of just "*Six* Flags." I wonder if East Texas looked as unpromising to him as the Dallas suburbs look to me. "I wish I had been nicer."

"What for?" Jessica's brushing her hair and she pauses and points at me with her brush. "We put him in his place. If he liked New York so much, he should have stayed there."

Mama turns and looks at both of us. "Now, Jessica, how'd you like it if someone did that to you?"

Jessica's brush strokes slow just a fraction and she glances at me. Yeah. How will we like that?

Daddy perks up. "It's the next exit." He signals. Relieved to see the van, one traffic light ahead of us, he smiles. We pass fast food, shopping centers. I don't really expect anything too soon. Too much town—no ranch yet.

"Here's my school." Daddy points to a sprawling building.

A few miles past it, we turn.

I'm a little surprised. We wind around following the van. I see an old guy with a flattop haircut and wearing Bermuda shorts watering his lawn. Two wagon wheels lean against posts on either side of his driveway, and an old rusty plow sits in a bed of petunias. I guess he thinks that looks Western.

Daddy pulls to the curb and stops right across the street from the wagon wheels. I turn and look at the ranch-style house with a tiny cactus garden, full of weeds and dead flowers. Ranch house, but no ranch. As Jessica and I crawl out of the car, my pinecone falls to the street. Jessica's foot crushes the cone flat. I slip my hand into my pocket, find the braid of Domino's hair, and squeeze it hard.

CHAPTER FIVE

"What do you think, girls?" Daddy doesn't wait to hear. He strides over to the truck and guides Uncle Richie as he backs up the van into the driveway.

"It's a . . . house." I can't hide my disappointment.

"Well, of course it's a house, dummy." My sister's looking up and down the street—for what? Other kids, I imagine.

The red brick house is built long and flat like any other ranch house. A person could almost reach out the side window and hold hands with someone in the ranch house beside it. I grouse, "So much for wide-open spaces."

Jessica snorts, "What'd you expect? The Ponderosa?" My sister scans the windows. "I wonder which one's ours." There are three: two small ones on the far left and right and a picture window just to the right of the doorway. All smiles and big eyes, she looks at me. I shrug. "Becky, what's *your* problem?"

If she thinks I'm going to play "Let's squeal and get all excited," she's got another think coming.

We walk over the yard and Mama sighs at the dead flowers dried crispy in the Dallas heat. "I guess they stopped watering once we bought the house. The neighbors must think this looks awful." She pulls herself together and brightens. "Come on girls, let's go look at your room. Just wait till you see."

Mama pulls the key from her purse and smiles. "The first

time to open up my very own house." She throws the door open grandly and gestures for us to come in.

"Ooooh, it's so nice and cool," says Jessie.

"Central heating and air!"

"It stinks in here and the carpet's ugly," I mutter. Our voices are all echo-y in the empty home.

Mama looks hurt and I feel bad right away.

Jessica elbows me. "Becky you're such a party pooper!"

"I'm sorry, Mama." I hug her and make myself smile. "Show us around."

Mama gestures to her right. "Here's the living room." Mud-colored drapes droop limply by the picture window, and dust specks litter the sunlight. "Those beige drapes are sort of dingy and dull, but we'll fix that. Over there's Daddy's study. It's supposed to be a formal dining room, but it's so tiny."

She grabs our hands and leads us down the small central hall. "Here's our kitchen and dining room and look at this den! I'm going to do it all in cheerful colors and I get to paint it anyway I want!"

"No Ma-maw to disagree," I put in.

"No. No Ma-maw." Mama sighs like she might be just a little sad about that. She grabs our hands again. "Let's go see those bedrooms." Mama wrinkles her nose and giggles like a six-year-old.

We run to keep up. We go out the den door and into a long hall. "I'm saving you girls' room for last." Mama points to a room at the end of the hall. "Here at long last is my sewing room. No more shuffling stuff back and forth off the kitchen table. And the master bedroom is across the hall. Daddy and I will have our very own bathroom." It's bare and lonely in there, and the carpet is an odd pinky beige, but my mother's eyes sparkle. "I've got special plans for in here."

"Where's the other bathroom? I'm going to need it here soon," Jessica says.

"Follow me." Mama sweeps us the other way. "Here's the main bathroom." Jessica and I poke our heads into the blue-tiled room and nod. We pull back and look at Mama.

She grins like she has the best surprise of all. "Right here is your room!"

Our room is almost as big as Mama and Daddy's. "A nice big closet," Mama points out like we're prospective buyers.

Jessica marches over and places her hand on the closet door. "I want this side," Jessica demands. My clothes go on the right." Then she stands with her hands on her hips by the side window. "And I want this side of the room."

"Well, if you choose the closet space, Becky gets to choose where she wants her bed."

From the doorway, I point at the other window, but I don't really care.

"Over there's okay."

Mama and Jessie look at the windows.

"What color curtains do you think? It's going to be fun fixing this up."

I've had enough. "I'm going to look around, Mama."

"Well, sure, Becky. Go explore." Mama and Jessie begin to debate color.

"Blue, definitely, blue." Jessica knows what she likes.

"Well, white would go with everything..." Mama's voice fades away as I stride off.

Who cares about stupid curtains? I don't care about what's inside this pitiful excuse for a ranch house. I've got to know what's out back. That's what's important. I go into the den and see a green curtain that reaches to the floor. I hear Dad's footsteps behind me.

"Pull open the curtain, Becky. It's a sliding glass door. You can see the back yard." Daddy can hardly wait for me to see and approve. He smiles at me and I smile back—maybe there is hope for this place.

I fumble a second, and then my fingers find the cord and I pull. The avocado curtain whisks aside, and my eyes must adjust to the bright sunlight. As I peer, I can feel the smile slide right off my face.

Daddy's hand is on my shoulder as he looks at the blond grass of a fenced yard. "Nice-sized, but it won't take too long to mow."

"No, it won't," I whisper. There's not even enough room for a tiny goat. I feel stupid. What was I thinking?

The doorbell rings and we both jump.

Daddy says, "The football players are here! The coach and the team are going to help us move in." He gives my shoulder a quick pat and runs to answer the door.

Tears begin to stream down my face and that makes me mad. I'm not a bawl-baby. I struggle with the sliding door latch to get outside. Those high school boys are *not* going to see me cry. I can hear them coming in and I feel desperate. I begin to shake the handle, when I feel a cool, smooth hand on mine.

"What's wrong, sweetie?"

I'm too ashamed to look up. I glance down and see neat white sneakers next to my boots.

"You want to go outside? I'll help you." It's a high school girl.

The door slides open and I rush out and crumple onto the back patio. The older girl sits and puts her arm around me as I cry. Long red hair tickles my arm and shoulder as I lean into her. "It's okay. It's hard to move to a new place," she says. "I know. Please, don't be sad. You're my new neighbor."

I sit up, swallow hard, and wipe my face dry against my shoulders.

"There you go. Here, I'll go get you a wet paper towel for your face." She pauses. "Nobody will even know."

She slips back quickly and hands me a damp, folded towel. I look up into her kind blue eyes. Tiny cinnamon freckles fleck her creamy nose and cheeks. "Your hair smells good," I whisper.

"It's my fruity shampoo. I'll let you try some. My name's Audrey. My mother lo-o-oves Audrey Hepburn." The girl flips a lock of her red hair. "I don't look a *thing* like her."

"My name's Becky."

"And your sister's Jessica. We've heard all about you. My boyfriend is helping you move in."

"He's a football player?"

"That's right. And I'm a cheerleader."

"You're *nice*." I don't mean to sound surprised, but I am.

"Cheerleaders can't be nice?"

"Well, yeah. But they're popular."

Audrey smiles and shrugs. "I just like to encourage people."

"Why do they only cheer for sports? What about smart kids or singers or Four-H? They're important too."

"Well, I hadn't thought about that, but maybe I should start cheering for them too." She smiles, and I smile back. Audrey stirs a little. "Let's go find your sister, and I'll show you where I live."

I slide back the door and begin to push aside the heavy curtain. Suddenly, a big rough arm shoves me aside and grabs Audrey, and a deep voice crows, "There's my girl!"

CHAPTER SIX

"Billy!" Audrey pushes a big blond guy. "This jerk is my boyfriend." She slugs his forearm. "Stop that, I hate it!" He chuckles and tries to kiss her, but she's having none of it. She shoves him away, trying not to smile.

He's awful pushy. I see a big chunky class ring hanging on a rough chain around Audrey's slender neck. It doesn't look comfortable.

I look Billy in the eye. "That ring must be yours." I sound accusing.

He looks at me. "You been crying?"

I lift my chin. "Not to speak of."

My mother and sister walk in and I announce, "This is my Mom, and this is Jessica."

Billy hardly grunts, looking only at Audrey, but she reaches out and hugs Mama and Jessie. "Nice to meet you, ma'am! Hi, Jessica. I'm Audrey Baxter and this is Billy Markam." She whacks Billy and whispers, "Say hello."

"Uh, yes, ma'am. Sorry. Hi."

The doorbell rings.

"That may be my mother. We live right down the street from y'all." Audrey is right.

A tired, worried-looking lady is at the door, holding a small foil-wrapped loaf. It's only when she smiles that I can see she and Audrey have the same kind eyes.

"Hello, I'm Susan Baxter, your neighbor down the way?"

"Come on in Mrs. Baxter. I'm Elizabeth Ramey. Call me Liz."

"Call me Susan." Mrs. Baxter notices Billy and smiles a tight careful smile. "Hello, Billy." I bet she doesn't much care for him either. I don't blame her.

Billy nods at her. "I'll go bring in some more . . . stuff."

Mama says, "Girls, why don't you go on outside, so these boys can get us moved in."

"I'll get out of your way too, Liz," Mrs. Baxter says. She gives Mama the little loaf. "If you like, Audrey and I would be happy to help you unpack."

Mama nods, grateful.

"I'll be back later," says Audrey's mom.

"That would be wonderful."

Jessica, Audrey, and I sit on some boxes watching the sweating boys and coach troop back and forth across the lawn. Our mother stands at the door directing traffic. "Yellow tagged boxes in the kitchen, blue in the living room, red in the den."

"So organized!" Audrey says.

"You have no idea," I say. "She arranges all the clothes in rainbow order. Red blouses, orange, peach, yellow . . ."

"Our mother probably invented *R.O.Y.G.B.I.V.*," says Jessica.

Audrey tells us, "Now, a 7-Eleven is within walking distance. You saw the high school."

"Are there any kids on our street?" Jessica wants to know.

"Only me and Kenny—and there he is." A boy about my age rides by on a bicycle with an old banana seat, and he sticks his tongue out at us. "Ignore him. He probably thinks you're both cute, but he doesn't know what to do about it." Audrey yells, "Kenny Wright, you come over here!" The chunky boy cautiously walks his bike over to us. His knees are skinned up over the blue stripes on his dingy tube socks. "Becky and Jessica, this crazy boy is Kenny. Kenny, this is Becky and Jessica Ramey, our new neighbors. You go on now. And be nice!"

Kenny walks off looking back at us with an ornery grin. The tip of his tongue starts to show between his lips.

"You stick that tongue back in your mouth or I'll weave it into the spokes of your bicycle."

Kenny looks at her like she just might try, but then he chuckles.

"I used to help my mother babysit him. He's a pill. His grandfather lives in the house with the wagon wheels out front. Retired cop—keeps his police scanner on all the time."

The high school boys start to poop out a little. They're leaning on the truck and horsing around with a faded red plastic bat. Kenny's granddaddy swaggers over. "You boys see the Super Bowl last year?"

"Yes, sir!"

"Well, I was there! Let's polish this off and you guys can come see the home movie I took," he hollers. "Got a Dallas Cowboy shirt signed by Tony Dorsett too."

That gets 'em going. Coach too. Our flat-topped neighbor calls Kenny over. "Boy, come help me with this coffee table."

I wonder if the table would mash down the man's hair if he carried it on his head or would the bristly hair hold it up like a bed of nails? He catches me staring and grins. "Good afternoon, ladies."

"Hi, Mr. Wright." Audrey says, "This is Jessica and Becky."

"Welcome to the neighborhood," he booms.

Kenny makes another horrible face at us, rolling his eyes back into his head, and his granddaddy thumps his ear. Thwack! They squat and lift the furniture. Kenny scowls as he backs up the steps, carrying my mama's table, and I scowl back. He had better not scratch it.

"Y'all will have to speak up around Mr. Wright. He's deaf as a post and shouts all the time," Audrey says.

Three young girls walk by us. They eye us silently, but then light up and smile when they notice Audrey. She waves, and they wave back.

"Who are they?" I ask.

"Those girls live a few streets over. They go to your school. You'll meet them."

Jessica and I look at each other, worried. "They weren't too friendly," Jessica says.

"They're just shy and in a hurry. They're going to Girl Scouts. You two in Girl Scouts?" Audrey says.

"No, Four-H. Jessica sings," I say.

"Becky rides horses. That's all she thinks about—horses."

"You have got to meet somebody. I've got a little cousin who is cr-razy about dogs—she . . ." Audrey doesn't finish, because Billy is here. He reaches down and takes her hand and pulls her to her feet and then to him.

Some man stands on our lawn looking at them, his eyes flat. The tall man with gray sideburns doesn't approve of that hug. A neighbor? Audrey's dad?

Billy sees the man and steps back. "Hey, Dad."

"Billy, we leave in five," Mr. Markam announces. He turns back to my dad who tries to grab a box, so he can escape and carry it on into the house.

Daddy is wearing one of his counselor faces: the trying-to-be-polite-to-the-annoying-parent face. Some football dads are the worst.

Mr. Markam is determined to have Daddy's attention. "Like I say, Billy has a lot of potential." He leans down and flicks some grass off his alligator Western boots. "There are a lot of coaches trying to lure him in, and we'll be depending on your guidance."

Or to make sure Billy's grades squeak by. Daddy says some athletes get away with too much. "Get away with too much trouble and too many bad grades." He says that a lot. Granddaddy doesn't agree, but he's a coach.

Mr. Markam holds out something in his hand. "And welcome to the community. If you folks need any legal advice, here's my card."

Billy watches and when he's satisfied his dad's not looking, he gives Audrey a quick smooch. Billy walks over to his father like it's no big deal.

Audrey's eyebrows raise a fraction. "Billy's daddy is a lawyer."

"Where do you live, Audrey?"

She looks a little sad. "Across the street and down a bit. The little house with the green door." An old blue Plymouth sedan with a faded red fender sits in the driveway.

"Is that your car?"

"*Our* car. It's all we can afford since Daddy left. It runs. Mostly. Gets Mom to work. That's all we need, I guess."

Jessica juts out her dimpled chin, and her blue eyes narrow. "Well, I'm sure glad you're our neighbor."

"Me too," I add.

When you're in a strange, hot, dried-up, unfriendly neighborhood, if you got somebody like Audrey, you got some hope.

CHAPTER SEVEN

I could eat that big breakfast Mama made, but it'll just come right back up. It's the first day of school, and I won't know a living soul on that bus except my sister and Audrey. My stomach's in knots, and I'll toss my cookies for sure.

"Today, I better stick with dry toast, Mama."

Daddy's already gone. He left early, all dressed up in a shirt, one of his old fat ties, and a sport coat. He came in and kissed our foreheads while we were still in bed. Jessica grabbed his tie and wrinkled up her nose, but Daddy just laughed. He looked young, kind of excited and happy and scared all at once. I guess first days are hard for counselors too.

Jessica got right up and showered and started in on her hair. I could hear her bellow even over the blow dryer. She's already gone through three 'dos'—four counting the one she had Mama fix. Jessica took that ponytail right down and tried something else.

We stand at the front door for Mama's inspection. I'm wearing my pink Easter dress that Mama made from a Gunne Sax pattern. My sister says I look just like the TV Laura Ingalls, except without the buckteeth. Jessica is playing it safe with a sky-blue blouse and denim skirt. She hasn't let Mama buy us many school clothes until she's sure of what other girls are wearing. We've been slipping through the department stores like spies sizing up enemy territory.

"You both look real sweet," Mama says.

Jessica shrugs. "Of course, *you'd* say that."

Mama takes my chin in her hand and makes me look at her. "Remember first impressions count. Put your best foot forward." She whispers, "You just be friendly, and you'll make friends."

We hug Mama, but we make her stay in the kitchen. Mama looks back at the eggs and bacon and toast. "Well, I guess I'll see if Susan Baxter wants brunch today."

We peek out the door. Audrey and Kenny are up the street waiting at the bus stop. We weren't coming out if Kenny was there by himself. We walk on over watching for Audrey's reaction.

"Hi, you two. Turn around—let me look." Audrey adjusts Jessica's hair clip a little. She winks and her thumb and fingers signal "Okay!"

Jessica's shoulders relax, and I feel my face ease into a smile. I check the ruffles at my neck, my wrists, and my skirt's hem to make sure they're all fluffed out.

"Where should we sit, Audrey?" I whisper. I don't want anybody to tell us to get up and move. We'll have to look for another seat, afraid someone will tell us the next seat's not for us either—with everybody watching.

Audrey says, "I'll put you right in front of me and my best friend, Theresa."

I hear the growly rumble and smell the oily diesel fumes before the bus rolls around the corner. My heart thumps and my stomach does another queasy flip. Audrey leads us onto the bus like we're the new owners.

Jessica and I say hi to the bus driver and the red-faced man smiles back, surprised. Doesn't anybody ever say hi to him?

"Y'all, these are my new friends, Jessica and Becky Ramey. Tell them your names."

I hear a few kids on the bus mumble their names: Beth, Chad, Bucky.

A sunburned, blond boy named Kyle says, "Hi, Audrey. Hi,

y'all."

Audrey says, "Kyle's a freshman receiver on our football team. He helped you all move in the other day."

I nod, but my head is in such a whirl, I doubt I'll remember any of their names.

Kenny's sitting by one of those other boys. He elbows his friend and then turns to Jessica and me and turns his eyelids wrong side out. The pink, shiny part matches the wet tongue hanging out of his mouth.

Jessica says, "Gr-ross."

I won't give him the satisfaction. I say, "You're going to stretch them out. Then you'll have saggy old man eyelids when you're in high school. Look just like a basset hound."

"Nuh-uh," Kenny says. He elbows his friend again, because Chad laughs. Kenny opens his mouth like he'd like to say something smart back, but he just can't think of anything.

Audrey laughs too. "You tell him, Becky."

At the next stop a scowling high school girl with lots of deep red lip gloss gets on and plops down next to Audrey. "I want to be back in bed." She grabs her long brown hair, twists it to the side and lays her head on Audrey's shoulder.

"Reesy, I want you to meet my friends."

"What friends, where?"

"Right in front of us."

The girl opens one sleepy eye and says, "They're kids."

"Theresa, this is Jessica and Rebecca Ramey. Theresa's a cheerleader too."

Theresa sits up and looks at us like we're road kill.

Audrey leans her head on her friend's shoulder and pushes out a cute pouty lip. "Be nice Reesy Cup. Say hi to Jessie and Becky."

Theresa rolls her eyes, but she smiles. "Hi."

I put out my hand. "Hi. Nice lip gloss. I don't wear it yet." Theresa takes my hand and shakes it, and she smiles a little bigger, but only on one side of her mouth.

"I like your uniforms. Back at our old school they had to

wear red and white—like a candy cane," Jessica says and looks up at the ceiling like she thinks our hometown is dumb. That's loyalty for you.

Theresa looks down at her sky blue-and-white-pleated skirt and shrugs like she's bored. "Well, at least one day a week, I don't have to think about what to wear." The girl stretches and reaches for her purse. She opens it and digs around and comes up with breath mints. Theresa pops one in her mouth and gives one to Audrey and then says to us, "Here, hold out your hands," and gives us some too.

Kenny calls out, "What about me?"

"That's what I'm saying. What about you?" Theresa growls.

Kenny backs off.

Jessica and I look across the aisle at the other bus riders. The kids look back, measuring us.

I point at the fourth seat back, and tell Jessica, "That was where Tabby and I sat on our old bus." I wonder who she's sitting with today. Will she ride Patchwork after school? And what will I do? No chores, but no horse either.

The bus pauses and a bushy-headed boy gets on. Jessica and I look at his loud silky print shirt and then at each other, but we press our lips together, so we don't smirk. If he's a popular boy, he might get away with wearing it. The slender boy smoothes his hair while he looks for a seat, but the wiry mess springs right back out. The other kids are snickering and whispering. He slouches, and I can tell that shirt's going to give him trouble.

I look back at Jessica and she mouths, "Bad idea. Real bad idea."

I glance around the bus. A couple of girls are wearing sundresses, but no one has an outfit like mine. I ask Jessica, "Does this look all right?"

She shrugs and her forehead wrinkles. "I think it'll be okay."

The bus jolts to a stop; we've pulled up to a flat-faced

building with faded green metal trim. The front door yawns ready to swallow us up. We're on our own now. Jessica whispers, "Bye," but Audrey and Theresa are talking and don't even look up.

Theresa frowns. "What do you mean you don't feel right?"

We're off the bus before I can hear Audrey reply.

A herd of girls, wary-eyed, step toward the front door. I bet if I stamped my foot, they'd spring off like a bunch of white-tailed deer. Thing is, I'd probably spook myself too.

That Beth girl says, "Hey, you in the eighth grade?"

She's looking at my sister, head tilted to one side.

"Yes." Jessica tilts her head and watches Beth back.

The sturdy girl smiles, but only a little. "Follow me. Our wing is this way. Who's your homeroom teacher?"

"Cox."

"Me too."

Beth leads the way and I stumble after them, because I don't know what else to do. The shiny floors smell buttery with wax. Colorful bulletin boards and bold posters say welcome, that school's begun and everything's fresh and clean and exciting. Room after room has smooth dark green boards with carefully printed lists. How long will that last? How long before somebody marks on the craft paper, and the borders on the bulletin boards curl up like they're retreating? Soon the chalk trays will be filled with the dust of assignments hardly anybody does, wrong math problems, and detention lists. My stomach does another tumble. Hope my name doesn't go up on some board.

Beth and Jessica take a sudden right, and I bump into Beth when she stops inside a classroom full of older kids. They're all staring at me like I'm a mouse at the lions' watering hole.

Beth's forehead wrinkles up. "Kid, you better get to your class. This isn't even your wing."

I back out, the teacher closes the door. I am lost.

CHAPTER EIGHT

The hallway's empty and my footsteps echo against green metal lockers that are lined up, shut tight, and full of secrets a kid like me cannot know. A banner at the end of the hallway brags "'78-'79 Eighth Grade is Mighty Fine!" A girl carrying a stack of papers leaves Jessica's classroom and hurries past me to the classroom across the hall.

As she returns, I clear my throat and say, "Can you tell me where Mrs. Goforth's room is?"

"The sixth-grade wing. Where else?" She brushes past me to her class and shuts the door.

"Well, nice meeting you too," I say.

I look to my right and to my left. To the right would take me to an outside door, so I head the other way. A lanky, freckled boy leaves a room, walking with long purposeful strides; he's carrying a note—to the office, I guess.

I run to catch up. "Hey, can you help me? I'm lost."

He pauses. "Okay, where you supposed to be?"

"Mrs. Goforth."

"Oh. *Goforth. You* better hurry. Goforth hates for anything to mess up her routine. Here's seventh-grade section." He points at two double doors without slowing down. "There's the gym." We come to where two hallways cross and the tall boy jerks his head to the right. "Hurry, go this way. Name's on the door. Don't say anything. Don't disagree. Find somebody big or some-

A Thing of Beauty

one bad to sit behind. Maybe she won't notice you. You might be okay." The boy checks his watch.

"Thanks. I'm Becky."

"I'm not going to tell you my name, because I'll tell you right now I won't remember yours. Besides, you're a sixth grader."

I watch him rush away. "Well, aren't you just the best Welcome Wagon ever."

Two older boys are heading my way. I can tell by their sly grins that they're up to something. One boy's braces glint evilly and spit bubbles shine in the corners of his mouth.

"You lost? Whose room you in?"

"Goforth."

They shoot each other shifty smirks like I won't even notice. "Well you're supposed to be by the swimming pool on the second floor," says Metal Mouth.

How stupid do they think I am? We told the same dumb lie to new kids back home. You'd think this city school could at least come up with something original.

I make my eyes go all big and innocent. "Well, that tall boy was going to the office, and he said we're all supposed to be lining up to hear Roger Staubach. He's giving a motivational talk in the gym. Two other Dallas Cowboys are coming too."

The boys frown, uncertain. "Staubach, the quarterback?"

"I guess so." I shrug, still showing the girly big eyes.

We all see a lady heading our way, and Metal Mouth and his sidekick get themselves in gear and hustle to a classroom. The lady wearing a red suit looks over her glasses at the boys' backs and says, "Yes, that's right, fellas. Keep moving along, now." Her short iron gray hair glistens, perfectly groomed. She turns to look at me and I take a big shuddery breath. "I'm Mrs. Buckley, principal at this fine institution of learning. Now how can we help you, young lady?"

"I'm Rebecca Ramey and I'm supposed to put my best foot forward, but I'm lost."

"Well, I believe I can help. Who's your homeroom

teacher?"

Mrs. Buckley ushers me down the hall and pauses before my classroom door. A white sign with tall black letters says GO-FORTH. It looks like a command.

"Now don't you worry about a thing. Everybody gets lost some time." The principal raps softly and then opens the door.

A woman with puffy hair sprayed hard and shiny is reading aloud, "Number two: stay seated and silent." Her dark eyes squint in annoyance, but she carefully manages a smile, a polite mask. "Mrs. Buckley."

"I've brought you a student. Rebecca is new and had some trouble finding her way here. I'll let you get back to your orientation." Mrs. Buckley winks at me as she closes the door.

"Well, I'll have to rearrange everything," Mrs. Goforth sighs.

She hasn't looked at me once, but the cautious students look at us like something's about to explode.

"I had your desk all prepared, but I moved it out of the way. Where am I going to put you?"

I look at four girls in the front and they reach and link hands. "Noooo, don't move us now!" one whispers, pleading.

No room for a newcomer, I think.

"That will be enough, girls." The teacher purses her lips thinking. "Chad, move your desk back and shift that desk behind you in front of yours. You—what's your name? Rachel, sit there."

Every desk has a nametag with a name written in perfect cursive, taped to the corner. Goforth directs me to my desk and points to my nametag. "Rachel…"

"Rebecca. Rebecca Ramey."

She cranes her neck to read my label. "Rebecca. This is the Palmer method of writing. Use it."

The teacher straightens and checks her watch. "At this time, we're going to the gym for an orientation."

We line up and file out. Chad steps on the back of my heel and I stumble, so the kids around me giggle. I elbow Chad's belly when he shoves forward. Now laugh at that!

Mrs. Goforth goes through the wedged-open gym doors to the bleachers and directs the students to sit. She makes one of the front seat girls sit by me. The girl looks up at the two rows above us, longing to be by her friends, not by a new kid. She has an overbite and she's a mouth breather, so that makes her face look extra mopey.

I look at her turquoise prairie dress and clear my throat. "That's a nice outfit. Did your mother make it?"

She looks at me like I slapped her and bugs out her eyes. "What are you trying to say," she yells. "Who do you think you are, coming here and making fun of people's clothes?"

Mrs. Goforth marches over, "Amy, what is wrong with you?"

"She insulted my dress," Amy says.

"This is uncalled for—we do not make personal comments about another person's appearance, we do not yell, *and* we do not elbow people. Yes, I saw that. You two can't behave on the first day? I can't deal with this now. Both of you go to the office and wait."

Mrs. Goforth marches us toward the hallway. Two older boys are desperately peeking through the glass in the door, and one of them is Metal Mouth.

"Richard, what are you boys doing?" Mrs. Goforth asks.

"Is Roger Staubach here yet? Why do the sixth graders get to hear him first?"

"What are you talking about? This is PE orientation," Mrs. Goforth turns to the tall lady gym teacher. "Miss Powers, do you know anything about Roger Staubach?"

A short broad-shouldered man bursts through the locker room door, "Hey, what is this about Staubach coming?" His whistle swings wildly from his blue-and-gray lanyard.

I grab Mouth Breather Amy's hand and head for the office. The secretary is frantically shuffling forms and attendance slips. She waves us on to Mrs. Buckley's office.

Mrs. Buckley looks over her glasses. "Now what?" she

whispers. "Ladies, what do you need?"

"This girl said my dress looks homemade."

"And?" Mrs. Buckley looks at me.

I shrug. "My mother made *my* dress. I thought hers was pretty. I was just making conversation."

"Okay, girls. Go wherever it is you're supposed to be right now. I must take care of this Roger Staubach rumor. Has Coach Parks and the whole seventh grade in an uproar."

I take off out of there fast, and Amy's right behind me.

"You got me in trouble," Amy says.

"You were the one pitching the hissy fit," I say.

Amy stalks up to her friends and looks down at me, superior and scornful. "Her mother made her dress." Amy narrows her eyes. "Hey, you. What kind of jeans do you wear?"

"I don't know. *Blue*?"

She leans forward like she's going to make a killer blow. "We wear Calvin Klein.'"

"Well, good for you. *I* wear Rebecca Ramey."

CHAPTER NINE

The last bell rings and I'm caught in a flash flood of kids carrying me along toward the front of the building whether I want to go there or not. Jessica and I spot each other, and she grabs my arm and pulls me along to our bus. "We've got to go jeans shopping right away!" Jessica hisses in my ear.

I look at her. "We've got jeans."

"No. We've got Wranglers and they will not do. Not even Levis will do. It's got to be Calvin Klein or no jeans at all."

"Oh, yeah." I shake my head. "Calvin Klein. I heard about him today."

"We can't wear anything else."

Jessica and that Beth girl sit and spread out their stuff, taking up a whole seat. I settle for the one in front of them.

"I met so many people," Jessica says. "You make any friends, Beck?"

I snort. "A couple of enemies, more like."

The bus pulls into the high school bus lane, and the high schoolkids climb on. The bushy-headed boy from this morning flops down beside me. Not many seats are left. That shirt was trouble all right. One button is half torn off and the seam under his right arm gapes open.

Audrey and Billy get on the bus, and it's like royalty arrives. Everybody watches them. Bushy Head's shoulders stiffen when Billy brushes by us. Maybe Audrey's boyfriend really hated his silky shirt. Billy takes Audrey's hand and guides her toward the back. He leans over a bus seat and stares at two middle schoolkids sitting there until they get up. The boys move all red and embarrassed to the front.

The bushy-headed kid sighs. His day must have been about as bad as mine was.

"Are you new here too?" I whisper.

"Yeah. I'm always new. Military brat."

"My dad's the new guidance counselor."

"Yeah? Mr. Ramey?"

I nod smiling.

"Is that right? He helped me today. He's a nice guy." The teenaged boy smiles, and I wonder if anyone noticed that he's cute. "How was your day?" he asks.

I tell him about getting lost, making Amy mad, and about the Roger Staubach rumor. He laughs when I tell him I started it.

"I may have to start my own rumor. Shake up things around here a bit. The revenge of the new kids." He looks at me and his face relaxes into a crooked grin. "I'm Frank."

"I'm Becky." I'm not alone, so I feel a little bolder. "They wear stupid jeans around here."

"That's the fad right now. They dead sure don't wear shirts like mine—my mom thought it was, (and Frank draws little quotes in the air with his fingers) *fashionable*."

"Go buy a new shirt—and get a haircut. Maybe they won't recognize you," I suggest. "Your new disguise for starting rumors."

The boy shifts his book bag onto his shoulder. "Thanks a lot, kid. I guess. See you around. This is my stop."

"What'd you say?" Billy hollers. "I couldn't hear you. Your shirt's too bright."

"It's too loud, Billy. Too loud," Audrey says. "If you're going to be hateful, you might as well say it right."

"What's wrong with you?"

"Nothing." Audrey squeezes past Billy's big legs. "I need

to check on the new kids." She tries to slide up before the bus starts, but it lurches forward, and she almost falls. She pulls herself over into my seat.

"You okay, Audrey?" Jessica asks.

"Yeah, I'm fine. I just feel a little crummy. Becky, when we get to our stop, could you take my book bag? My stomach's upset, and I may need to get in my house fast."

"Audrey, do you have Calvin Klein jeans?" Jessica asks.

Audrey leans her head on her hands. Miserable, she mutters, "Yes, Vanderbilt too. Mama spends too much on my clothes. She shouldn't use the credit card so much."

Billy thunders down the aisle and squeezes in by us and I'm about mashed.

"What's wrong? Are you mad? Are you okay?"

Audrey fans her face a little with her hand. "I'm all right, just carsick. I just need to go home and lie down." She takes his hand and squeezes it. "Call me later, okay?"

Our bus stops and Audrey rushes down the bus steps and down the street. Jessica takes Audrey's bag and I carry both of ours. Audrey fumbles with first one house key and then another. She looks sick and frantic, so I grab the keys from her hand and unlock her door for her.

"Thanks," is all Audrey can squeak out as she bolts into her home.

"We'll check on you later," Jessica calls out.

Audrey only moans.

We burst in the front door and rush for the kitchen. "Mom?"

Mrs. Baxter and Mama are sitting at our table. You can tell they've been talking and Mrs. Baxter's face goes from secret-adult-talk face to the talk-to-the-kids face. "Well, hello there, girls. Your mother and I just came back from a Tupperware party."

"Yes, we had a great time and I met a bunch of ladies on our street." Mama flips through the pages of yellow, orange, and brown rubber bowls in a catalog.

Jessica announces everything all dramatic. She can't just tell anything. "Oooh, Mrs. Baxter. Audrey is sick—sick as a dog. Becky and I had to help her."

She and Mama look at each other. "I better get her to that appointment."

"Feel free to call Clifford later, Susan."

"I hate to interrupt after a long day at school—even guidance counselors need a break."

"No problem. He's glad to help."

Mrs. Baxter nods and gathers her purse and order form.

Jessica starts in about the clothes. "Mama, we have to take back those jeans. Calvin Klein. It has to be Calvin Klein, or our lives are over."

"Consignment shop, Liz. Take them to the consignment shop. I wish I had," Mrs. Baxter says to the door as she closes it behind her.

"I refuse to pay that kind of money for blue jeans," Mama says.

"Mama, you don't understand. We cannot wear those jeans you bought. The other kids will make our lives miserable."

"They tore a new boy's shirt at the high school," I warn.

"Tore his shirt? Well." Mama pauses. "I haven't taken the tags off the jeans and I still have the receipts. But I'm not making any promises. Let's check out a consignment shop, first. We just might make it before closing."

"Used clothes, Mama?" Jessica says. "That's as bad as Wranglers. What if they can tell?"

We hop in the car and I call out the directions written on a junk mail envelope, while Mama drives too fast. She wants to catch the shop before it closes.

Jessica sits in the back seat with an anxious frown and crossed arms. "I'm not wearing anybody's old, sweaty clothes. I can tell you that right now."

Jessica refuses to get out of the car, so Mama and I go into the shop without her. A headless mannequin wearing a rust-colored skirt and blouse stands guard by the door.

"That's a great fall outfit, and it makes the shop look jazzy. I bet they won't give it up," Mama whispers. She fingers the sleeve of a blue silk suit, turns over the tag, drops it, and shakes her head. "Pret-ty, pret-ty, but not in the budget." We stroll toward the kids' rack.

I murmur, "Not much left. It looks like all the kids' clothes have been picked over."

"See," Mama says, "all your classmates probably got here ahead of us."

We step out of the shop and Jessica is outside leaning on our car looking hot and mortified—afraid someone will see us come out of a used clothes place.

A pink car squeals into the spot next to our car.

"That lady sells that makeup, doesn't she, Mama?" I ask.

"Yes, that lady sold a whole bunch of that makeup to earn that car, and that lady looks upset," Mama whispers.

She's right. The woman throws open her door. Her high heels pound the pavement like she's trying to break it up. Two girls sit in the foundation-colored car screaming and wailing.

"What are you doing, Mother? Mother, you can't do this to us!"

"Mother! This is so stupid!"

The angry lady's nostrils flare. "You ungrateful, demanding, selfish, spoiled 'outfits.' You two are going to hear me now." She stomps to the car's trunk, opens it and takes out an armload of bright colors and denim blue. Her sprayed-stiff big hair looks like a helmet as she storms up the sidewalk. Mama and I step aside.

She sees us. "You here after clothes?"

"Nooo, Mother. We'll be good!" the sisters wail.

"You bet your sweet hind ends you will be good!" the lady calls back.

Jessica's eyes are huge. She looks from the mother to the girls who look back at Jessica with angry, resentful eyes.

"What are you looking at?" the older one says.

The woman turns to my mother and shoves the whole

pile into her arms. "Here take these. You'll save me a trip, and I won't be able to come back and get them." The woman stomps back to the car and hollers at the car window, "You better hush, or I'm taking the stereo and TV to Goodwill. Next stop, Kmart!"

The squalls and wails fade away as the pink car rushes down the street. Mama looks at this armload of clothes like it could have something dangerous or catching. Cursed clothing.

CHAPTER TEN

We round the corner and we all look toward the Baxters' house. Nobody's home yet.

"I hope Audrey's okay," Jessica says.

Mama takes a deep breath and pauses, an odd, long pause. "Yeah, me too. Gather up the loot—that's what it feels like—the spoils of war."

Jessica carries the jeans and I take the rest and pile them on the dining room table. Mama splurged on take-out and she frowns at the tacos like she's having second thoughts.

Daddy shakes his head when we tell him about the crazed pink car lady.

"I feel so guilty, Clifford. Like we're taking advantage."

"Sounds to me like the woman knew what she wanted."

"I'm going to call the shop and see if they know where or how I can reach her."

Jessica is pawing through the jeans, and she stops and whispers, "Nooo, Mama."

Daddy shrugs. "I'm not sure what that's going to accomplish, but go ahead, if it'll make you feel any better."

Mama's coral-nailed finger pulls the telephone dial around again and again, and Jessica hugs the jeans to her chest. I scoot my chair over, so I can hear all I can.

Mama says, "Hello, I was just at your shop and a woman… Yes, she had a Mary Kay car."

I don't need to be up close. Neither does Jessica. Mama holds the receiver out from her ear.

"Lady, do *not* bring those clothes back here. You keep them. We've done gone through this before and we are not doing it again. If the clothes are gone, we do not have to deal with those women. Enjoy." And then a click.

Jessica grabs a pair of jeans and a dark red blouse and heads for our room before our parents can change their minds. Mama squints at the label on another pair. I can see CK stitched on the hip pocket.

"I think these are all going to be too long, Becky, but you can try a pair."

Mama's almost right. They're only a little too long, but they squish me too much. No give at all. I can wear 'em, but that's about all I can do in them. I hand the jeans right back.

"You can *have* those britches." I say.

Jessica comes back looking pleased. Her hands stroke the letters on the hip pockets.

Daddy says, "Turn around." He shakes his head. "They'll do for a little while, but you're almost too big."

"That's the way they wear them, Daddy."

"That's the way some people wear them—not a Ramey girl."

"And that burgundy blouse is a bit mature," Mama says. "I'll set it aside for later."

"You could wear it." Daddy says.

"Yes, I could." The corners of Mama's eyes crinkle in a smile. "We really ought to share some of this with Susan and Audrey."

Jessica gasps in protest, but Mama holds out the palm of her hand.

"Stop right there, Miss Greedy, you do not need all these clothes."

Jessica huffs and grabs the phone, "I'm going to call and tell Beth." She starts in telling her friend all about the mom and the girls. "I'm not kidding. Calvin Klein and some blouses. Oh, yeah, Audrey barfed all over her bathroom when we got..."

Mama snaps, "Jessica, you do not need to go telling other people's business."

Jessica frowns, makes her ponytail swish, and her blue eyes roll. "I'll call you later, Beth."

She starts to snatch an embroidered chambray shirt from me, but Mama grabs it and holds it up to my shoulders. "Share. Becky gets some too."

"Blue's not her color," Jessica says.

"This blue is everybody's color. Maybe *I'll* need to take some clothes back to that shop." Mama takes a blouse and folds it.

Jessica looks down. "Sorry."

"That's better," Daddy says.

Daddy's tie is undone, and his jacket is rumpled. He leans back, and sips iced tea from a Taco Bell glass.

"How was your day?" Mama asks.

"The usual. Crazy, but more of it. Kid tried to change his schedule—not with us—by himself. Tried to white out the classes he didn't want and type in new ones."

"That's bold," Mama says.

"Uh-huh. And it almost worked."

The phone rings and Mama lifts the receiver just ahead of Jessica. "Susan, I was just thinking of you. We just got the most unbelievable . . . yes, Cliff is here." Mama raises surprised eyebrows and looks at Daddy. "Sure, he'll be right over." She shrugs. "Susan would like to talk to you, Clifford." They walk to the door whispering.

Jessica takes off with another pair of jeans and my chambray shirt, and I'm right after her. One good yank on that blond ponytail and I get my shirt back. "Don't you do that again," I warn. Jessica slings me down on my bed, but I have a death grip on my blouse. "I'll tell!" I grab a pair of jeans off the floor and whip them at Jessica's bare leg.

"Ouch! You brat! You're so selfish. I just wanted to try it on."

I tell her, "No way, Jose."

The phone rings and Mama calls out, "Becky?"

I go to the kitchen, still hugging my embroidered shirt.

"Becky, Daddy needs you to take his address book to him at the Baxter's." Mama looks serious. I know not to ask questions. "Come right on back."

"Save me some tops, Mama."

Jessica crosses her eyes and wrinkles her nose at me behind Mama's back.

I put my shirt into Mama's hand. "Take care of this for me, please." I give an I-showed-you look to my sister.

Mama gives Jessica a pair of Vanderbilt jeans. "Go try on these, Jess." I think Mama wants to dodge questions. Jessica's too jeans-crazy to even notice. She's under a spell.

CHAPTER ELEVEN

I can see my dad through the window screen. The careful, concerned way he leans forward and listens to Mrs. Baxter makes my heart speed up a little. I know he'll never tell me what's wrong with Audrey.

Audrey's my friend, so I slip up and listen. I am a quiet girl. That's how I know things my parents don't expect me to know. I hold what I know closely like a little bird or kitten, so adults cannot see it or hear it. Folks can't hear my heart beat fast, and they won't hear me cry.

I can't see Mrs. Baxter, but I can hear her angry voice. "Help? Markam called and informed me he'd help her get an abortion, but that's all he'd do. Billy's talented and nothing can stall his football career. Besides, he says, she has a choice now. Audrey can get an education. They can have a real life. Like he really cares. She can't marry him. That's not happening." Her voice grows tight and squeaky. "Besides he says Billy doesn't want to—who's to say he's the daddy?"

Audrey's mom sobs for a good while, and Dad asks a question I can't make out. I'm hearing what they're saying, but it's like hearing a news report about some people far away. Some girl somewhere is pregnant, and I'm sorry for her, but I can't quite take in that it's Audrey.

Susan's voice grows stronger, more frantic. "To tell the truth I can't see any other way. We're broke, dead broke. It's not cheap dressing a cheerleader. People expect things. I didn't want this divorce to ruin her life, make her live poor. I'm in over my head. One more month and we could be evicted."

Dad tries again. "Have you thought about talking to Billy's mother? Maybe she'd be more helpful."

"Oh, she's been out of the picture a long time. Don't feel sorry for her. She and Markam are pretty much cut out of the same bolt of cloth. She took the little girl and left when Billy was seven. I'm sorry for him, but I did everything I could to keep Billy and Audrey apart. I forbid her to ride in his car to school, so he just started riding the bus with her."

My dad looks down for a moment and then says, "Have you called Audrey's father?"

"I'd rather die. He'll blame me, but he won't help." Susan laughs, but there's nothing happy about it. "Who do you think arranged our divorce? Markam. Heck, he does his own family dirty. His brother's children are living like refugees. Beth Markam rides the bus. Your girls probably know her."

Dad's address book slips from my sweaty hand like a slippery fish and hits the porch. Thump! Dad's head jerks around and his eyes open wider, and then my dad makes his face look calm and professional. I better play along.

"Ah, Susan. Becky's here with my address book. Excuse me a minute."

Daddy steps out onto the crumbling concrete step and puts his arm around my shoulder. "Thank you for bringing this. Let Mama know I'll be home in a minute." Daddy ushers me across the street. "Rebecca, we'll talk later. These people are in a real spot and they need to feel their business stays their business. Got it?"

I nod. "Jessica already told Beth that Audrey barfed."

Daddy frowns. "Hmmm." He pauses. "Don't say anything to your sister, and we'll talk more about what you've heard. I'm depending on you Rebecca Jane Ramey." He squeezes my shoulder and I know he needs me to help him. I won't say one word to my sister, no matter what she does or how much she begs.

I watch my dad until he opens the Baxter's green door and I think, *I won't let you down.* I cross the street and walk to our house, feeling strong and important.

And then I hear her whisper. "Becky, Becky. Over here." Audrey crouches by our next-door neighbor's fire thorn bush.

I look around and then join her behind the shrub, doing my best to avoid the wicked spikes. Audrey sits leaning against the brick with the swaying orange berries hanging over her head. If she moves only a little, one of those thorns could tear her cheek. "I guess you heard them arranging my life for me."

I don't want to say anything wrong. It seems right to just sit by her for a moment. I look at her from the corner of my eye. "Do you feel okay, Audrey?"

"I feel stupid." She lays her hand on my arm. "Don't ever be this stupid, Becky." Audrey hugs her knees to her chest and leans her head forward and cries.

I put my arm around her. "Don't cry, you're my new neighbor."

That makes her smile a little. Audrey straightens, dabs her eyes dry with a moist wad of tissue, wipes her nose, and pats my hand. "Becky, do you think I could use your phone—alone?"

"Sure."

"I'm going to need some privacy."

My scalp prickles and I'm not sure why. "Okay."

"Check and see if your mother is busy."

I feel funny about going and checking, and I can't think why it should matter. I can hear Mama's sewing machine in the back room. Jessica's singing along with her *Sound of Music* record.

I return to Audrey, and she jumps when I speak. "Nobody's using the phone."

"And your mom and sister?"

"They're busy."

"Where's your phone?"

Why doesn't she just come inside and see?

I feel like I'm passing on dangerous information. "There's

one in our kitchen and one in the living room."

"Maybe I'd be out of your way in the living room," Audrey suggests.

Audrey enters our front door silently, and it seems wrong to not follow her example, but it feels dangerous to be quiet. I point to the living room phone and Audrey nods. "Let me know if anyone's coming. I won't be long, and I don't want to put your folks out."

I feel weird, but Dad said their business needs to stay their business. I stand in the little entryway, standing guard, yet overhearing Audrey dialing the phone.

"Billy? . . . What do you mean, 'what am I going to do?'" I glance over. Her eyebrows jolt upward. "What are you talking about? Grant is Theresa's brother—of course he's always at her house." Audrey's fingers rake back her long hair. "When have I ever lied to you? You're the only. . ." Her fist tightens around her hair at the base of her neck. "Is that what you think of me?" Her hand releases the ponytail like it became something disgusting. "No. No, don't bother. I'll take care of myself."

Audrey's leans back in the chair and closes her streaming eyes. "I gotta think, I gotta think." She sits up, rubs her neck, and dials again. "Theresa? No, Mom doesn't know where I am. She did? What did my mom say? Did your mother look for me?" Audrey chews her bottom lip and wraps the cord around her finger.

"That's right. She won't check again." Audrey glances up at me and then shifts her body away. "I'll meet you there."

Audrey gets up and walks to me. "Becky, I have to step out for a while. If my mom calls over here, tell her I said I'll be okay." Audrey leans down, brushes my hair back, and smiles at me until I smile back. I feel like there's something I should do, but I don't know what it is. Audrey's eyes look up and past me. "Hi, Mrs. Ramey. I just borrowed your phone. The house is really coming together."

"Thanks." Mama looks concerned, but she doesn't know what to do either. "Audrey, is there anything I can do for you?"

"No, Mrs. Ramey. Just the phone. Thanks." Audrey turns

and waves at us as she steps back to her house.

Mama stands, rubbing her shoulder for a moment and then closes the door when Audrey steps onto her porch.

Mama puts me to work, taking out the stitches from a crooked hem. Twenty minutes later, Daddy and Mrs. Baxter rush through into the kitchen.

Susan braces herself against the doorjamb. "Please tell me she is over here."

CHAPTER TWELVE

Mama's horrified expression is all that Susan Baxter needs to see. Her girl is gone.

"Susan, she came here and used the phone and then she left. I watched Audrey go back to your house."

Mrs. Baxter closes her eyes, biting her lip. Daddy stands with one hand on her shoulder and with a crease on his forehead that grows deeper.

Mama says, "She was talking to Becky when I walked in."

I look down at the dull gold floor tiles, and I feel like everyone is looking at me.

Mr. Wright steps in. "Pardon me for not knocking." He looks at Daddy. "I've looked all around both homes. She's not here."

Daddy nods. "Liz, what's Jessica doing?"

"Her homework. She's got quite a bit."

"Tell her you're across the street." Dad sweeps the air with one hand. "Seeing about Tupperware—something. We'll talk about this over there. Rebecca, come with us."

Once we're in her living room, Mrs. Baxter sits forward in a green chair, and looks at me as though I might know the only thing that will get her daughter back.

Daddy sits on her worn couch and I sit facing him, nibbling at a cuticle.

"Don't chew your nails, Becky. What did you and Audrey

talk about?"

I sit on my hands and keep them there. "I was going home, and I heard her whisper my name."

We hear the door open and all look over—it's my Mom.

I look back at my Dad. His hand is gentle on my arm, but his eyes don't blink, and they don't smile.

I try to swallow, but my mouth is dry. "Audrey was behind that sticker shrub next door to us."

Daddy looks up at the ceiling. "She was hiding, Becky. Didn't that tell you something?"

"Clifford," Mama murmurs.

"She was upset." Tears ooze and hang on my lower lashes. "She said you all were arranging her life and she wanted to use the phone." I lean forward and whisper. "You said their business needed to stay their business."

Mr. Wright squats down beside me. "You did good, Becky. You did good." He pats my knee. "Who did Audrey talk to? Do you know?"

"Well, first she called Billy, and they argued about her telling the truth and then she told him she'd take care of herself and hung up."

Mr. Wright nods his bristly flattop and smiles, approving. "And then?"

"She called Theresa, and I think Theresa said Mrs. Baxter had called her mom, and then Audrey said she'd meet her—Theresa—somewhere." I look over at my dad and his eyes are closed and he's shaking his head. I blew it. "Audrey told me to tell her mom she's okay and that she was just stepping out."

Mr. Wright slaps his knee and we all jump. "Well, there you are. She's at Theresa's. The old cop stands up and says, "Susan, Audrey knows you've called there before and she figures you won't call there again."

"Should I try to go get her?"

"No, let her cool down. You trust Theresa's people?"

"Oh, yes."

"Then let her stay. Thirty years on the force—I've seen it

over and over. Believe me, she'll be back."

I escape the couch and stand by my mom. I lean my head against her shoulder and say, "I'm sorry."

Mama strokes my hair, and whispers, "Why didn't you tell me?"

"I didn't think there was anything to tell. We watched her go home."

Mama takes in a sharp breath. "Well, that's right."

"Liz, can I show you something?" Mrs. Baxter asks. She's holding a beautiful peach and ivory dress with embroidered ribbon on the sleeves. The bodice laces up like it would on a gown from a fairy tale.

My mother touches a cuff. "Cluny lace."

"Audrey would look like a princess in this," I say.

Mrs. Baxter smiles and tears up again. "Yes, she would." Miz Susan looks at my mom. "I found this pinned to the dress when I checked her room. Do you think this could mean anything?"

Mama reads the note. "Take it back! I won't need it!"

"After Billy's dad called, I tried to tell her she should just move on. She could still have her life, her homecoming." Mrs. Baxter swallows. "I showed her this—I just couldn't resist buying it. She got so angry. Said I shouldn't have spent the money, and she's right. It's a sad thing when the child is more responsible than the mother."

Mama looks at the note and puts her hand to her mouth. She looks at Mrs. Baxter's anxious face. "I don't think it means...anything." And she glances down at me. "She wouldn't have made plans with her friend if...you know. But let's show it to Mr. Wright and Clifford."

My parents send me back home, and I know I won't hear another thing about Audrey from them. I let them down. I decide to forget the homework and just get in bed. I hear Mama and Daddy when they come back from the Baxter's, but they don't even come say good night

※ ※ ※

It's been three days. First day nobody on the bus notices that Audrey's gone, but after that the crazy rumors start. Some people say Audrey eloped with a college guy. Billy's ears turn bright red and he says, "Who? What college guy?"

Bus gets real quiet after that. Beth raises her eyebrows and whispers to my sister, "Theresa's brother Grant goes to college."

Some kids say a serial killer got Audrey. Jessica doesn't think that's true, and I *know* it isn't true, but it sure gives me the shivers. Theresa overheard the talk and yelled, "Shut up! Don't be stupid. Nobody kidnapped anybody." I guess she doesn't want to hear it anymore, because she told the bus driver that her mother's going to drive her for a while.

Billy stayed away from the bus for a day, but today he rides it home singing nasty songs about women who do guys wrong.

Kenny's tired of it, and he stands up and yells, "You shut up, Billy. Audrey was a nice girl!"

I whisper, "She *is* a nice girl, Kenny."

Nobody wants to risk saying anything else. It's all too sad and awful. We all sit hushed the whole route, thinking scary, lonely thoughts.

And I can't breathe a word of what I know—not even to my sister.

CHAPTER THIRTEEN

"Rebecca, you've just got to be more positive." Daddy's late for work, because Mama made him stay for this talking-to. His knee is jiggling up and down and shaking the whole kitchen table. "What do you mean, your new school stinks? What don't you like there?"

I stare at my spoon as I stir my milk and cereal. Where do I start?

"Mrs. Goforth's concerned."

"She doesn't like me. The kids are bad in my class. She thinks I'm bad too. The only reason she called is she found out you're a school counselor."

"You don't know that."

Daddy doesn't want to hear it, but I know I'm right.

"Mrs. Goforth says part of the problem is that you don't copy down your homework instructions."

You'd have to be able to hear the directions to write them down; Mrs. Goforth won't repeat them, and I can't see the ones in the far corner of the blackboard. If you ask for them again, she looks at you with eyes as black and spiteful as a wasp's—the same temper too.

"Have you made any friends, Becky?" Mama rests her chin in her hand and glances at Daddy.

Audrey. I made friends with Audrey. I shrug, and Mama looks down and her hand covers her mouth. My mama makes friends fast. I disappoint her.

"Do you sit with anybody on the bus?"

"With Jessica until she made friends with those eighth-grade girls."

"You didn't sit with her back home, before."

"I didn't have to. I sat with Tabby." I look up from my cereal at my parents and then I look away. I feel like there's a wrestling match inside of me. My mean blaming side versus my loser side. The blamer says it's Daddy and Mama's fault I'm lonesome. The loser knows that I'm to blame. I'm the only reason this move isn't just perfect. Daddy loves his new job. Mama loves her first house. Jessica loves her new choir and her new friends. I don't love anything here; I'm a loser.

"Who do you sit with at lunch?"

I stare at the sugar bowl like an answer might crawl out from under the lid. I don't want to say I sit at the Nobody table. That's where you go when nobody knows you or wants to sit with you.

"Oh, Becky." Mama brushes my hair back from my face.

"Becky, it's not going to get better unless you try."

I open my mouth, but Daddy holds up his hand. "Don't tell me what you can't do. Look for what you can do." I stare ahead at the sugar bowl and press my lips together hard until they hurt.

Daddy stops and takes a deep breath. I feel his big hand gently grasping mine. "All we ask you to do is try. Today, before you come home, I want you to do three things: come back with the name of one kid, write down tonight's assignment, and Mama says you have a book report coming up. Go to the library and pick up a book."

"I'll try, Daddy."

"You go out there and have a great day and do us a good job." Daddy sounds like a coach trying to rev up a losing team. *Do us a good job.* He couldn't have made a harder assignment.

Jessica comes rushing through to grab her books, and I'm glad for the interruption. "Come on, Becky. The bus will be here in five minutes." Jessica likes to say bye and rush out early so the other kids won't see our parents. Our folks are okay, I guess, but we're too big to need them around. I feel better if I know Mama's looking out the window—just to be on the safe side. Aunt Louise keeps sending clippings about serial killers and kidnappers and that kind of makes a person edgy.

Mama can't resist giving one more order. She calls out the door, "Becky—you find that girls' restroom and use it. You're going to make yourself sick holding it all day."

"Mama!" Jessica and I fuss at the same time.

"The whole bus could hear you." Jessica rushes away to the bus stop so no one knows this is our house.

While we stand waiting for the bus to roll up, Jessica grabs my shoulder and turns me around. "Good gravy, Becky. Your tag's hanging out. Can't you dress yourself? You're gonna embarrass me to death." Jessica tucks in the tag and grabs for my arm, but I twist away.

"Quit it, Jessie."

She frowns, looking me over. "Well, at least your stockings match your skirt." She straightens the collar on her knit shirt—what a priss—and strokes the little embroidered alligator, her coolness insurance. She doesn't know Mama recycled the alligator from a Goodwill bargain and put it on a Brand X shirt.

The bus rolls up and Jessica climbs on first. I'm praying for a decent seat. No such luck. Beth and another girl I've seen, but don't know, wave at Jessica and scoot over to give her room to sit. No seats left up front. That means I must get past Kenny and Chad and sit a lot closer to the stupid, loud, rowdy boys than I care for. Just as I'm almost to the last empty seat, Chad sticks out his leg and I go sprawling. Books, binders, papers fly out from my opened backpack and under seats. The boys laugh mean, barking laughs, but a ninth-grade girl tells them to shut up and helps me gather my stuff and jam it all back in my book bag. It's a moment or two before I can check the damage. My skirt is dirty and there are big holes in the knees of my pink stockings opening wide like a wailing baby's mouth.

"You boys knock it off now." Our bus driver glares at the boys one by one. "I've thrown boys off this bus before and I'll do it again. Chad, you're on report right now."

Jessica and her friends storm over to check on me and the bus driver says, "You're going to have to sit down now, girls."

"Yes, sir. We're coming." Jessica looks at my legs frowning. "Can't you watch where you're going? Well, you'll just have to go to the girls' room and take those ruined stockings off." She rushes off shaking her head like it's my fault. At least she slaps the back of Chad's sorry head on the way back. He won't tell on her, because her friends' narrowed eyes dare him to say a word.

When Frank gets on the bus he frowns at my wrecked clothes. "Are you okay, kid?"

I shrug. "Yeah." No point in whining.

"Stinks, doesn't it?" Frank mutters. He sits across the aisle and stares out the window. He has his own troubles.

I limp to my class and drop off my book bag. I don't want to, but I go over to my teacher's desk. "Mrs. Goforth, I fell on the bus. I have to go to the girls' room, please."

Mrs. Goforth sighs and looks up at the ceiling like I just ruined my hose to personally inconvenience her. "Well, go on and hurry up."

Trouble is, I have no idea where the restrooms are, and I don't want to ask. I walk down the green-tiled hallway, doing my best to look like I know what I'm doing. I spot the water fountain and I figure the restrooms must be close by and I'm right. I rush into the first one, and I stop and stare. There are a couple of the oddest-looking contraptions on the wall I've ever seen. They're not sinks and they're not potties.

Someone behind me clears his throat. "They're called urinals." It's a tanned, skinny boy from my class.

I about jump out of my skin, tear out of the boys' room and dash for the girls' room. All I can do there for a second is cry. I will never ever hear the end of this. Rebecca Jane Ramey almost used the boys' restroom. I don't think my life can get any more miserable than this. I peel off the shredded stockings and wipe down my scraped knees. I wash off my face and look tough at my red eyes in the mirror. I may have to go back into that hateful classroom, but nobody will see me cry.

My bare feet already feel sweaty and nasty in my shoes, but I march down the hallway like I mean to face down anybody who dares make a smart remark. I stand in the classroom doorway frowning so hard I can see my eyebrows. Nobody even looks up. I slip back to my seat glancing at each face on the way. No smirks, no giggles. The tan skinny boy is busy pawing through his pencil case like he doesn't know I'm here. I ease into my seat and my language arts book is open at today's assignment. Who got that out for me? Doesn't matter, because Chad knocks it off on his way to the tissue box.

Mrs. Goforth's wandering through the room, hovering like a hornet ready to strike. "Do you all have nothing but cotton between your ears? Everyone should have had their thank-you letter homework out long ago." She leans over my desk and pulls my work over, and then pushes it away, when she sees my letter's all done.

Would you be happier if I hadn't done it? I think. I'd like to write her a thank-you note. *Thanks for my queasy stomach and my headache at the end of the day. Thanks for helping me with my torn stockings. Thanks for the clear directions. Thanks for nothing.*

Nobody else has written the notes, but the good front-seat girls. The bad or dumb or quiet kids sit in the back and most of them spend the period copying work while Mrs. Goforth teaches the front-seat people. I usually hide my work and turn it in at the end of class, so none of the boys pesters me into letting him copy it. Sometimes I forget to turn my homework in at all. Maybe that's why I'm in the back with the jerks and dummies and a boy named Patrick who eats his own boogers.

I take the eraser tip of my pencil and draw barrel racing clover leaves with it on my desktop. Daddy promised we'd go to a rodeo or Cowtown, but now he says we're too broke or he's too busy. I remember his orders and scrawl the homework on my forearm before we pack up.

The bell rings and everybody rushes out because they're glad to leave Mrs. Goforth, and then slow down because they remember it's PE.

CHAPTER FOURTEEN

Kids avoid Mrs. Goforth because she's mean, but we're flat scared of Miss Powers. She is tall, taller than Daddy, taller than the boys' basketball coach. She stands by the gym door with her big blond curls and big nose and big blue eyes that don't miss a thing. I look at her standing as cool and calm as a statue with her clipboard and I realize all that's missing is a torch and spiky crown. Miss Powers looks just like the Statue of Liberty.

We change into gym clothes and line up. The boys and the girls are together today. Miss Powers announces, "Listen up. Boys' gym teacher is out sick. Mr. Parks planned dodge ball for you boys today, so it's what we will all play. But it's going to be played my way. No head shots, no hard hits, or you're out. If you're hit below the waist or somebody catches your ball, no whining or arguing—you're out. I've got plenty of locker room chores for people who can't play by the rules."

Chad doesn't have anything to lose. He's already in trouble over the bus. He makes sure I see his nasty I'm-gonna-get-you smile as he shoves past me on the gym floor. We're on opposite sides and he thinks he's gonna give the new kid some more trouble.

My team lines up waiting for the balls to hit. Most of us dodge the first round, but a sleepy-looking girl seems to run right into a ball so she can get it over with and go sit on the bleachers.

Kenny aims and hits two girls who are busy talking. "I got two at once!"

One by one, kids are hit or must sit down because someone catches a ball. Soon we're down to two girls and Kenny and Chad.

Chad throws a hard, fast ball at me. I dodge the ball, but it hits the dark-haired girl behind me and leaves a big red spot above her knee. She stumbles to the sidelines. Chad nods at me and takes aim again, but I step aside. He and Kenny team up on me. They throw, and I dodge—every time. Kenny's ball whizzes by my cheek. Chad reaches way back, and I can tell they've agreed to aim for my head. I run toward the ball, catch it, and heave it right into Chad's belly.

He drops to the floor and sucks for air like a beached fish.

Miss Powers strides over to Fish Boy and sets him on a bench so he can catch his breath. He sounds just like a circus seal. I've got a month of locker room chores ahead of me, I'm sure.

Miss Powers looks at me. "Rebecca, you must be playing by East Texas rules. Here we switch sides before we begin launching the ball at the other team. We'll let it go for this time. I think we're all learning some new rules today, aren't we, Chad? Like, don't underestimate your opposition?" I didn't think statues could smile, but I swear I think I see a corner of Miss Liberty's mouth curl up a little. "Game's over. Everybody get cleaned up." She helps Chad stand and has Kenny help him to the boys' side.

I can hear the girls whispering in the locker room.

"Did you see her throw? I think she's mean," says Amy.

The dark-haired girl disagrees. "Chad, had it coming—look at my leg."

"Well, I'm just saying, she's quiet, but watch out. I saw her giving dirty looks to everyone in the entire classroom."

They fall silent as I walk around the corner.

The lunch bell rings at 11:00—way too early if you ask

me. I don't even want to look at what they put on my tray. One lady puts down a crispy corn dog and golden tater tots, but the next one slops green beans all over them. Back home the cafeteria ladies would keep all the dry food separate from the sloppy food. Plus, they would give me an extra roll, because they know I love them just like my daddy did. I'm not back home, so I keep my mouth shut and head for my seat in the Nobody zone.

I walk past the popular girl table. It is shiny, and the girls laugh and chatter while they sit there. They stop talking when I pass. The beat-up Nobody table is in the far corner of the cafetorium. I don't think it gets wiped down much. Grease coats the surface like sadness.

I hear a tray clatter down across the table from me. It's the tan, skinny boy. He always wears an old pale blue Western shirt, three sizes too big for him over his T-shirt. When the wind catches it, the shirt billows out and looks like a ghost chasing him.

He forks a green bean and looks at me. "Do you always tour all the restrooms in a building?"

I glare at him over the soggy tater tots.

"Don't worry. I won't tell anybody." The boy pauses. "Good shot in PE. Chad won't try that again."

"Thanks. He'll get back at me sometime, I'm sure."

"Maybe not. Next time he chooses sides, he'll be sure to pick you to be on *his* team."

"I thought I'd get in trouble. Miss Powers is cool."

"She's better than cool. She's magnificent. She's like a Greek goddess. Like . . ."

"The Statue of Liberty."

"Yeah—just like that. Good observation, Rocket Launcher. Rocket Launcher Ramey, I'm Rusty, Rusty Burnet."

"Why do you wear that shirt? It's nice and all," I lied. "I just see it a lot."

The tan boy flushes darker. "It's my brother's. I miss him. He's in the county jail."

"I'm sorry."

"It's okay. It could be worse. He may only get manslaughter. At least our mom doesn't get harassed and troubled anymore." Rusty pulls out an old paperback Western and flips through its pages. "You like Louis L'Amour?"

"I don't read much."

"You oughta try . . . uh-oh. We better move—food fight's about to start. That stringy-haired teacher on duty never learns." Rusty shoves his book into my hand.

A stray tater tot hits our table and another hits Rusty's shirt and slides down into his pocket. Kenny smacks my blouse with a handful of slimy green beans. Mrs. Goforth's hand-out-of-nowhere catches Rusty's wrist as he gets ready to lob a mustardy corndog across the room.

"Everybody, *everybody* who has any food whatsoever in their hands will march to the office now. Hold your hands out!" Mrs. Goforth demands. "You too, Rebecca Ramey. I see those green beans."

"But I was just wiping them off my blouse."

"You heard me." A teacher shouldn't sound so satisfied at a time like this.

I guess they called home, because Daddy came and picked me up.

"Well, Rebecca, you have certainly made an impression today. On the good side, Miss Powers wants you on her basketball team, and a cafeteria lady spoke up for you. On the other hand," Daddy pauses and puts his hands on the steering wheel. "Sugar, you look like a wreck. Did anything good happen today?"

"I knocked the wind out of the boy who made me fall and ruin my stockings. Nailed him right in the belly in PE."

Daddy sighs and lets his head fall back against the headrest. "Did you do *anything* Mother and I asked you to do today?"

I take a deep breath. "I went to the restroom today—the boys' *and* the girls'. I wrote my homework assignment down on my forearm. I met a boy named Rusty—his brother is in the county jail. Oh, and here's a book: *Heller with a Gun.* By Louis L'Amour."

Daddy leans his head forward onto the steering wheel a moment, then sits up straight and breathes in deep. "Well, then. We can't call this day a total loss."

CHAPTER FIFTEEN

"I'm going to take you on home, but I have to run by my office first, okay?" Daddy says as he puts the car into gear. I look at my daddy out of the corner of my eye. He's showing a little gray above the Ramey square jaw, but at least he doesn't have a big belly yet. On the bus, Theresa told us that the high school girls like to watch him jog on the track after school. "Your Dad's cute," she said. I don't want to hear that.

Jessica said, "Gross. Y'all are crazy. You don't know what we know. He makes the bathroom stink."

Daddy turns the steering wheel and cruises over to the high school. He pulls into the farthest staff parking spot in the hot sun. Daddy sees me glance back at the shady parking places and grins. "New guy gets the hot spot."

"How about a soda from the teacher's lounge?" Dad asks. He strides to a door and says, "Wait outside so you don't alarm the teachers." Daddy whispers, "They're afraid students will uncover all their darkest secrets if kids are allowed in. Coke okay?"

Soon Daddy hands me a cold bottle and we head to his office. I sit in the student chair and look around his new room, while he flips through papers on his desk. Some things look the same as his old office. Daddy still has a Texas state flag and his Texas A&M diploma on his wall.

"Where's your Aggie brick, Daddy?" Uncle Richie painted a brick maroon and lettered "Aggie Bowling Ball" in white and gave it to my dad one Christmas.

Daddy lifts it off a stack of papers and sets it back down without looking up. "Never figured out how a die-hard Republican like Richie could root for the University of Texas and not for the Aggies." My granddaddy says TU is nothing but a nest of wimps and liberal Democrats. They're still mighty fierce football rivals.

Daddy's phone rings. "Clifford Ramey, speaking. Ah, Mrs. Russell." Daddy waves me away and I know to go outside to the chairs by the secretary's desk.

I sit and the cracked orange vinyl on the worn chair pinches my leg. I'm alone because the secretary is at the copier. Nobody's business must stay too private here, because I can still hear Daddy.

"Mrs. Russell, had you thought about Texas A&M for Roger? Well, sure, Prairie View A&M would have some fine opportunities for . . . Sure, there are other schools as well. I'll do some checking and get back with you. I hear a click and then "Man!" Daddy gets up and goes to the office next to his. "Hank, I consider myself an insightful counselor for my minority kids, but today I cannot win. This mother just called me and chewed me out for not suggesting a historically African American institution for her son. This morning I got blistered *for* suggesting a historically black college."

"We shouldn't assume, Clifford."

Dad looks up sharply, then sighs, and nods.

Hank's deep voice chuckles. "We are not necessarily meant to win with any parent—ever. "Just ask them what they want, give it to them if you can, do your best by the kid, and know you still may lose. Oh, yeah. Don't forget your duty with Carl."

Daddy steps out of the man's office and mutters under his breath, "New kid on the block gets all the fun jobs." I get up and watch in the guidance office doorway as my father jogs down the hall to a classroom and returns escorting a pouting, greasy-headed boy. The boy drags his heels as they walk to a frowning, unshaven man waiting in a car right outside the school entrance. I see the new boy, Frank, from my bus, and he and the boy nod at each other. Frank's bushy hair looks greasy too.

"Can't that boy go anywhere by himself?" I ask when my dad returns.

"Evidently not," Daddy says. "Not without getting in trouble. Gather up your books. I think we can leave now. I'll just grab my stuff."

The secretary rushes back from the copier and is furiously stapling papers, when a tall pale kid in a button-up shirt walks up to her desk. "I have an appointment with Mr. Ramey. My folks should be here."

Dad comes out of his office. "Ah, Tim, you're here. Are you ready for this?" Daddy looks at me and whispers, "This shouldn't take too long."

A lady with fluffy blond hair steps into the office, all business. I get a whiff of overpowering Emeraude cologne as she breezes by. She is gripping a calendar notebook and is wearing those weird upside-down-looking glasses with the temple pieces attached down at the bottom of huge lenses. Her feathery hair is all in a ruffle around her head, but fiery eyes swim behind those huge lenses—kinda like a cutesy poodle that'll bite the first chance it gets. She glances back and sighs at the tall man behind her. "Are you coming? Come on!"

Dad greets them. "Mrs. And Mrs. Agnew? I'm Clifford Ramey."

The slender boy stares ahead like he knows he's facing a battle. An older lady in a hippie blouse enters the office, and she catches the boy's attention and he smiles a little. The mom sniffs and shakes her head. Whatever her deal is, she doesn't like that old lady teacher.

Daddy ushers them all into his office and closes the door, but the sound still carries. "Tim, let's begin with you. What are your goals for today?"

"Less hassle . . . less of everything. I want to drop student council, All the AP courses except for Mrs. Lawson's. Probably tennis and maybe track. And I am sorry, Mom but I am dropping band."

"You are dropping out of everything during your senior year. What about those universities? What about our goals?"

"You mean your goals, Mom. I am tired. I am done. My knee is shot. My stomach's a wreck, and I'm only in the first nine weeks."

"You have got to be kidding me."

"I either drop stuff . . . or I could just drop out of high school period, Mom."

"Mrs. Agnew, what is your big goal for your son?"

The smell of cigarette smoke begins drifting into the waiting room along with the high reek of Emeraude. "Pardon me, my nerves. I want him to have a successful career . . . and to receive a degree from the best university to put him there."

"He's just come out of the hospital and is recovering."

"Yes." The mom seems irritated.

"Mrs. Lawson, you have stated that Tim will be able to make up the summer work for AP English, but that he needs some margin to do so."

"Correct."

The mother breaks in, "It seems to me that Mrs. Lawson just needs to adjust her expectations for busy students."

"Let's not get off track. Pardon me, while I open the window. I hear Tim saying he needs some margin in his life. And he feels these activities need to go away to achieve that. And according to the doctor's note, this seems to be the doctor's opinion as well. Maybe if Tim can just drop a few of these activities, he'll find some relief."

"But the competition . . . the best universities are looking at full participation in every activity."

Dad interrupts, "The fine university that Tim has selected does not. They like what they see."

Tim's dad says, "I told you . . ."

Mrs. Agnew says, "I will be taking this to the board of education."

"You do what you need to do, ma'am. I think Tim and his health are telling us he wants and needs something different."

The angry lady stomps out of the office as her husband mouths "Sorry." Tim flashes two V for victory fingers as he goes by.

"Thank you, Cliff. Thank you," Mrs. Lawson says. "Hoping for the best."

"No problem, Miss Lawson." Dad's phone rings again. "Sorry, ladies. I swear, Becky this is the last thing."

Dad goes back to his desk and sits. He's so tired, he doesn't realize his door is open. "Oh, Debbie. Hi. Tomorrow's the big day."

Even from where I sit, I can hear the girl cry over the phone.

My dad says, "No, now don't worry. Yes, I'll be in the courtroom too. Don't worry. Don't let them buffalo you. Remember, you know what you know. Right?"

I don't know if she feels better, but I can't hear the girl's desperate voice anymore.

"All right. See you tomorrow."

I don't know who that girl Debbie is. I don't know what her troubles are, but she's lucky my daddy is on her side. I feel better for her just knowing that.

Daddy no sooner hangs up the phone than it rings again. "Hi, Liz. We're on our way." Daddy stops and draws in his breath. "Do they think it could be Audrey? I'll be right there."

Daddy gathers his stuff in a rush, and calls to the secretary, "Emma, I have to leave now. Take messages." Daddy lowers his voice. "Just tell Hank, it's an emergency."

CHAPTER SIXTEEN

"Daddy, is Audrey okay?" I can't keep the shakes out of my voice.

Daddy checks his rearview mirror and sighs. "I hope so, Becky. I don't know."

"Daddy, Audrey's a good girl."

"I'm sure she is." Daddy pushes the turn signal and frowns. "Look, Becky, I don't know what's going on. But the police have found . . . something. Mr. Wright wants Mama and me there while he talks to Mrs. Baxter. I want you to go home and stay there."

"Daddy, you better tell me if something's wrong."

"I will tell you."

Daddy glances over and sees the tears welling up. He reaches over and grasps my hand. "Sugar, it may be nothing."

"I'm praying for her, Daddy."

"That's good. You do that. I will too."

Mr. Wright is waiting for Daddy on our lawn when we pull in.

Daddy says, "Becky, go on in now and wait for us."

Mr. Wright talks way louder than he thinks he does—Daddy says the old cop is probably half deaf from hearing too much gunfire on the shooting range. I won't have to listen hard to know what he's saying.

Mr. Wright leads Daddy quickly across the street, hollering for the whole neighborhood to hear, "Clifford, an old buddy from the department called me. They've found the body of young woman in a trailer park."

Now I wish I were deaf. Daddy tries to shush him, but it's too late. I run inside, shut the door, and sit in the living room and hug an old flat throw pillow to myself and say over and over, "Please, don't let it be Audrey."

I hear the back door open and Jessica call out, "Mom? Where is everybody?" Her sandals click against the floor and then pad quietly on the worn carpet. "Becky. Where did you go today? You okay? Why'd you leave school?"

My eyes are squeezed shut, but I feel Jessica beside me. "Becky, what's wrong?"

I swallow hard. "Something's bad happened. A girl's dead. It might be Audrey."

"Wow." Jessica's forehead wrinkles up like she's scared but then my sister crosses her arms. "Well, she shouldn't have run off like that."

"Shut up, Jessica. Just shut up! You don't know what you're talking about." The phone rings and we about jump a mile.

Jessica and I both reach for the phone, but I wrestle it away from her. "Hello, Ramey residence."

"Becky? Is that you?" It's Audrey. I drop the receiver and then scramble to reel it in by the cord. "Becky, are you there?"

"Yes. Where *are* you? Are you okay?"

"Yes. I'm okay. I can't reach my mom—can you go get her? The phone's busy."

"Stay there. Stay there. Don't hang up. Promise me, you won't hang up?"

"Yes, Becky. Go!"

I tear across the street without looking, and Kenny almost sideswipes me with his bicycle. "Look out, Ramey! My granddaddy could still arrest you for jaywalking."

I pound on the Baxter's door.

Daddy and Mama open the door. Daddy glares at me, outraged and unbelieving. "What did I tell you, Rebecca? Go home and stay there!"

Mama says, "You get home now!"

"Mama, it's Audrey. Audrey's on our phone. She couldn't get through to her mom."

Mama and Daddy stand openmouthed as Mrs. Baxter pushes past them and runs to our house.

We all follow and gather about Audrey's mother and watch her face go from joy, to fear, to confusion. Mrs. Baxter hangs up the phone, stands for a moment, silent, and Mr. Wright puts his hand on her shoulder. "She's okay. Audrey hid out at different places, but she's safe now at her aunt's." She looks at my Mom. "Audrey says she's decided and she won't come home until her dad and I get things straight. She was at that trailer park, where they found that young girl. She saw the vans from the television stations—that's why she called. She didn't want me to worry." Mrs. Baxter collapses into my mother's arms.

※ ※ ※

Audrey means what she says. Her mom must cut up the credit cards and get a second job, and her daddy must pay more to help. They sat at our table and worked it all out. Daddy said our house was neutral like Switzerland. Audrey would not look at her sheepish daddy with thinning red hair.

She said, "You put us in this spot, Daddy. You knew Mama couldn't handle money."

I tried not to hear this time. I didn't like it, and even my room with the door shut wasn't far away enough. I could hear Audrey yell, "Don't you dare blame her! The mother of your child lives off peanut butter and crackers half the time. You got your divorce and we got broke! How do you think I paid my lab fees? With my lunch money. Your cheerleader daughter qualifies for free lunch, but I don't take it. How do you like that?"

Lucky Jessica was at Beth's.

Audrey's moving up north to Sherman with her daddy, so her mother can get on her feet. I guess she'll have the baby up there. I don't think her stepmom's too happy. She didn't like it none when I asked was she Audrey's sister, her looking so young and all. Audrey looked at her stepmother without blinking and said, "Tracey, I'm sorry your new kitchen floor has to wait, but my father has to pay for his grandbaby."

Word must have gotten around that Audrey's back, because Billy's Trans Am cruises down our street real regular. Mama says she's seen him drive by every other day since Audrey disappeared.

Audrey refuses to see him.

Theresa and her brother helped Audrey load her things into her dad's sedan. My sister watched them out our window. "Becky, Billy drove up!"

Billy got out of his car and slammed the door and shoved Theresa's brother. Grant wouldn't fight. He just shoved Billy back. "Don't make a bigger fool of yourself than you already have, Markam." Audrey stomped into the house and slammed the door.

Jessica looked at me and said, "He just loves her so much." My ma-maw says watching soap operas will make a person stupid, and my sister is living proof that it's true.

We watched as Billy went to the door and Mr. Baxter answered. "Billy, I believe my daughter has made her feelings clear. You just take this now and go on."

Billy took his class ring and threw it across the lawn. He roared off in his car and left about half the rubber on his tires on our street. That fool who calls herself my sister went and found that ring. She doesn't know I see her take out Billy's ring and gaze at it like it's Cinderella's glass slipper. Except the slipper went on the girl, not on the boy, and Cinderella was probably a half-decent catch and never got anybody pregnant.

"Audrey's daddy is keeping them apart," Jess says. Dream on, dummy.

Jessica would give a whole load of designer jeans to know what I know. I'm sorry I know it, because some secrets just stink.

CHAPTER SEVENTEEN

It doesn't feel right going and cheering for a rival football team. I ought to be back home leaning on the fence on the sideline by Uncle Clayton. We'd talk horses and cheer for Dub and our old team. I ought to be giving Granddaddy his "Good luck, Coach" hug.

Daddy says we should be loyal and support Jessica at this home game. She's singing the National Anthem with two other middle school girls. Mama says it's an honor that the girls were invited. Jessica's a wreck. My sister changed her clothes three times and her lip gloss five times. Said it had to match her outfit.

Mama and Daddy and I climb up the bleachers, like mountain climbers looking for a campsite. A few folks nod and say "Hi, Mr. Ramey" to Daddy, and Mama spots a few neighbor ladies and waves. Back home we'd know every other person we'd see, and a good many of those would be relatives. I feel like I'm on the wrong side of the stadium, because no one's wearing red and white like we would back home. Folks are wearing sky blue sweatshirts and jackets. Daddy spreads a blue throw on our laps. If it weren't chilly football weather, I'd push it off.

Mama sits up extra straight, biting her lip. Jessica looks up into the stands and spots us and turns away when she sees us. The girls gather around the mike and they start off a little wobbly, but then they grow stronger. Jessica's voice sails over the stadium bleachers, and she stands taller as she comes to the high part. "Oe'r the la-and of the fre-e-e, and the home of the bra-a-ave." My sister smiles a little, because she knows she hit the highest note strong and true. It feels like folks were holding their breaths, feeling sorry, but hoping for the young girls, and then they were all happy the trio got it right. Claps and whistles explode around us, like the crowd knows it's a great start and maybe even good luck for the home team.

Jessica comes rushing up the aisle toward us with laughing, excited girls behind her. Voices all along the way call out "Good job! That was great!" Daddy and Mama and I hug her, but she pulls away quickly.

"Daddy, can I have some money?" Jessica fidgets, wanting to run off with her friends.

Daddy pulls out a five and says, "Take your sister and share." Jessica looks a little annoyed and Mama looks a little panicky. Daddy says, "They've got to make friends sometime, Liz."

I practically run down the bleachers to catch up. Jessica's friends don't really want me to come along. Once we're at the concession stand, Jessica tries to get away with giving me only two dollars out of the five, but I won't have it. "Daddy said 'Share'!"

She huffs and looks up at her bangs.

I hear a voice behind me. "I'll give you fifty cents, Becky."

It's Rusty. I'm so glad to see someone I know; I don't even care that Jessica runs off with my half dollar. We get in line at the stand, with moist hot dog and burger smells tempting us.

"What are you going to get, Becky?"

"A bottled Coke and package of Tom's peanuts to go in it."

"Peanuts to go *in* your Coke bottle?"

"Don't knock it until you try it."

"Okay, guess I'll order that too."

Rusty watches me as I bite open the package of nuts and funnel them down the neck of my soda pop bottle. He shrugs and does the same.

We click our bottles together in a toast. "Chug and crunch," I say. I take a small mouthful, and the sweet cola fizzes around the salty nuts. "You have to tuck the nuts in your cheek while you swallow some of your drink. Don't choke."

Rusty almost took too big a swig, but he coughed a little and did all right. "Not bad. Where'd you learn that?" Rusty asked.

"Did it all the time back h . . . where we used to live. My Aunt Janet showed me. Makes a real good snack."

"Um-*hum*!" Rusty mumbled, his mouth full.

I guess younger kids everywhere spend most of a football game walking around and around the sidelines, seeing who's there and what they're doing or wearing. On our first round, Rusty and I see Miss Powers in the bleachers. Looks like she's trying to ignore Mr. Parks. The boys' gym coach has a long piece of grass and he's pestering her with it, trying to make her think a bug is on her shoulder.

"You know what Mr. Parks looks like?" Rusty asks.

"What?" I say.

"One of those Stretch Armstrong dolls. Just look at him—real broad shoulders and long blond hair over his ears."

I look over at Mr. Parks and I grin. I can just imagine some little boy stretching the teacher's arms way out. Suddenly, Miss Powers turns around fast and pushes him, and Mr. Powers falls off his seat and onto his neighbor's foot. Rusty and I laugh real big over that one.

"I think Mr. Parks likes her," Rusty says.

"Miss Powers? No way. She's a head taller than he is." I feel annoyed, but I don't know why.

"He doesn't care," Rusty declares.

"She won't have him."

"We'll see," Rusty says.

"Hey, Burnet. Let's race." It's Patrick, the booger boy, calling to Rusty. "Kenny and Chad are waiting over here."

I follow the boys just beyond the visitor goal post to watch.

Chad looks at me challenging. "Why don't you race too, Ramey?"

I shrug and line up with the boys. Jessica was embarrassed I wore jeans to the game, but I'm glad I did. Some dad I don't know hollers "Go" for us and we're off. I feel my legs pounding and my Coke and peanuts sloshing in my stomach. Still I pass the dad at our finish line and only Patrick is even close behind me. Chad's wheezing and Kenny's puffing. Rusty doesn't look so happy.

Boys make me tired. "I'll see you all later," I call over my shoulder, with Patrick begging for a rematch. "Nope, I'll barf if I race again."

I pass Miss Powers and she calls out, "Some of the basketball team are looking for you tonight."

I nod and start to head back to Mama and Daddy's seat, but I see Daddy by the stand with a cardboard holder with two tall drinks.

"Hey, baby. Are you having a good time? You feel all right?"

"Yeah, I'm fine," I lie. I shouldn't have run after that snack. "I saw my friend Rusty and some other kids."

"Oh, yes. Those girls have been looking for you," Daddy says, nodding to a group of tall eighth graders from my school. He heads up the bleachers and leaves me alone.

I turn toward them, and they spot me. They stride toward me like they're on a mission. A towering girl with a big Afro and clear, smooth black skin leads them. "Hey, little girl, you Becky Ramey?"

My eyes narrow. "I don't know how little I am, but I *am* Rebecca Ramey."

"Uh-*huh*. Miss Powers says you should play ball with us." She doesn't sound impressed. "I'm Daniesha Journey, and I *am* a center on our junior high team." She steps closer looking down at me, sizing me up.

I swallow, but I do my best to not blink. "Okay."

"That you over there racing with those rowdy boys?"

"Yes."

"You go any faster than that?"

"When I don't have Coke and peanuts in my gut."

The other girls snicker and Daniesha turns and stares them down. She turns back to me and frowns. "You go to church?"

"Yes, I do." At least we're looking for a new one, so that wasn't exactly a lie. "Do you?" I ask.

"Indeed, I do. My father's the pastor of the First A.M.E." Daniesha's frown gets deeper. "Don't you ever smile, Rebecca Ramey?"

I narrow my eyes again, so I don't blink.

Daniesha puts her hand on her hip. "Do *not* give me that spaghetti Western stare! Like you're all tough and bad."

I feel my eyes widen despite myself.

A tall black girl with deep dimples laughs. "We oughta call her Eastwood. That's her name: Eastwood." She is the very tallest of them all, but she wears a necklace that says "Pee Wee."

"Okay, Eastwood," Daniesha says. "I guess we'll put up with you at practice. Do not consume any Coca Cola or peanuts."

I watch the cluster of tall, strong girls walk away. One freckled girl looks back at me over her shoulder. I don't know if I passed the test or if they'll even speak to me again, but at least that's over.

Suddenly I hear yipping. Just past the stand, two men are chasing a little white dog dashing around the north end of the field. He dodges them, and the two stout men can't even grab the leash the frightened pup trails behind him. They'll never catch him like that.

I pick up a lone French fry off the concession stand counter and crouch down and whistle. The little terrier pauses, and he seems glad to see me. He edges toward me with his little carrot tail wagging, and I stay as still and calm as I can, offering him the fry. He must decide I'm all right, because he ignores the fry and jumps up and puts his forepaws on my chest. I pick him up and feel his frantic heart beating in his warm little chest. I don't know why, but I feel tears sting my eyes and I realize how long it's been since I've been around any animal. It feels so good that I must make my chin stop trembling.

"Is he yours, little girl?" one of the men said.

"No, sir, but I'll walk around with him and find his owner," I offer.

"That sounds like a good idea. He was running loose, and we couldn't catch him."

I recognize the dark-haired girl from my homeroom. She brightens when she sees the little dog. "He's so cute. Is he yours?"

I shake my head no. Amy and the other girls with her frown at me and pull her away, but the dark-haired girl waves bye.

The little fellow licks my cheek and I notice his tags. One says his name is Angus. "I bet if somebody went up to the announcer and told him to say there's a little dog named Angus by the concession stand, the owner would come," I suggest to a boy who stopped by to pet the dog.

The boy agrees and begins to climb up the bleachers, but before he can get halfway there a girl my age cries out, "Angus!"

I can see tear streaks on her face, but I won't say anything. Angus wriggles from my arms and bounces and then jumps up into her arms.

"Thank you so much. My little brother was supposed to watch him while I went to the ladies' room, but he got bored and tied Angus to the bleachers and he got away. I was so upset." Her chin trembles. "I was afraid I wouldn't see him again."

"What is he? Some kind of Scottie?"

"Close. He's a West Highland Terrier. They're from Scotland too. Maybe you could come over and play with us sometime. He likes you." The girl smiles.

"What class are you in? I've never seen you at school before."

"Oh, I'm not *from* here. I'm with the other team," explains the blond girl.

A Thing of Beauty

"Oh." I can't keep the disappointment out of my voice.

Just when I thought I had met someone.

"Well, maybe we'll see each other another time," she says. "Thanks," she calls back, heading to her side.

I watch her leave and look across the field. I guess I ought to watch this game. I check the score to see we're three points behind.

I notice Billy Markam moving into formation, first time I've seen him since Audrey left town. Every day Jessica and I look for his car in the parking lot on the way home and wonder if he's talked to Audrey. Jessica thinks it's the most hopeless, romantic thing, and I bite my tongue.

I don't like Billy—not one bit, but I can't ignore him. Not on the football field. He strides through the turf and chalked lines like it's home, like he's certain what needs to happen for his team. His teammates look at him, and it's as though he gives them some of his power, just standing there.

It's our play. The center snaps the ball to Billy and he fires it to a receiver.

The boy gets tackled.

The loudspeaker crackles, "Number Seven, Kyle Roberts hit hard behind the line of scrimmage. A loss of three yards on the play."

Nobody gets too worked up. Even the old paunchy guys in their ancient letterman's jackets stay seated. Kyle glances over at Billy, who shakes his head. It's okay.

The boys in sky blue and white cluster again and then reform.

"Ball at the twenty-seven-yard line. Markam gets the snap . . . pitches right side to Moore."

The wiry young guy runs hard, but he gets swarmed under.

"Moore dropped in the backfield. A loss of three on the play."

This time, folks are standing and the coach is pacing. Billy's confident, even cocky, walk doesn't change. It's like my daddy says when he's sick and tired of some athlete, "Wrong like only a jock can be."

They're in a for-sure-Tom-Landry shotgun and it looks certain: Billy's going for another lateral pass. The boys in black and gold make a beeline for our receiver, but wait... Billy never threw the ball. He still has it and he's tearing down the field. He breaks a tackle and cuts to the outside. It looks certain the safety's gonna nail him, but the crowd roars when Billy sidesteps the guy in a black helmet.

Now Billy's just running—running for the joy of the power in his legs and the air in his lungs—like a colt in spring sunshine. When I tell my grandfather, he will say it's true. It's a thing of beauty, a thing of beauty.

And just when I think nothing more could happen, some kid with broad shoulder pads and a little ol' hiney cuts across the field. He's on the light side—probably warmed the bench for a good while, but he's built for speed. The kid's run is a desperate thing. If it bursts his lungs and breaks his heart, this boy aims to bring down Billy Markam. And who wouldn't love to be on that field too and just run, run, run with them?

"He's to the twenty, to the ten... One man to beat!"

We can't cheer, we can't talk, and we can't breathe until it's done. The little guy launches himself at Billy.

"Billy Markam's hit at the goal line..."

But the ball is locked tight and safe in Billy's arms.

"Makes it in!"

The boy gets up and he and Billy stare at each other in wonder. The kid almost had him, and until this moment, Billy never knew it.

The crowd erupts, and I know this is one for the records. I cheer, I scream. I shake my fists in the air and I even do a Texas Aggie whoop and then I turn and see Theresa. Somehow, I feel guilty.

Audrey's friend mirrors the moves and she mouths the cheers along with the other girls, but it's a sour thing. The cheerleader smiles, but it's a bitter smile like she laughs at herself for cheering for Billy of all people. Theresa claps and cheers as he runs to the coach, but that sly, bitter smile does not fade.

I don't really like Theresa all that much, but I think we both miss Audrey, so I move closer. Maybe she will see me and say hello.

Theresa glances at me, but she only nods. She looks back at Billy and the girls clustering at the sidelines and screaming and him just eating it up. My sister's jumping up and down in the big fat middle of it all, just hoping Billy will notice. I move a little closer to Theresa and she surprises me. She puts her arm around my shoulder. "It didn't take him long to forget her, did it, kid?" And I know she means Audrey.

CHAPTER EIGHTEEN

"I just don't see it! 'The group in the woods is . . . are hiding.'" I shove away that stinking language paper like it is spoiled milk. "I don't *know*." The purple ink on the moist page reeks of failure.

Miss Powers pushes it back across the desk. "Look at the sentence again."

I cover my eyes with my hands. "I hate verbs." And I hate having to stay after school, even with a nice teacher.

Miss Powers sighs. "You're tired."

I nod and peer at her between my fingers.

"How would you like to go on a field trip with me and the other basketball girls?"

"I don't think they like me."

"You all better learn to like each other, if you're going to be a team." Miss Powers pauses. "I'm taking you all to my dad's place west of Fort Worth." She raises her eyebrows. "We have horses."

I lean forward. "What kind?"

"First the sentence."

I groan, but I look. And I see it. "*Is* . . . the verb . . . it's *is*."

The corner of her mouth twitches. "Why?"

"Take out 'in the woods.' The subject is 'group.'"

"Got it." She nods. "Now you do the other sentences."

"But the horses. What kind of horses? Did you barrel

race?"

Miss Powers shakes her head. "Nope. Cutting and roping. You barrel race?"

"Not since we moved. My cousin Missy—she coaches me barrel racing. She talks about taking me to Cowtown Rodeo, but she hurt her knee, and this year's her son's senior year and he plays football. So that takes up weekends. Daddy promised we'd visit my grandparents soon and I could ride then, but we haven't done it once."

"Ah. I'm sure he's busy."

I snort. "Too busy to keep promises."

"You still writing your cousin? That's good practice."

I look down and push aside the paper and shake my head. "She doesn't write back anymore." Tabby wrote twice the first week, and then later to say Chad was mean and she hoped I hit him again in PE. The first letter she said they were for sure going to the Queen's Tea at the Rose Festival, but she didn't say "Wish you could come."

Miss Powers said "Hmm," and then she was just quiet and sad with me. "You know what? You ought to write to yourself."

"Huh?"

"Keep a journal. Always helps me straighten out my thoughts. Something to think about." Miss Powers looks at the door. "Your Daddy's here."

"You ladies ready to call it a day?" My dad's wearing his sweatpants. He runs while I get tutored on Tuesday.
"I believe so. Becky has two more sentences, but she can finish them at home."

I sigh, relieved. "I always get it when you explain it. I wish you were my language arts teacher. Why don't you teach that instead of PE?"

"I was an English major. I keep applying, but I guess they think a basketball player should only teach PE." One eyebrow rises a little. "For now, I tutor."

"You teach everything good, Miss Powers."

"*Well,* Miss Ramey. I teach well." She pauses and smiles at my father. "Mr. Ramey, would Becky be available weekend after next? I always take my basketball team to my father's ranch close to Weatherford. Team building, I guess you'd say. Mr. Parks takes the boys team as well."

"I'll have to check with her mother. You say at a ranch?"

"Ple-ease, Daddy."

"We also take them to the art museums at Fort Worth. There are two really fine ones—just so the kids are well-rounded."

Miss Powers is smart. If that doesn't make the mothers happy, I don't know what will.

"The kids have a great time. Fishing at my dad's 'tank' and with your permission, horseback riding."

Daddy glances at me and hesitates.

Miss Powers smiles. "My dad gives Western riding lessons. Our stock is tame. It would be nice to have another experienced horsewoman along, though. Horseback riding is new to most of the girls."

"Well, I believe her mother had planned a big excursion to North Park Mall with her aunt and cousins..." Daddy starts.

I grab his hand and whisper, "Please, oh please, oh please..."

Daddy looks up at the ceiling and then down at me. "But I can see this is an opportunity Becky can't pass up. We may have to sell Mama on this. It might help her feelings if you'd read a book or two and turn in every scrap of language arts homework between now and then."

※ ※ ※

Dear Journal,

This is my first time to write in you. I get to go to the ranch! I faked reading an Anne of Green Gables *book and I did most of my language arts homework. Jessica said she would tell me the answers if I washed and dried all the dishes. I agreed I was that ~~desperit~~ desperate to go. I got gypped though, because after a while I figured out pronouns and the anta-whatchamacallits by myself. Mama said the dishes haven't looked this good in a while and it was more peaceful too, because we girls weren't fighting. Jessica is a slob. When I rinse and dry, I have to keep sending stuff back because Jessica leaves crud in the forks and lipstick on the glasses.*

Dear Journal,
Anne of Green Gables isn't too bad. It stinks to get stuck in a strange place with stuck-up people. I ought to know. I'm going to black my sister's eye if she doesn't stop reading my journal. That's a promise, Jessica.
Speaking of stink, that military brat kid, Frank does. Stink, I mean. Nobody wants to sit by him on the bus anymore. It's too bad. He's nice once you get to know him. Frank's jittery though. Bounces both knees and makes the whole seat shake. Somebody ought to ask him what's wrong.

CHAPTER NINETEEN

It's a red dawn and Mama and Daddy both come to see me off at the school parking lot.

If Mama could back out, she would. "Becky, please be careful." I don't think she thought I'd keep my part of the bargain.

"I know how to ride a horse, Mama."

Mama asks, "What am I going to say to your cousin when you're not here for our shopping trip?"

I say, "Tell Tabby to do what I do. Write a letter and see if anybody answers."

Daddy puts his arm around me and walks me to the school bus and says, "These people raise horses and those are valuable animals. Only ride the horse they give you."

"I know how to act, Daddy. I'm not going hurt a horse."

One of the big girls calls out to me, "Eastwood, hurry up!"

I escape to the bus and get on quick, before anyone thinks I'm a little kid who still needs her mommy and daddy.

My folks call out "Have a good time." I nod and give a little wave to my parents, but then I turn around. I glance back, and they grow smaller and sadder as the bus pulls away.

I settle in and reach for my little blue diary.

Sept. 22

I'm not going to say Dear anything anymore it's stupid, because I am writing to me. Jessica won't read my secret, personal thoughts or correct my grammar anymore, because I have a plan. Anyway, it's Friday and we're on our way to the ranch.

I stop writing and look around the bus. All the older girls are paired up and sitting in front of me. They're all too big to sit with a sixth grader.

I can hear the boys behind me singing Lynyrd Skynyrd songs and it makes me think of Uncle Richie. They are flat wearing out "Sweet Home Alabama." Somebody's voice cracks on the 'sweet' part and the boys laugh and snort. "SWEE-eet, SWEE-eet!" they all squeak over and over. I'm ready to slap them. Daniesha frowns and looks out the window.

I stick my pencil in my mouth and give it a couple of good bites. The more chewed up a pencil, the less likely somebody will take it—especially my sister. As I close the blue book and put it into my book bag, I feel someone lurch over and plop down beside me. It's Rusty.

"I guess we're both just tagging along," he says.

"Yeah." I look at Rusty. "How come you're coming? You play?"

"Nope. I haven't had my growth spurt yet. I will." Rusty doesn't let people get under his skin. "I do statistics and I'm learning to be a trainer. Coach says I'm part of the team too." Rusty looks past me at the sky. "It's looking black out there."

The sky is boiling with dark clouds. It's not like East Texas. The trees sheltered us from seeing too much sky. Here I feel helpless and in the open with no place to hide. From the flat horizon on up we're surrounded by huge clumps of grumpy clouds as dark as charcoal. Lightning flashes and thunder booms before we can say two-Mississippi. Even the big boys and Daniesha jump. Raindrops hit the bus windshield in big noisy splats. Hope that rain doesn't cause trouble and keep us from riding.

Soon we drive out of the storm, and the only raining clouds in sight hang over the horizon like dark combs.

The boys are too hoarse to sing anymore, and we girls just might throw 'em out the emergency door if they try, so we start looking at cars.

A green Camaro whizzes by and a boy named Bucky yells out before anybody can, "I call that one."

"Nuh-uh, I saw it first," some guy with a deep voice growls.

"I called it," Bucky says.

"I call the Beemer!" says a boy with pimples.

Three girls scream "I call the Lincoln!" and we all laugh.

I look ahead and see horses. "That's what I want!" A young bay mare is frisking along the fence. I reach out my hand and open and close it like I could grab her and pull her to me. "Horsie, horsie, horsie," I call out.

"Horsie?" Daniesha says, eyebrows raised.

"That's what my cousin and I would play on trips. We'd call 'horsie' when we saw one. It's kinda dumb, I know."

"No dumber than calling out cars you can't even drive yet —at least you can ride a horse." Daniesha smiles.

"Eastwood's too little. She can't ride any horse," the freckled girl says.

I frown at her. If looks could kill . . . well, she'd be dead and buried.

Pee Wee calls out, "Ooooo, Eastwood's giving Julie a Dirty Harry look now."

One of boy growls, "Feelin' lucky, Punk?" Everybody laughs, except Rusty.

I don't say anything—sure as I do, I'll fall off my horse or something. They'll just have to see.

Miss Powers stands and peers out the window. "Look at that sky now, kids." It's a brilliant blue with only a few gray clouds and lots of puffy white ones. "A blue true dream of sky," Miss Powers whispers.

"You mean true blue, Miss Powers?" Freckles asks.

"No, it's a poem."

"You make that up just now, Coach?" Daniesha asks.

Miss Powers smiles. "No . . . E.E. Cummings." She closes her eyes and begins to recite this odd poem.

Coach Parks grins, looks back at his team, and says,

A Thing of Beauty

"Fellas, we're going to get poetry *and* art museums on this trip." As soon as he says it, I can tell he regrets it. Miss Powers stands up tall and majestic and goes and sits just in front of the girls. The two coaches had each been sitting on a front seat behind the driver, joking back and forth.

Rusty whispers, "Coach Parks is going to be so-rry."

"Serves him right," I say.

The bus slows on the Farm to Market road and turns onto a blacktop lane.

Miss Powers says, "Okay, folks we're almost there. Girls, gather up your belongings. We'll bring in your things first, and then we'll get on the trail."

Mr. Parks announces, "We fish first, guys. We'll ride tomorrow."

Soon we see the entrance and we pass under a sign that says Blue Sky Ranch. We pile out of the bus and look about us. The coaches introduce us all to Miss Powers's parents and her older brother. Her tall, graying father tells the boys to gather their gear and follow him to the bunkhouse. "We ladies will stay in the family room of the ranch house," says Miss Powers.

I drop off my bag as fast as I can and rush toward the stables.

"Wait a second, Miss Ramey," Miss Powers calls out. "Don't forget your helmet."

"Oh, shoot," I say.

"Yes, ma'am. Everyone wears one."

A little boy struts over to our coach, and he has a wad of something tucked in his lower lip. Miss Powers says, "Chuckie, what do you have in your mouth?" She pulls down his lip. "Raisins! Girls, this silly little boy is my nephew. He's four years old and way too big for his britches."

His grandmother clucks her tongue. "Chuckie, either eat those things or spit them out. You're going to rot your teeth. He thinks it makes him look big like those fool boys dipping snuff."

"Chuckie, that's nasty! You'll get sick and your teeth will turn brown and fall out," Miss Powers says.

"They will not." Chuckie frowns. "I'm going to ride with you today."

"Not today, Chuckie. We've got one more kid than we thought. Becky here needs to ride," says Miss Powers. "You can ride with me on my horse."

Chuckie buries his face into his grandmother's side, then peeks out and scowls at me.

"Well, be that way," says Miss Powers, walking off.

A string of horses is tied up outside and ready to go for us. Miss Powers directs each girl except me to a horse. "My dad is bringing one for you."

Chuckie glares at me while I help some of the girls adjust the cinches on their saddles. Miss Powers says, "Ignore him. He's just mad because you're stealing some of his thunder. He likes to help the girls."

"I want to ride," Chuckie mutters.

"Another time," his grandmother says.

"The horse you'll ride is over here, Becky," Mr. Powers says. I see a buckskin gelding tied to the fence. "My daughter says you've had some experience."

"Yes, sir. A bit," I say. I go to get acquainted with my horse, and the buckskin tries to bite me. "No, you behave." I smack him on his gray-beige shoulder to show him who is boss.

"I'm sorry, Becky," says Miss Powers's dad. "I don't know what's gotten into ol' Pat today."

Chuckie says, "He tried to kick me today."

"Ah! That's why Pat's riled up. Somebody's been pestering horses," says Mr. Powers.

"I believe he's okay now, sir," I say. Pat seems to like it when I scratch his neck and withers. I take my time and let him get used to me, before I swing up into the saddle. Just when I'm thinking he's ready to be good, that ornery plug tries to run me into a cottonwood tree.

Miss Powers's dad and brother watch me, foreheads wrinkled.

"No, you don't!" I tell my horse. I make him stand still

until he settles down, and then I make him head to the line of girls and horses ahead of us.

I hear the men laugh softly behind us. "She lined him out okay."

When Pat and I catch up, the girls turn and look at us. "I told you Eastwood couldn't ride," says Freckles, laughing.

I narrow my eyes at her. I guess Pat doesn't like to be teased either, because he tries to bite Freckles's horse.

"That nag almost drew blood!" Freckles storms.

"Well, if you feel left out, I could let him bite you too," I say.

Miss Powers says, "Girls, let Becky pass to the front so Pat calms down."

I walk the buckskin for a while, but then I move him on into a jog and then a lope. Maybe Pat needs some orneriness exercised out of him. My braids bounce and whip my shoulders to the rhythm of the ride. Lope, lope, lope. I slow him back down to a walk, and it's then I take the chance to look about me. Not so many trees here except by the muddy creek with water the color of broth in a pot of red beans. It's grassland with that "blue true" sky above us, and with plenty of room to ride. At the side of the trail is a clump of the last pale pink evening primroses. Pat and I just stand and enjoy the quiet and now we both seem content. Maybe he's felt cramped up and lonely too. I'm almost sorry when the girls catch up.

We're back at the stables and the ride is over. I kind of regret I didn't make Pat walk the whole way to stretch out the time. Mr. Powers and his son show the girls how to unsaddle the horses. Some of the girls are a little uneasy about brushing the horses, so I help. A girl named Jen comes close to getting kicked. "Don't walk behind a horse like that," I warn. "Come up by his shoulder."

"Thanks for your help, Becky," Mr. Powers says. Then he smiles. "You girls want to see something beautiful?" He leads us to a stall with a little chestnut mare with a white star between her dark eyes. "Her new owner is coming after her tomorrow."

I can hardly take my eyes from her. Her powerful, muscular hindquarters show she's built for barrel racing. Her back's short and strong and her cinnamon legs are straight and clean. "She's got nice big feet," I murmur.

"Somebody's got an eye for horses." Mr. Powers smiles.

I feel my face grow warm. "I just know what my Uncle Clayton would say."

Chuckie starts hanging on the stall door. Mr. Powers frowns. "Chuckie, leave that horse alone now."

For a moment, he just looks at his granddaddy. He makes it snappy and climbs down, when he sees his daddy heading for him. "Hardheaded!"

"Well, ladies, let's head over to the kitchen for some lunch. Those boys ought to be back from fishing," says Coach Powers.

The lunch is just sandwiches, but it hits the spot. We all really worked up an appetite. The boys smell fishy, and they laugh and brag about what they almost caught. Rusty got himself a bass, but it finned him. Ouch!

"You won't hold a fish wrong next time," Coach Parks says.

Daniesha watches me while she nibbles at a chip.

"What?" I say. "Why are you looking at me?"

"You are good with horses. Why don't you ride horses instead of play basketball?" Daniesha asks.

"Takes money. Daddy acts like it takes millions. Can't afford the horse and can't afford to keep it. Makes my mother happy. She's afraid I'll get hurt."

Daniesha says, "You could get hurt playing basketball."

"Yeah, but Daddy says with basketball, he only has to pay to feed me. We could never afford a really good horse anyway."

Coach Parks leans forward in his chair. "You'd be surprised. A lady in California wins all kinds of barrel races with a little ol' mutt horse called Geronimo. There's all kinds of ways to afford riding for a girl that's willing to work."

I smile at Mr. Parks. Suddenly, that sawed-off coach looks sorta handsome to me.

"Heck, move on over here and you could do chores and ride here any old time you wanted," Mr. Powers says. "You want to watch me walk that little mare?"

"Yes, sir!"

"Well, head on over there. I'll catch up."

I open the door, and Chuckie slips out ahead of me, running. He stops and juts out his jelly-smeared jaw as he looks back at me, before he hurries into the stable and slams the door.

CHAPTER TWENTY

I walk from bright sunshine into the darker stable, and my eyes squint to adjust. I don't need bright light to see that Chuckie is hanging on the stall door again.

"You better get down from there," I say.

"You're not the boss of me!" he says and to prove it, Chuckie opens the stall and gets in.

"I'm gonna go get your granddaddy," I say.

Chuckie's eyes grow big, and he shuts the stall door. The mare doesn't like it one bit. I can hear her thump against the walls, and then I hear Chuckie cry out.

I rush to the stall. The mare is on one side, and a trickle of blood runs down from her knee, and Chuckie lies pale on the other side holding his shoulder. I reach for the halter to calm the mare, but she balks and rears up. My feet slip on you-know-what, and I can't break my fall. My head slams against rough wood, and I feel myself collapse and slide sideways like a rag doll. When I finally open my eyes, I'm face down in dirty straw. I sit up groggy and confused. Mr. Powers is calming the mare outside the stall, and Chuckie's grandmother is looking over the little boy.

"I don't want to go to the doctor," Chuckie wails.

"Well, you should have thought about that before you went pulling stunts. Let's go call your mother." Their voices sound fuzzy and far away.

A Thing of Beauty

Mr. Parks feels the lump on my head and Miss Powers looks at my pupils and brushes the dirt and straw from my face.

"It's that girl's fault," Chuckie calls out.

That wakes me up. That's just what my daddy will think. Nobody else was there, so no one's sure. The Powers would like to believe us both, but they're uneasy and uncertain.

We meet my parents at the Amon Carter Museum in Fort Worth, and the look in my father's eyes says the whole trip was a mistake. Miss Powers told them what she knew. My father feels my lump and worry lines crease his forehead. "Becky, that horse might be seriously hurt. What did I tell you?"

It isn't fair. He didn't ask my side of the story, and my daddy's gone and judged me. My mother looks at me like she'd like to stick me right back in a preemie incubator. I don't look at them and I don't speak to them. They didn't believe in me enough to ask for the truth, and I'm not going to volunteer it.

They'll never let me on a horse again. I just know it. I don't have any kind of luck. If I needed a bucket of manure, I swear it would turn into roses.

The boys and girls watch my parents and me in the museum lobby, and their serious eyes seem to say "She's in trouble." I bet they're disappointed that the trip was cut short, but more weather was rolling in and besides, Miss Powers thinks I need to see a doctor.

My parents are stiff, but polite to my coach. They thank Miss Powers and then walk me to the car where Jessica waits. She looks at me like my trouble and disgrace could be catching.

"I don't care how much you wanted to ride . . . that was so impulsive, so irresponsible," my dad says. That's what Daddy says about the bad kids at school. That's what he says about Cousin Wes—and he's in prison.

We don't have to wait long at the pediatrician. Our bearded doctor says my head will be okay, to just rest. The only consolation is that Jessica and I both must have a tetanus booster shot while we're in the office. I roll up my sleeve and smirk at my sister's pale face, even when the shot pinches hard.

Jessica hates vaccinations and nurses. My sister pitches such a fit that the nurse pins back her arm to give Jessica her shot. That great big thirteen-year-old makes such a scene that for a second my parents forget how ashamed they are of me.

I don't say anything when we get home. I just go lie down, looking at the tiny peaks of paint on the wall by my bed. The phone rings, but I don't move. A few moments later, my door opens. I know my parents are standing there. "Becky, why didn't you tell us?" my mother says.

"Why didn't you ask? What difference does it make? You both get what you want. I don't ride horses again—ever," I say without turning over.

My dad clears his throat. "That was Miss Powers. It seems we got the wrong impression."

"Is that right?" I say. I don't intend to make this easy.

"That little boy's collarbone is broken. He didn't want to go to the doctor, but he finally had to admit that he was hurt." I feel my mother sit beside me. "He said you were trying to help him and the horse."

"The horse is okay. Only a minor scratch," Daddy says.

I turn and look at my parents. "Well, now that's a relief." And then I turn my back and close my eyes.

"Becky," my mother says, "don't be like that."

I sit up and look at my parents. "Like what? Irresponsible and impulsive? You think I'm a baby. You didn't believe me. Miss Powers's daddy trusts me. He said I could work for him and ride his horses anytime."

My father kneels by my bed. "We're really sorry, sugar"

I lie back down and roll over. "My head hurts. If you don't mind, I'm going to take a nap."

Later, I hear a gentle tap on my door. It's Miss Powers, Daniesha, and Freckles. They bring me a pink carnation in a vase and a Charlie Brown card that all the kids signed.

"Look inside the card," Daniesha says.

"We picked out postcards from the museums just for you," says Freckles.

A Thing of Beauty

One card has a portrait of a lady with curly hair. "That one made us think of you," Daniesha says.

Miss Powers says, "It's a self-portrait of a French artist, Le Brun."

"Yeah, the guide said she did her own thing. She painted herself in everyday hair instead of all powdered and piled up like Marie Antoinette's," says Freckles.

"Rusty picked out this card from the Amon Carter. We'll have to take you back there sometime," says Miss Powers.

I smile as I look at the postcard of the Remington sculpture. "A bucking horse. I guess that would remind me of this trip. *The Wicked Pony*," I read.

My father sticks his head in the door and my smile vanishes.

Miss Powers stands up. "Well, we better let Becky rest now, girls."

I look at my father and turn over and close my eyes. I feel my father sit down beside me on my bed. I feel his hand touch my hair, but he stops short of patting my head. He tucks my covers about my shoulders and tiptoes from my room.

Mama says Daddy's trying hard to make it up to me.

Two days later, Mama says, "Go look in the garage, Becky."

I open the door from the kitchen and all I notice in the dim garage are old paint cans and oily gas fumes. And then I spot spokes shining faintly next to the wall.

I reach my hand around and flip the light switch. A blue ten-speed bicycle leans against its kickstand. I walk over and run my fingers over the shiny fender. I can smell fresh car wax.

"It's not brand new, but Daddy shined it up and put on new tires and a new seat. It belonged to the secretary's daughter. It's as good as new. The girl just outgrew it."

My dad stands in the doorway, watching my reaction.

"What do you say, Becky?" Mama says.

I pause and look at him. "Thank you." I squeeze the gearshift on the handle bar, experimenting.

"Take it on out for a spin." Dad lifts the garage door and I roll the bike down the driveway and onto the street.

Kenny rolls up on his old bicycle and says, "Wow! When did you get that?"

"Just now."

"Can I try it?" Kenny asks.

"Not until I do." I don't want to look too excited, but I'm restless and ready to move and explore.

Kenny pulls a Queen of Clubs card from his pocket. "You want to make some racket? Let's put this in your spokes."

"Sure, why not," I say.

We take off on our bikes making a satisfying "rat-tat-t-t-tat" as we go. Kenny and I tour the neighborhood, and he shows me where Kyle and Bucky live. I spot Beth by a house with one taped-up window on the side. Her lawn is overgrown, and weeds are tall around a rusted lawn mower. She doesn't look at us, and ducks inside like she'd rather not talk. Kenny and I pause by the entrance to our development, and he points to a trailer court across the highway. "That's where they found that dead girl. Rusty? You know Rusty?"

I nod.

"He lives in that green trailer at the end."

"No kidding."

Kenny and I make the same loop for a few days, and I get to where I can just about guess how many loops it will take me before I need to be home in time for supper and homework.

❈ ❈ ❈

Sept. 29

Kenny was grounded today and that's okay. He doesn't want to go anywhere on his bike he just wants to do stupid stunts. Well, he did one too many and now his tire is busted and he's behind on homework anyway. I did some traveling on my own.

A Thing of Beauty

Mama doesn't know and I'm not telling. I was back in time for supper and when she asked where I went, I said, "Just out on my bike like always—five loops' worth." I didn't say five loops' worth where.

A German shepherd chased me, but I outran him. He wasn't the kind of dog you could make friends with. Ears all back and teeth showing.

Five blocks away from home I saw Chad, sitting on his front porch counting out money. His hair is so long now, it hangs over and around his aviator glasses.

He looked up and said, "Hey, Ramey, you got some money?"

"A dollar."

"I have two dollars and I dug out some quarters and dimes from the couch and Barcalounger, and I sneaked a dollar from my sister's purse. If you put in your dollar, we could have some pizza," Chad says.

"Won't your sister be mad you took her dollar?"

"No, she gets into my money all the time. If she gets a slice or two, she'll be all right." He stacks the quarters and dimes to be sure his count is right. "Mom's at work and she won't care. We're both tired of frozen dinners."

"Wow, you get to just fix what you want," I said.

I smiled, and Chad caught me. "What're you smiling at?"

"You look just like you're wearing a helmet with goggles."

"Really? Cool."

Boys. Who else would think that's cool?

Chad's sister walked our way, but Chad didn't look worried. "I got a dollar from your pocketbook, so we can get pizza. Becky's eating with us. She chipped in."

"Okay."

"Man, it would be World War III, if I got into Jessica's money," I said.

"She's in my homeroom. Your sister is kind of . . . dramatic, isn't she?" Chad's sister said.

"You got that right."

The delivery guy came, and Chad's sister dug up another fifty cents from the old car up on blocks in their driveway. "Those guys depend on tips," she said.

We sat on Chad's front step and ate pepperoni pizza and washed it down with lime Kool-Aid. It spoiled my dinner, but I didn't care.

I've got wheels now.

CHAPTER TWENTY-ONE

If I can hear myself think in this bus, I can finish my homework and be free to roam all weekend. It's getting dark early, so if I want any time on my ten-speed tonight, I've got to get this busywork out of my hair. I count the seats. If I calculate right, I'll be upwind of Frank and won't smell him too much, but I'll get full benefit of the quiet zone all around him.

Frank gets on, and I'm off by only one seat. I just shift up one and everybody else bunches up a bit toward the back waiting until the weird army brat gets off.

"Hey, Becky," he says.

"Hi, Frank." I glance up at him. His eyes look glassy under his greasy mop. He flops down by himself and then leans forward to see what I'm doing.

"Doing your homework early. That's great, kid. You do that." He flops back and looks out the window.

I hear Beth whisper to Jessica, "Dang, he stinks!" Several kids pull the necks of their T-shirts up over their noses.

Nobody teases Frank anymore—since last week. They're afraid of him.

That day Kyle and Bucky were talking about world history class and bellyaching about a quiz on the bus ride home.

"Why do we have to talk about Vietnam? Why do they

have to keep going on and on about it? It's over and done with."

Next thing we knew, Frank had Bucky by the collar, screaming at him. Bucky's twice his size, but he didn't lift a finger, because of the crazy look in Frank's eyes. "What do you know about Vietnam? Does it look to you like Vietnam is over?" Frank said through his teeth, pointing to four round bruises lined up on his cheek. Frank shoved Bucky away. "It ain't never gonna be over." He walked back to his seat without another word, breathing hard, staring ahead. He got off two stops before his own and the bus driver didn't stop him.

Kyle murmured, "A fist made those bruises on his cheek."

"He's nuts," Bucky said.

Some days Frank doesn't ride at all. He lines up with the other kids at his stop, but then he walks off as the bus arrives, and most people are glad he does.

Today, Frank gets off a stop too early without speaking. I put my sweater over my head like a hood to muffle the noise and finish up my last five math problems.

I beat my sister out the bus door and into the house. "Mama, we're home. Here's my homework," I call out. I peel off my school clothes and put on a T-shirt and some Wranglers.

My sister lies on her bed weeping, because she gave Billy his ring and he didn't even look at her or say thanks. She called to him out the bus window and handed it to him. He shrugged and walked away and now she's bawling. She's hopeless.

"What did you think he was going to do? Ask you to marry him?" I say.

"Shut up, Becky!"

I go to the kitchen and drink some water from a jelly glass.

"Don't you want a snack?" Mama says. "How was your day?"

"No. Fine," I answer. "I gotta go, Mama, if I'm going to get in a good ride."

"Be back before dark," I hear my mother call in the distance.

"Well, she's sure getting in some exercise," I hear my dad

say.

Today's an experiment, and I think I can carry it off. I won't be able to stay, but I think I can make it to Rusty's trailer park and back before sunset. I might just run into him. I want to try, because I think he likes me. It's the kind of thing I'd like to talk over with Tabby, but she's not here and she doesn't know him. I also kind of like Coach Parks. I'd like to run that past my cousin too. Like how old does she think he is and how old would Coach be when I am done with college?

I roll past the 7-Eleven store windows and catch my reflection and I sigh. Will I ever be cute enough for anybody to love me? Could anybody love a lanky girl with crazy, witchy hair and a jawline as square as a brick?

I'm pretty sure Rusty likes me, because when I told him about my new bike, he said, "Cool! Maybe we could ride bikes sometime." He also asked did I like the postcard he picked out. He smiled when I said both postcards were tacked up on my wall. It might mean something. It might not. He wrote more than any other boy did on my get-well card. "Get better REAL soon!" If Tabby were here, she could ask Chad, who could ask Kenny, who could ask Rusty does he like me?

I look over my shoulder, and the sun is still well up over the trees. If I pedal fast and steady, I'll make it to the trailer park and back home with time to spare. I make great time, until I get to the four-lane road. The schoolkids are home, so nobody much worries about slowing down for the crosswalk in front of the elementary school on the other side. It takes a lot longer than I expect, cars whizzing by without looking at my ten-speed and me. "I'll just have to pedal faster going back," I tell myself.

A red pickup truck honks at me as I rush across, but I make it. I walk my bike past a tan trailer and I hear a voice, "You really ought to be more careful. You could get hit, you know."

I look at the girl who says this and we both blurt in surprise, "You're in my class!" and then we giggle.

Her name is Sunny, and she's one of the invisible kids—

always there, always silent. She could be in with the smart good girls, because her work's A-plus right and A-plus neat, but she stays to herself in the class, in gym, at lunch. I've heard her voice one other time.

Sunny's short blond hair is parted in the middle and swept back in little wings so perfect, her hair almost looks molded like a Ken doll's. She always wears the same outfit: a skirt and a button-up blouse with puff sleeves and with a tiny ruffle and a bow at the neck. Only the pastel colors change from day to day.

When Amy first noticed this, she whispered, "She must go buy the same thing in every color."

And then Sunny looked at her and blinked. "Don't you? It really makes sense—don't you think?"

Now Sunny is in cut-off jeans, except her jeans are hemmed off more like. She's toweling dry a Chihuahua that's yapping and growling and looking bug-eyed at me.

I park my bike and just stand there and offer my knuckles for Bug-eyes to sniff and he calms down.

Sunny smiles, approving. "Cortez doesn't usually make friends that fast."

We talk dogs, those that yap, those that don't, and then Sunny says, "Rusty told me about your horse accident. Are you okay now?"

"Yeah, I guess. My parents aren't."

"Rusty really likes you."

I look at Sunny's mild blue eyes. She isn't teasing at all and it's like she's reading my mind.

"He thinks you're cute too. He saw your Mom, and he said you're only going to get cuter," says Sunny. "He says he may marry you once he gets through college."

I like that, and I don't like it. That's nailing down things a lot faster than I care for. You want to keep your options open at eleven. This kind of chases off those Rusty daydreams.

"Don't say anything. Rusty will be embarrassed."

"Believe me, I won't," I say.

"I have another Chihuahua—she's Cortez's wife and she may have pups tomorrow. I won't get anything done this weekend. They could come at any time."

"You want help?"

Sunny smiles and shrugs.

"I could come right after breakfast." I'm not sure she wants me here.

Sunny nods. "Of course. You better leave now though. I don't know where you live, but you only have about ten minutes before the sun goes down." Sunny gets up and pushes Cortez inside the trailer door. "I'll see you across the street." The serious blond girl guides me across the street with her hand up and she stares down a pickup driver who slows to a stop at the crosswalk.

I pump my legs like crazy to make speed. Dad frowns when I glide up into the driveway, but I've made it just in time.

Tonight, I can hardly sleep for thinking, "Puppies tomorrow!"

CHAPTER TWENTY-TWO

Next morning Mama sits down, puts her chin in her hand, and watches me eat my pancakes. "Sugar, are you happy here?"

I shrug. "It's okay, I guess."

"Just okay. Are you making friends?"

I play with her hen and rooster salt and pepper shakers. "Yeah, I've got friends." I change the subject. "I thought you didn't like 'country' things. Your whole kitchen is farm stuff."

Mama's made red-checked napkins and cushions, and then blue chambray place mats and appliance covers with red-checked trim. Antique canning jars full of dried noodles and beans huddle on the counter. Mama even has this cream pitcher that looks like a cow and the milk pours out of its mouth. I can't look at it when I use it, or it'll turn my stomach.

"I never said I didn't like farms." Mama sprinkles sugar over her pancake and cuts off a bite. "I just don't like some things about farm life. Maybe I keep all this around to remind me of what I don't have to put up with anymore."

"Are *you* happy here, Mama?"

She sighs and cuts off another bite of pancake. "Yeah, I am—mostly." She pauses. "Moves are always hard to make, and there are always things you don't expect."

A Thing of Beauty

Mama and Daddy take a lot more time over the bills than they used to. Mama buys a lot more frozen turkey legs than she did back home.

"At thirteen cents a pound they're a buy," Mama says. She and Daddy talk more and more about her going to work full-time. Mama's trying out Avon, but she's having a hard time dredging up customers.

Jessica's in the den practicing vocal scales so the house isn't fit to be in. "Oh-A-Oh-A-Oh-A-Oh-E-Oh-E-Eeee." Bit by bit she just keeps going higher and higher until I want to scream. Suddenly Jessica stops and pounds her fists on the piano bench. "This old thing is tinny and out of tune!"

"So, tell me about your friends," Mama says a little louder.

"You know, the basketball girls, kids at school. I gotta go Mama. Kenny wants me to help him put on his new tire."

It's time to get to those puppies.

Jessica roars and pounds the piano bench again.

I'm hitting the road.

I help Kenny put his new tire on his bike, and I put up with him for a few loops around the block, then I tell him I need to run by home. I go by our house, so it's not a complete lie.

I shiver a little in the fall air. I should have worn a jacket. It's early enough there's not much traffic on the four-lane. Sunny's on her doorstep, and she smiles in relief when she sees me walking across the crosswalk.

"Something's definitely started. Have you delivered puppies before?" She opens the door and leads me to a cardboard box in her bedroom. Sunny's eyes are usually calm and quiet, but today they dart from me to the pregnant Chihuahua.

"I've seen puppies, and calves, and I once saw a colt being born. It pretty much takes care of itself. Being born, I mean," I say.

Sunny twists a small ring on her pinky. "I hope Mrs. Cortez hasn't been unfaithful with some big dog."

I look in the box. "Maybe with another Chihuahua, but not with any big dog. She looks about right to me."

Sunny frowns. "I need to get the kitchen cleaned up and my dad off to work."

"Well, go on and do what you need to do. I'll sit with her awhile," I say.

"Da-a-d?" Sunny calls. "You've got to get up now. I'll have just enough time to braid your hair."

I hear someone shuffling around in the next room. A big man lumbers by and into the bathroom—and he has hair down past his hip pockets.

I hear a flush and the sink running for a moment. Sunny calls out, "Ready for your hair?"

The tall guy comes out and sits on Sunny's bed. He holds a tiny blue elastic in his big fingers, so it's ready for the end of his braid.

Sunny points at me with the hair brush, before she tackles the tangled brown waves. "Dad, this is Becky. She's a nice girl from school and she's going to help me with Mrs. Cortez."

Her dad looks at me with faded blue eyes as vague and washed out as his work shirt. "Cool," he murmurs.

Sunny makes short work of that braid. "Your lunch is on the counter." Sunny watches him leave and then turns back to see my reaction. "We don't look alike. My grandmother can't stand him. She says I look like his best friend."

"That's pretty rough coming from his mother," I say.

"Oh, she's my mom's mother. My mother works for a feminist lobby in Austin. She left my dad so he couldn't oppress her."

I raise my eyebrows. I'm not sure that foggy-looking man could oppress much of anything.

Sunny is still eyeing me. She takes another breath and plunges back in. "My grandmother sends us money, but I only buy clothes and we save the rest for college. Dad and I pay our own bills. I'm going to be an accountant and make lots of money, and Dad will live with me in a big house and be my gardener."

I put on my dad's encouraging counselor face. "Sounds

good."

Sunny lifts her chin and says in a rush. "And one more thing, my real name's not Sunny. It's Marshall Sunshine. I was born in Marshall and, well, Dad said they were all stoned and it sounded good at the time."

"Hmmm. Well, that kind of works out okay. I was born in Longview and my granddaddy calls me 'Ranger.' I shrug. "There's some old story about me wandering off when I was little and him finding me out by the barn."

"Marshall Sunshine and Ranger Rebecca," Sunny says smiling a little bolder.

"Yep," I say, but Sunny's mild eyes grow doubtful, concerned. "We won't tell anybody," I tell her. "It's our secret."

Mrs. Cortez must be made for having babies, because she pushes out three brown pups without much fuss. Mr. Cortez comes over to inspect, and his wife lifts a wrinkled lip and shows her teeth at him.

"Oh, look, she's smiling," Sunny says.

"That's what you think," I say. "She'll bite his head off, if he doesn't back off." Mrs. Cortez gives a chipmunk growl to show that's true. "We better let them have some peace and quiet."

Sunny says. "I've got to go tell people their puppies are born. I wish there was a fourth puppy, so you could have one."

"That's okay." I'd like a little more dog than that anyway.

Sunny and I walk to a trailer next door, and two girls sit on the step making something with little papers. I catch a whiff of strawberry and wonder if it could be their bubble gum.

Sunny's all business. "Mrs. Cortez has had her pups, so you all can pick up yours in six weeks."

I watch one little girl roll up a paper and make neat twists on either end. She smiles, proud as she pops it into a Tupperware container. "What are they making?" I whisper to Sunny.

"Joints. They pull in a little cash from high school girls and a couple of neighbor ladies. Their uncle gives them the grass at a discount since they're family."

"How old are they?" I ask.

"I don't know. The little one goes to the elementary school. Older one's repeating seventh grade."

Well, I won't be bringing up that story at the dinner table. My mother would have a cow. She'd lock me up in my room tighter than Tupperware.

I shiver a little, and it's not from the cold. "Did you know that girl they found dead?" I ask.

"Oh, yeah. Domestic dispute—it was her boyfriend did it." Sunny wrinkles her nose. "Cops don't know. Now folks think that guy who died outside Rusty's trailer was his mom's boyfriend? That wasn't a domestic. He owed somebody a lot of money. Cops pinned it on Rusty's brother because he said he'd *like* to kill this guy. He didn't do it though." Sunny talks about this like she'd talk about soggy tater tots in the lunchroom.

I see a guy with wild, matted hair standing on a doorstep knocking and I recognize his jacket. It's Frank. He sees me, but he leaves and ducks around a corner, and he doesn't say hi.

I push my bike as we walk up to a trailer with starched lacy curtains in the windows and bright yellow mums by the door. Sunny is on the step, knocking at the door while I wait below. Suddenly, I feel two hands grasp my handlebars and I pull back. I look into the narrowed eyes of an older boy tightening his grip on my bicycle. He tries to jolt it out of my hands.

"Nice bike. Why don't you let me try it out?"

I hear gravel crunch behind me, and then my father's voice. "Why don't you just let go of my daughter's bike and take off?"

I don't know if this boy knows my dad, but he lets go and walks away quickly.

My father doesn't look at me as he takes hold of the handlebars. He walks back to the Impala, opens the trunk, and puts in my bike. He says in a flat voice, "Get in Rebecca. We're going home."

As I get into the car, I see Rusty standing by his green trailer. He raises his hand to wave, and then lets it fall to his side. I look at Sunny, but she's looking at her shoes. I think we all know Ranger Rebecca is grounded.

CHAPTER TWENTY-THREE

My father stares straight ahead. "Your mother is at home crying. She took the call from one of my student's parents. His son recognized you and thought we ought to know where you were. Do you know how embarrassing this is?"

"You didn't say I *couldn't* go there," I mutter.

"I notice you knew not to ask," Dad says. "You can't just wander the countryside like you could at home. That neighborhood could be—*is* dangerous."

Mama's bawling all right and she's made up her mind. "We have to settle on a church and join it now." I guess I'm a sinner now, and church is her last hope. I was just getting used to seeing Sunday night TV. For the first time in my life I got to lay out from church and watch all the Disney shows without being sick. The only good thing about church were the Sunday school treats, Vacation Bible School crafts, and birthday cards from our teachers. Uncle Richie worships on the lake; I'd just as soon worship on a horse, thank you very much.

We've looked off and on since we moved. We've tried first one church, then another. It isn't like back home, with dozens of tiny churches on every other corner, half of them split off another. Daddy says you can always tell when a church is a split by its name: Harmony, Unity, or Friendship.

We drove several miles to that old church in Dallas with a huge youth choir that travels all over. We felt swamped and lonely all at the same time. Then there was that big church with the preacher who didn't like for people to watch television or for ladies to wear pants—ever. He just kept calling, and finally Daddy ran him off by saying that everybody ought to do like people in the Bible and all wear robes. Daddy said, "Tell you what, Brother. Let's you and I wear kilts." That preacher didn't call again, and my folks put off looking. Until I was bad.

Anyhow, here I am Sunday night, sitting outside this little church building while my parents sit and talk and laugh with the preacher and his wife. We went this morning and came back for the evening service. Jessica made a big hit. Mrs. Lewis heard her sing and Preacher Lewis's eyes lit up when he heard that Jessica plays the piano. I'm the bad kid, so I'm not much to brag about. Mama sits and whispers with Mrs. Lewis, and it's probably all about me.

I sit on the step and watch teenage boys play basketball in the church parking lot. They don't invite me to play and I don't ask. The Lewis's little twins burst through the door.

The little girl bellows, "Form of... iceberg!"

The little boy yells, "Shape of... lion!"

And then they scream, "Wonder Twin Powers Activate!"

I was trying hard to be unhappy, but a smile breaks out anyway. "I thought the girl was the animal."

"No!" they both say.

"I'm the animal!"

"I want to be water. You be the blue monkey that carries me!" the little girl says.

The little kids are blond headed, but they have brown eyes like puppies. They run around turning into stuff, and sometimes I grab up the little girl and run around with her.

"So where are the other super heroes?" I ask. "Where's the Hulk?"

The little boy hunches over clenching his little fists, his

face turning purple. "I'm the Hulk," he roars.

Next second, he's a Wonder Twin again. There's no rhyme or reason to it. I find a piece of old Venetian blind cord and I offer to be Wonder Woman, so now they're bad guys and I lasso them. And then Jessica comes out.

"Y'all are so cute—just like Donnie and Marie Osmond," my sister says.

The twins run up the church steps and onto the porch like it's a stage. The little girl strums an air guitar and they sing "A Little Bit Country, A Little Bit Rock 'n' Roll." And the first line's all they sing over and over. It's all they know.

Jessica tries to teach them the rest, but they just sort of slur it all out, "Blah, blah, blah ... Oh, Oh, Oh ..."

I offer to lasso them again, but now they only want to sing with Jessica.

My parents and the Lewises look out the door smiling. "If you can teach them five more words besides the first two lines, I'll be grateful," Mrs. Lewis says.

Daddy sees my frown and says, "You should see Becky play basketball."

I look away like I don't hear him.

I feel the little boy grab my leg. He growls, "She's Wonder Woman!"

"She's Space Monkey, Glick!" the little girl screams.

The teenage boys all laugh, and I turn red and look away.

When I look back, the boys are smiling at my sister.

Jessica is about the worst thing to happen in my life.

CHAPTER TWENTY-FOUR

Sunday, November 19, 1978

Why doesn't my father listen to me? I don't have anything here. Nothing to do. No horses. Nothing to take care of. And now I don't even have my bicycle. I made my first real friend, Sunny, and I can't even be around her. He didn't believe me when he should have, and he doesn't keep promises. It's "I'm busy or I have to work, or I have something at church." He promises stuff, but "I promise" means "I'll tell you what you want to hear and hope you forget it."

❊ ❊ ❊

I can hardly wait to be at my real home eating real Thanksgiving food with my cousins. I might not get to ride Domino, but I'm going to brush him and feed him, and clean his hooves.

Daddy fueled up the car on Tuesday and rode into school with the math teacher, so he would miss the gas lines and we'd be ready to go. We'll still have a delay. It's Wednesday night before Thanksgiving, and we're spending the night with Granny Beauchamp in Waxahachie. We go down to get her, so she can have Turkey Day with all the Rameys. Mama says Granny doesn't have anybody but us.

Daddy's sitting at her green Formica table sipping a glass of Ovaltine. "Granny, Liz and I don't want to run you out of your bed."

"Oh, yes. The girls and I are going to have a slumber party on the hide-a-bed, so you two just get yourselves on into my room." Granny's skinny, but she's wiry and fierce with a big black beehive hairdo.

"Your granny ain't but one way." Daddy sounds half admiring, half aggravated.

She bustles out of the laundry room carrying her yellow company towels to the bathroom.

"Daddy, she'll snore all night," Jessica whispers and she's right. I might sneak on to the recliner.

"Just get her telling stories. It'll delay the snoring *and* you'll fall asleep. I promise," Daddy says.

I don't want to hear any more stories. I've already heard dreadful tales of girls who are careless around horses or who go wandering in strange neighborhoods. Granny B. started in as soon as we walked in the door.

Granny B. hustles into the room with a handful of bobby pins and a roll of toilet paper. "Come here girls. You're going to help me wrap up my beauty shop do."

She gives Jessica the pins.

"Jessie, you take the end of the toilet paper and pin it here." Granny pats the side of her black do. "Now you hold it there a little, so it doesn't rip out. I want to use this potty paper more than once. Now, Becky, you ease it on up and around—easy does it—so it doesn't break. About three rounds should do it. For once in my life I can have my hair done once a week, but I've got to make it last. I'm not made of money."

I wind the last bit of TP around Granny's heap of shiny black curls, and Daddy laughs.

"So that's how you preserve the skyscraper!"

"Clifford Ramey, you and I are fixin' to go round and

round." Granny wags her short, red-nailed finger at Daddy. Daddy rushes off like he's in a panic, but he peeks around the corner and grins. "You *better* run," Granny warns. She smiles, because she loves for Daddy to pick at her.

Jessica and I look at each other. We are sleeping with a woman who has her head wrapped in toilet paper.

After Granny checks our teeth and our nails, we settle down. "Granny, tell us about you and Mama and the calves," I say. I don't want to hear any more 'bad girl' tales.

Jessica sighs because we've heard the calf story a million times.

"Well, when your grandfather passed, he left your mother and me with twenty-one pregnant heifers—and thirteen of those calves had to be pulled. The two of us were stuck with pulling them."

"That would be so cool," I say. "Delivering all those babies."

Our mother is at the doorway, and she shakes her head. "Once you've delivered five or so in the rain, it loses its charm." She and Granny look at each other.

Granny cuts her story short. "Well, I made the best deal I could on the land and the cattle, and your mother and I bought this place."

Mama smiles, "You made it look real nice, Granny."

"Yes, *we* did." They smile, sharing memories they don't tell us. "Well, ladies, we want to get an early start. Let's turn in," Granny says.

Seems like we just drift off good, blocking out Granny's snores, when Mama's waking us. I wake up on the floor, freezing with only a pillow, because Jessica crowded me off the hide-a-bed.

Granny B. supervises and frets while Daddy packs her casseroles. "I'm bringing some klobásy too, just in case folks get tired of turkey." She went over special to Ennis to a market for the Czechoslovakian sausage. Mama says Granny's always going to bring lots of food, so she does her full share. That's just her way.

Once we are crammed inside the Impala, Granny starts in on more tales. Jessica turns her head toward the window and snuggles into her pillow, so she doesn't have to hear them. Granny tells us about picking cotton all night when she was eight, about her daddy putting out a grass fire by their barn.

"Tell us a new story, Granny. Something scary."

"Well, there was that school explosion..." Granny begins.

My daddy glances sharply at her in the rearview mirror.

"Granny, that's not a fun story," Mama cautions.

"Not too much... Granny B.," Dad adds.

Granny insists and her eyes flash like a prophet's. "It's a part of their history."

Jessica sits up. "What school blew up?"

"1937. New London School—finest rural school in the country. State-of-the-art. Gas leaked into a crawl space and the whole thing was demolished. The whole block was littered with the remains of poor little children. Teachers and staff died too."

Jessica looks out the window as if she'd like to wish this story away. I shudder. "Did any children survive?"

"Precious few. We'll never know how many died exactly. All the school records were blown away. Folks might not have remembered a new child at all. You are in the sixth grade, Becky? Almost the entire sixth grade perished. Can you imagine that?"

Mama jumps in, "But it was wonderful how the community pulled together and pitched in to rescue the injured. Oil workers, doctors, farmers, mothers, businessmen—everyone worked together—risking their own lives. It was heroic really."

"Adolf Hitler sent flowers and a note of condolence," added Granny. "Every building of any size was used as a morgue. There weren't enough hearses to go around, so some parents loaded the caskets and flowers into the backs of pickups."

"Morgue?" I whisper.

"Place for dead bodies," Jessica murmurs.

Somehow the thought of a little casket, uncovered and vulnerable to wind and rain gets to me. I swallow. "Did we know anybody that was in that?"

"Your grandparents."

"Ma-maw and Granddaddy."

"And Uncle Clayton and Aunt Louise. Don't ask any of them about it. They won't talk. Nobody talks about it." Dad says, and the case is closed.

Mama tries to leave things brighter. "But the kids got the best of care in a brand-new hospital in Tyler."

Jessica brightens. "Tyler. Tell us about the Tyler roses, Granny." Thank you, Jessica.

Mama smiles and winks at us and Daddy sighs, relieved.

"Well, I wasn't so sure about this Texas Aggie coming to visit your mother." Granny raises outraged eyebrows and her voice sounds high-pitched and argumentative. "I didn't know him. All I knew was that your mother's college roommate was trying to set up her brother with my precious girl."

"Aunt Janet was your roommate?" I ask.

"Uh-huh." Mama nods.

Granny sits forward. "Well, your daddy came by way of Tyler, and here comes this Aggie bringing *me* six dozen roses in every color: red, white, yellow. Back then you could get roses for thirty-five cents a dozen at those roadside stands. Guess he knew what side his bread was buttered on." Granny reaches up and pokes my father in the shoulder. Daddy chuckles.

"Didn't you get any flowers, Mama?"

"Oh, yes. Two dozen pink sweetheart roses," Granny puts in. "Poor old Janet, lost her best friend and favorite brother in one fell swoop. She can't win. She always was the family goat. Majored in home economics and married beneath her."

Daddy looks over at Mama shocked and she shrugs. "Well, it's kind of true. Tracey is the baby, and you're your mother's pet, and Janet's in the middle."

"You really think I'm the favorite?" Dad asks.

Mama and Granny chorus "Yes!" They laugh, and I check

Jessica's reaction. She grins, agreeing.

Daddy sighs. "I love to see both my sisters. I really do. I just don't want to be in the same house with both of them."

"And your mother," Mama adds.

"And my mother."

"The price of being the peacemaker," Mama says.

Daddy shakes his head. "I guess."

"Shoot, you'll just hide out and watch football like the other men," Granny says.

Jessica groans. "Oh, no. Thanksgiving football."

"Texas state religion and its annual holiday." Daddy laughs.

CHAPTER TWENTY-FIVE

We pull up in Ma-maw and Granddaddy's driveway as the first light is shining rosy in the deep blue behind the trees. Our grandparents are out the door and ready to hug us before we even leave the car. Daddy pops the trunk and Granny reaches in and gives our Ma-maw two apple potholders.

"You didn't have to do that, Wanda. It's so good to see you. Look at all that food!" Ma-maw catches me on the run. "You and I are going to have a talk, missy." She kisses me on the head, but I know I'm in for it.

Jessica pecks Granddaddy on the cheek before Mama loads her arms with a grocery sack of supplies. Granddaddy gathers me in for hug and whispers, "What's going on here, Ranger? Are you having a hard old time there?" My daddy and grandfather glance at each other. Maybe Granddaddy will take my side and talk Daddy into giving back my bicycle.

Granny B. was right. The girls and women will be in the kitchen while the men watch football. I sneak into the den every chance I get to check scores and take a break. Ma-maw pulls me back in and has me search through the chopped walnuts for shells, so no one breaks a tooth on the Waldorf salad. Ma-maw's cat weaves himself around and around, rubbing against my legs while I work. Jessica places tiny marshmallows in neat rows on the sweet potatoes. She tried to get away with dumping in the white lumps and calling it good, but Granny B. caught her and made her do it right. Tigre finds a stray marshmallow and his orange paws bat it about the floor.

When Brittany and Tabby come in, we hug them, but Jessica and I feel like strangers around our cousins. Brittany has made new friends, and she acts bored when Jessica talks about her new choir. I tell about my trip with Miss Powers, but only about riding old Pat. That's still a sore subject.

Ma-maw says, "She tried to protect a young boy from a frightened horse."

"And nearly got a concussion," Mama adds.

"Our little Becky," Aunt Janet says.

I frown. "I'm not little anymore, y'all."

Tabby interrupts, "I finally won a belt buckle in barrel racing," but then she clams up. Does she have a sore subject too, I wonder? I felt jealous though, and then I felt bad.

Old orange Tigre huddles at our feet, his pointed ears moving first one direction and then another.

Jessica tells everybody about the Mary Kay lady and all those clothes. Ma-maw and Granny B. laugh, but Aunt Janet doesn't.

She says, "Yeah. Designer jeans fever has hit here too." Tabby frowns and picks up a squashed marshmallow and throws it away.

Brittany mutters, "Wish that lady would show up here." Tigre's ears go back and, uneasy, he dashes away.

"I wouldn't wish that," I declare. "I say those clothes are cursed. Jessie is already outgrowing them and now she's just greedy for more." Jessica pokes me, but she knows it's true.

Aunt Janet and the girls set Ma-maw's table, while I begin folding paper turkey napkins in the kitchen. I hear my grandmother whisper to my mama, "Richie got laid off, so he and Janet are struggling right now. Don't say anything."

We hear gravel pop in the driveway and doors slam. It's

Aunt Tracey, Uncle Ethan, and their boy, Walden. Mama says Aunt Tracey was the baby and the most worrisome child in the family. She went off to college, became a vegetarian Buddhist, and married a Yankee environmentalist from Vermont. Ma-maw worried even more when they left off being Buddhists and became Jesus people, but she breathed a little easier when they became Episcopalians. It's not Baptist, but it's some better. Aunt Tracey teaches English at Rice University so Ma-maw's proud.

Our grandmother says, "Ethan, what are we going to do with you? Wearing shorts and sandals in this November weather!"

Uncle Ethan hugs Ma-maw and laughs. "You call this November weather? This is summer in Vermont. Besides, I'm wearing socks with my Birkenstocks."

Uncle Richie can't keep from needling Aunt Tracey's husband. "Saved the environment, yet, Ethan? When you get done with the speckled owls and the spotted fish, you might see what you can do for the working man," Richie says.

Aunt Tracey hugs Daddy and asks, "How's that new job? We were so sorry we couldn't come to the picnic before you left."

Aunt Janet grumbles, "I'd hate to think what I'd hear if I ever stood up Clifford." Ma-maw frowns and my aunt hushes.

Granddaddy hugs Tracey and says, "Here's my baby girl!" He ruffles Walden's hair, and says, "You still playing that soccer, boy? No future in it—you come let your granddaddy show you a real football game."

Jessica and Brittany get to sit at the grownup table and Tabby, Walden, and I sit at the card table in the living room. Good thing is we can see the games, but bad thing is the men will be crowding in to watch before dessert's even over.

Granddaddy asks my dad to do the blessing. When he looks up he says, "We found a good church, Mother. Pastor Lewis is real excited about meeting H.J."

Ma-maw says, "Well!" Her pastor never asked to meet

Dad's black preacher friend.

"Liz, did you make your green Jell-O salad—with the nuts and fruit and cream cheese?" Uncle Ethan asks. Mama sends the platter around and my uncle says, "Yes, one of the three main Texas food groups: Jell-O, meat, and potatoes!"

"I notice you eat your share of it," Mama says.

"Ah-yup."

Aunt Tracey elbows him, "Of course you do. Anything's better than Yankee Barbeque—ketchup and burger!"

For a while the grown-ups talk about President Carter and him making peace between the Arabs and the Israelis. Aunt Tracey says, "I hope he know what he's doing with Iran. My Iranian students sure have some hard feelings. They're terrified of the Shah."

Richie snorts. "Socialists most likely."

Talking politics is getting dicey. Uncle Ethan and Uncle Richie are both turning red, so Daddy changes the subject. "So, seen any movies?"

"Too expensive. Have to float a loan to take your family," Richie grumps. "Anyhow, they don't do any good Westerns anymore."

Ethan says, "Well, who knows, Richie? They might make a movie about you."

"Shooooot," Uncle Richie drawls. "They'd probably get some city guy from New York to play my part."

It's time to clear away the food and dishes, and we're all sleepy and cranky. Walden tries to sneak off without helping, and Ma-maw calls him back, but Aunt Tracey lets him sneak away again. I don't really care, because all he does is whine about no cable TV or tape players. Aunt Janet looks at Mama and shakes her head. We girls don't even need to try get out of cleaning up.

Once we're done, all the ladies sit at the kitchen table and visit. Brittany puts a notebook in front of Ma-maw. Our grandmother says, "So this is that social studies project. Now what did you need me to do for you, Precious?"

"Well, we're doing our family tree and our heritage, and I'm supposed to interview my family. Granddaddy says we're mainly Irish." Brittany scans a worksheet of questions. "Let's see, who do you think I look like?"

"Hmmm." Ma-maw closes her eyes for a moment. "Somewhat like your mother, so you look a little like me too. Your eyes are like your daddy's."

"I have to do the same project in the spring," Jessica says.

Brittany blurts out, "What are you going to do for your family tree? You're not a real Ramey. You're adopted."

Jessica's eyes redden, and she swallows hard.

My ma-maw's eyes fire up. "Adopted? Like your grandmother? Like I am?" My grandmother reaches over and puts her hand on Jessica's shoulder. "Feels like a real Ramey to me." Ma-maw turns her glare on Janet and my aunt looks as if she feels like the biggest family goat of them all.

Jessica goes off to herself and reads near Granny B. Nobody's going to bother my sister there.

Walden hauls out these tiny painted lead people (wizards, elves, and I don't know what all) and tries to teach Tabby and me this fairy-tale game. It's getting good. I'm rolling the dice to get more powers, so I can beat a Medusa, when a voice says "Not Dungeons and Dragons!" Aunt Janet says this like she just stumbled on to a rattler. We jump, and little lead figures go everywhere. We're afraid we've lost Walden's wizard, until we spot Tigre swatting at the little blue-robed piece under the coffee table.

Aunt Janet takes a dim view of this game. "It's so dark and gruesome."

"I promise, Janet, there's no black magic involved," says Aunt Theresa, smiling. That really gravels Aunt Janet.

Tabby, Walden, and I play Chinese checkers to keep the peace, but when Tabby loses out to me, she gets up and flounces off. "Come on back, Tabby," Walden and I call.

"No thanks. I'm sure I'm not good enough company for you all. Not all of us can be rich or special. I'm not adopted or premature."

Those aren't the last hard words. We hear Dad and Granddaddy talk as they take down the card table. My father snaps, "Pop, I have it under control."

Granddaddy says, "Sounds to me like the cobbler's children are going without shoes. Something's on the child's mind, and you'd think a counselor would want to know what it is."

"Like you knew what was on my mind?" my father says. It gets real quiet. "Like you'd ever share what's on yours."

"Trouble with you, son, is you think a person can talk about anything. Some things should stay buried. Shrimp and Louise can go to those reunions all they want. That's not me."

Ma-maw asks for volunteers to take a plate to Aunt Ethel at her trailer. Jessica and I both jump at the chance. Jessica carries a foil-wrapped plate of food and I carry a dessert plate with sugar-free cake. We walk through the damp brown grass in silence.

"Home doesn't much feel like home, does it Becky?" Jessica whispers.

"No."

We knock and it's a minute before we hear Aunt Ethel fumble at the door. "Well, come on in here, girls."

"We missed you at dinner, Aunt Ethel."

"Well, I thank you, but that house was already too full of women." Aunt Ethel frowns at the little plate I carry. "Sugar-free dessert? Shoot! That ain't nothing to serve somebody on Thanksgiving. Are they fussing yet?"

"Some. More than usual."

"Uh-huh. Your aunts and their mom?"

We nod. "Daddy and Granddaddy too—about me," I say.

"Well, the shoe is on the other foot now. Your daddy wants you to do his sports just like his daddy wanted him to love football."

Jessica and I sink down and share the chair across from our great-aunt. Now, she knows the good stories.

Aunt Ethel sticks her tongue out at the dessert. "What

other sweet stuff did they fix?"

"Apple pie, pumpkin pie, pecan... Our daddy didn't want to play football?" I say.

"It was that black kid—that preacher. Tell me my sister put sweet potatoes on my plate."

"Preacher H.J. made Daddy stop football?" Jessica says.

"No. Not him. What's this in the dressing, oysters? H.J. got hurt playing football—bruised kidney. Becky, get me a fork from that drawer."

"But why did Daddy have to stop?" I ask.

"Oh, Clifford got all up in arms. The assistant coach pushed his friend to play hurt and Harold James lost a kidney. Goodbye to football scholarships for him. Your daddy took it hard and blamed your Granddaddy for not firing that assistant coach or yelling at the players for not covering H.J. Clifford. Said it was all racism. Why did Eileen let Janet use fresh cranberries instead of the good canned ones? Get me a knife, kiddo."

Jessica hops up and grabs one so Aunt Ethel will keep talking.

"Clifford was going to quit football completely, but your Ma-maw talked him out of it. He played, but his heart wasn't in it. He went all out for track and basketball, and your granddaddy was real hurt."

"And so, Preacher H.J. had to be a pastor," Jessica says.

"I guess that's what H.J. wanted. Your granddaddy helped get other scholarships, but he never let on." Aunt Ethel pauses. "You have to understand. Football is your granddaddy's life. He played on his high school team and his skinny brother Shrimp and their little brother Buddy would practice and practice, so they could play on the team like their older brother—Milt played at coaching them. Buddy and some others died in a tragedy and it's like Milton has been trying to rewrite history ever since. Help kids today have the life those kids would never have."

Jessica draws in her breath. "You were there. You were in that explosion."

Ethel looks from Jessica to me and pushes away her plate. "Eileen and I lost a sister and our parents. Our brother ran off. And most every friend I had died that day. I didn't ever want to come back to that place. I took off and married the young oil worker who dug me out of the rubble. You know how Louise worries your mother about checking your clothes? That was the only way they could identify her sisters—by scraps of their clothes. The bodies were—disfigured. Some parents had only body parts to bury. I don't know why I just told you that. You girls ought to run on now."

We try to hug her, but she waves us off, tears slipping down her face. Jessica cries too. I feel like I've had the wind knocked out of me. "Don't say anything to Mama."

"I know." And Jessica scrubs the tears from her face.

Uncle Richie and Dad are outside. Richie says, "Clifford, you mean well, but you *don't* know. Just how many friends have you seen blown up? And think about this: four years later a good many of those boys, your father included, enlisted for World War II." Richie wipes his eyes and nose. "And I don't know how they had the heart to do it."

We head back to the house, and Mama and Daddy already begin to pack the car. We don't beg to stay, but we hug our grandparents extra hard.

Ma-maw and Janet fix foil-covered plates without saying a word. Granddaddy and our dad keep their distance from each other.

"They still upset at each other, Mama?"

"Afraid so."

"Maybe President Carter needs to have a summit with the Rameys like he did with Israel and the Arabs," I say.

Mama sighs, "Well in both cases, it's a matter of long-standing family conflicts and I'm not sure either President Carter nor I have practical or permanent solutions."

CHAPTER TWENTY-SIX

I gotta go. I really gotta go.

It's chilly in our house, because there's an ice storm outside—during Christmas vacation. Daddy says this may be one for the records, because power is out in most neighborhoods. Couldn't happen on a school day. These city kids can have their Dallas winters. It's so damp and raw, you just feel chapped and chilled all over. My toes are cold even with wearing thick socks. The only earthly reason to get out of my snuggle sack is that I just have to go. Mama says somebody invented these sleeping bag things because the A-rabs are holding back oil. President Carter says we should all just keep our houses cold and wear sweaters like he does. It would be warmer back in East Texas, because the loblolly pines would shelter us and stop the wind. I'm cold, miserable, bored, and I gotta go.

I hear this big old dramatic sigh from the bathroom. It's Jessica. "I look like an alien," she grumbles.

The longer I wait, the more I'll have to go, and then that cold air will really make me desperate. I drop my *Black Stallion* book and wiggle out of the bag. I go to the bathroom door, and there's my sister inspecting her face. Jessica's squinting like she does when she's doing math—except there's just nothing new to calculate on the same old face.

"Mama, my chin looks just like a baby's bottom."

My sister juts out her jaw to make her chin a rounded knob of tiny pits, and frowns. I am wiggling, waiting for her to get out of the bathroom. I like my privacy, even if she is a girl too, and my sister.

Mama's face appears in the blue florescent glare. "Jessica Ramey, your face looks just like a little peach. Don't you pick at it. That dimple is perfectly precious."

Jessica huffs out a huge sigh and glares at Mama. "I wish I could fill in that dang chin pit." Jessica thinks she's big enough to try out cussing, but she's smart enough not to do the real thing around Mama.

"Don't swear, Jessica, and quit hogging the bathroom. Becky needs it."

"Come on, Jessie. I gotta go!" I plead.

Daddy calls from the den, "I got some Spackle in the garage. Fill that rascal right up."

Jessie wanders out of the bathroom and into the den. I hear our old couch creak. "Dad-deee. That's not funny."

"We could fill out your chin with peanut butter and then you could have a snack for later."

I laugh.

"Becky, I hear you in there giggling on the pot," Daddy calls out.

I come out still giggling. "Got a snack for me, Jessica?" Jessie is still trying to scowl, but her lips are curling up at the corners. She's leaning her forehead on Daddy's shoulder, hiding her face on his sleeve, and little puffs of laughter escape from her nose.

"Don't you snort any boogers on to my Aggie sweatshirt, girl."

Jessie sits up and pokes his shoulder. "You are so bad, Daddy."

"Hey, I'm just trying to help out here. We'll slap some Spackle on that chin cavern, and then Mama can spread on some of her Avon goop, and you'll be just gorgeous."

A Thing of Beauty

Now see, Daddy knows how to deal with my sister. Lately, Mama just makes Jessica crazy. She worries all the time and cannot leave anything alone. Daddy says she's a detail person.

I sit down on the other side of our father. He's wearing his ratty old sweatshirt, because it's a bad weather day. School counselors aren't supposed to be cool, but I'm still glad nobody else can see him.

Mama watches us laugh and make the couch creak. She is half smiling, half worry-warting. "I declare, Clifford, it just isn't fair."

They look at each other like adults do—knowing stuff they know and won't say—and Daddy makes her smile. "That's okay. In a few years, I'll be teaching her how to drive, and then *I'll* be the bad guy and *I* won't know anything."

Jessica frowns. "Go ahead, talk like I'm not even here."

"By the way, have you girls cleansed your faces? And toned and moisturized? You cannot begin skin care too early." Mama puts her hand on my chin and tilts up my face for a good looking over, and then reaches for Jessica's chin.

"Quit, Mama." Jessica turns her face away and scowls.

"Rebecca, pay particular attention to your chin and forehead and that little nose. You have skin just like your Aunt Janet's."

"Nobody knows *what* to do with *my* skin," Jessica blurts.

Oh, brother. Here she goes again.

"Jessica, what are you talking about?"

"Nothing. You people don't understand *any*thing." Jessica stalks off to our room.

"She's so moody." Mama shakes her head.

"She's so thirteen." Daddy shrugs.

I wait for a minute on the couch. If I give Jessica a chance to settle herself down, she may not mind if I come in. I have given up trying to predict what my sister will do. I really hate it when she squalls and cries about being ugly and stupid—which is about every other day, seems like. She sobs all hard, her nose is red, her face gets white blotches, and then her freckles really stand out. I can hide my tears. It's one of my best skills.

I get up and kneel by our Christmas tree and pick up some tinsel. Needles litter the carpet and half the ornaments have fallen off. When we pick up the decorations, we put them back any old way. Daddy says, "Time to just take it down."

"May as well," I say. Christmas was lonesome. We decided to have one to ourselves for once except for Granny B., and she drove up only for the day. It was fun getting packages in the mail, but I missed seeing my family's faces when we opened gifts. We didn't miss the squabbling.

I get up and flop down on an ottoman and sigh. "I wonder how Domino is doing. He's going to need extra feed and water in this weather. I bet he's cold and lonesome."

"He's snug and dry, I expect."

I saw Domino Thanksgiving before we left East Texas. Aunt Louise begged us to at least come by for pie and coffee. It got us away from the fussing, and we didn't mind that. I sneaked away to the barn. I breathed in deep, smelling the hay and spicy, warm animal odors. I groomed and patted the old horse and told him all my troubles and news. He looked at me with those warm dark liquid eyes and pricked up his ears like he understood. He looked older than I remembered, and so did Uncle Clayton.

It's like Daddy's thinking the same thing. "I hope someone can make it over to help Uncle Clayton with the animals," he says. "They've got heifers ready to calve. Hope that goes all right. The barn needs repairs, the fence. I'll have to get to it this summer."

I sigh. "I wish we could call somebody." Back home, all the Rameys would have swapped calls about how cold it is and is anybody's electricity out and does anybody need a generator? Ma-maw would invite us all over for chili or stew. Even if it were icy, we'd slip and slide over somehow.

"We'll call Ma-maw and Granddaddy on New Year's. Can't run up a phone bill, Becky."

I don't mention it, but I notice Daddy manages to call

his friend H.J. sometimes. Probably to tell on me and gripe about Granddaddy. Once I heard the preacher loud and clear tell Daddy "Clifford, it's high time you made up with your father." Dad looked shocked and sheepish. Then it got quieter while they talked about me and H.J.'s son Burgess. I guess even a preacher can have a problem child.

I pause, "Daddy, is Burgess bad?"

"No, baby. He's just going through changes like Jessica. Trouble is people can misunderstand, and he can get in terrible trouble."

"From white people."

Dad heaves a big sigh. "Yes."

"I guess you don't miss home."

"Yeah, I do sometimes." He takes in a breath and leans forward. "I've been meaning to check in with you. You heard some disturbing things from Granny B. You doing okay with that?"

"I'm okay. I'm glad I know. It explains a lot of things. Why March is the sad month. Ma-maw and Aunt Louise cry at a little of nothing, and Granddaddy..."

"Drinks," Dad finishes.

"Yeah. Did you know they used bad gas because it was free? But the government puts stink in gas now, so people can smell it."

"That's right. How do you know that, Rebecca?"

"Talked to my social studies teacher."

"If you want to know something, you are not going to stop until you do." Daddy shakes his head. "That's not a bad thing I guess."

"Now I get why Aunt Janet's stove stinks."

"And why your grandmother hates it." Daddy pauses and changes to his educator face. "School going better for you?"

"Some. Everything but Mrs. Goforth." I pause. "You all don't know it, but she's mean. She picks on kids if they don't have anybody to take up for them."

"Is that right?" Daddy looks at me. "Well, you won't always like everybody, but you have to learn to get along with them."

"She doesn't bother me much, because of you. But she watches for me to mess up, so she can hold it against me."

"So, don't mess up."

"Right." It seems like a good time to bring up my friend. "Daddy, Sunny is a good girl and she's real smart. Nice people that work hard can live in trailers. Aunt Janet and Uncle Richie live in one."

Daddy purses his mouth thinking. "I know that. Maybe your friend could come over here?"

I smile. Sunny and I eat together at lunch now, but it's hard to get in a good girl talk in with Rusty and Kenny and Chad there too. Besides all they want to talk about is Space Invaders. Obsessed, absolutely obsessed.

Daddy leans forward and pats my knee. "Becky, you will get to ride again, but it may take a while. I can't lie to you about that."

I look at him for a moment and then I nod. "I know." At least he's being straight with me.

"Do you suppose you could think about track?"

"Daddy, nothing personal, but it just doesn't do anything for me."

Daddy winces, but then he smiles, trying to be a good sport.

"Why don't you run? Do one of those marathons? I'll jog with you while you train," I say. "Cousin Missy scolded me and said I better stay in condition if I ever want to ride. I can run along with you."

Daddy smiles kind of crooked. "I may take you up on that."

"Daddy, you know what? Sometimes Jessica balks or jigs just like a horse."

"Jigs?" Daddy grins. "Are you calling your sister a horse?"

"Well, you know how horses dance in place instead of walking, when you want them to go? Like when their riders are too uptight?" I whisper in case Mama can hear us. "Mama's tense, so Jessica balks."

"Or jigs." Daddy chuckles. "You might just have something there."

"See, being around horses makes you wise."

"Ahhh. Rebecca, you don't give up, do you?"

"No, Daddy."

"You're persistent, I'll give you that. Go try your horse wisdom on your sister."

CHAPTER TWENTY-SEVEN

I peek around the doorway. Jessica is sitting cross-legged on her bed and wearing an afghan around her shoulders. She is frowning and strangling some throw pillow, but she doesn't fuss at me. Out of the corner of my eye, I see newspaper clippings of Billy lying by Jessica's foot. One article had his senior picture, and my sister clipped it out and put it in her wallet like he gave it to her.

Looking at my old horse stuff seems safe. I used to get a plastic horse every year. Mama says they're collectible. I used to keep my Breyer horses out for pretty, but until now I haven't bothered to unpack them in the new house. Today I feel like getting them out—just to look at them. They are the closest I'll get to a horse for a while, but I might keep my Breyer horses to myself. Sometimes you must keep your important things secret, or the cool kids will tease so much you must throw them away. You must be careful in a new place. If you mess up or look weird, there aren't any do-overs.

When Jessie sits with her head bent down, her hair looks like a blond curtain. I can feel her staring at me. "What are you doing, Becky?"

"Just looking at my horses." I pull a bay and a paint horse from the U-Haul box in the closet.

She blows her dishwater hair away from her mouth. Jessie gripes about her hair; it's as straight as a horse's mane. Mama and I can hardly comb our dark brown curly mess.

I take a little breath. "Jessie?"

"Yeah."

"I think your chin's kinda cute. It's a different double chin—it's not fat."

Jessie gives a little laugh-snort. "And when I get old and fat, I'll have a quadruple chin."

We both giggle.

"Stop it. It really is okay. I mean it's pretty," I say.

"I guess it's all right. I just don't look like anybody—*you* know."

"Your hair's the same color as Uncle Richie's yella lab."

"Oh, thanks a lot. I look like the Ramey family *dog*."

"Yep, our Old Yeller."

I dodge the pillow Jessie heaves at me and move my pillows off my pink bedspread. Jessie's stuff is blue. One time we switched because those were the colors everybody always assigned us: pink for brunette, blue for blond. After a while, we switched back. That made Mama crazy, because she went and made us new pillows with our initials on them in our new colors. I told her, "That's okay, Mama. They can be for us to lie on when we visit each other's bed."

She smiled, but just a little. "That's real sweet, baby."

Jessica says those initial pillows are just one more example of Mama making a big deal over everything.

My sister sits there watching me while I make a paint Breyer horse prance back and forth. His back legs stay pretty much in place, while the rest of his body moves from side to side.

"What are you doing with that horse?"

"Pretending to cut calves."

"I never got the point of that. That's the stupidest event. Doesn't even look like the rider needs to be there."

"Just shows what you know." It's like a ballet or a chess

game between a horse and a calf. The hard work's done ahead of time—training the horse to maneuver a calf away from the herd without letting it get away. Wish I could see Miss Powers do it. Riders keep one hand on the saddle horn, and rein one-handed the whole time. "I'd like to see you try it."

"Well, I advise you not to put these country hick horses out in our room."

"I'd like to know why not?"

"Look, I don't know what it's like in sixth grade, but nobody wants to be around goat ropers in eighth. There are the bad kids, the smart kids, the popular kids, the musical kids, athlete kids and then there's the goat ropers. No city people like ropers and this is Dallas."

"Nuh-uh, we're a suburb."

"Close enough. Everybody thinks ropers are ignorant."

"Well, what about the basketball teams going to the ranch?"

"Y'all are athletes and you can get away with stuff, and even then, you only go once a year. We've got one chance to get it right. I'm musical and smart—you could be smart or an athlete—both even."

"I don't much care what these kids around here think. I'm Rebecca Ramey and I ride horses and anybody who doesn't like it can just lump it." I'm the tough, quiet girl, but I wonder what the kids in my class would say. I picture them turning to look back at me sitting on the back row.

At least people want me on their teams now, but will they still want me if I'm a die-hard goat roper?

Jessica shakes her head. "You'll be sorry. I can tell you one thing. *I* don't intend to be unpopular. If you must have that stuff, keep it out of sight when my friends are over."

I swallow hard and bite my lip.

"Don't you miss home at all, Jessie?"

"I miss Ma-maw and Granddaddy," Jessica murmurs and then her face flushes. "But I don't miss Brittany one bit."

"You both just want all the attention and make each other

mad. You sing, and she does drill team. She *is* snooty. It goes with her pug nose." I take my pointer finger and push up the tip of my nose. "I think she looks like Miss Piggy—poor Miss Piggy."

"Brittany has Miss Piggy's legs too. I told her so too." Jessica's mouth purses sideways. "She told me she doesn't know who I look like—I'm not a real Ramey." Jessica shrugs a little like it really shouldn't matter, but her eyes are starting to water, and her nose is getting red. She could cut loose and bawl any minute.

"Well, at least your kids won't inherit a pig nose."

Jessica smiles. Close call.

"Girls, everything, okay?" Mama's at the door.

"Yes, ma'am." I make my piggy nose again. "We're just doing Brittany imitations." Jessica pushes up her nose too and giggles.

Mama laughs, but she doesn't want to. "Y'all be nice. God doesn't like ugly." She spies my U-Haul box. "You girls already have the right idea."

"Nooo, Mama. Not unpacking," Jessica groans.

"Oh, yes indeedy. These unpacked boxes have haunted us for over five months."

Daddy comes in with a box and sets it on our floor. "Consider it a treasure hunt, a solution to many mysteries."

"Like where are my embroidery scissors?" Mama adds.

"Where is all my nail polish? You and Daddy won't let me buy any," Jessica says.

"Not when you've got bottles and bottles packed away somewhere. Happy hunting, ladies. I'll be back with more." Daddy heads off to the garage.

We kneel by the box marked 'stuff' in Jessica's handwriting—purple ink. Mama tears back the packing tape and begins digging through. "What on earth? Dirty socks and underwear?"

"Well, you told me to pack everything."

"*Not* dirty clothes. Well, here's your jacket, Jessica. One mystery solved. It'll have to be dry cleaned." Mama shakes her head. "The rest is old notebooks and stuffed animals. I thought I told you to sort things."

"Well, I did, sort of—it's all my stuff."

Daddy brings in two more boxes. One is marked "girl's books." The bottom one is mine, marked "gear." Daddy offers, "Why don't we keep this one in the attic."

I wondered where that box had disappeared to.

"No thanks, Daddy. I'll keep it with me. It's not in the way." I look through and find my spurs, carefully wrapped.

Jessica lifts some books, looks down, and crows, "My nail polish!" She lifts a shoebox and rattles the bottles triumphantly.

"Why were they in a shoe box?" Mama is the only mother I know who keeps all the shoes in their original boxes. She even makes sure the shoes match what the boxes say.

"You told me to pack my nail polish, so I did. I had to put them in something."

"Well, where did you put your shoes?"

"I don't know. They're around here somewhere."

"My point exactly."

Daddy calls down the hallway, "Liz, I think I found a craft box."

"Put it in the sewing room. I'll be right there." Mama stands up. "You two unpack these and put things up—someplace sensible."

"What are you looking at me for?" Jessica huffs.

I hang up my favorite Western shirt. It's pink with tiny ruffles on the yoke. Jessie is looking me over like she was looking at her face earlier, calculating. "You like horses just like Uncle Clayton does. Your eyes are green like Granddaddy's too."

"What difference does it make? I got eyes. That's all I care. Daddy says I like horses, because young girls have big eyes and long legs just like colts do."

Jessica shoves her nail polish shoebox in her desk drawer, while I stack my box of horses and my box of gear and push them into the closet.

And then Mama screams. Makes us both jump.

"My scissors!" She comes to our door shaking them like

some TV trial lawyer would a murder weapon. "Why are my embroidery scissors encrusted in glue and stashed away in a half-ruined shoe box?"

"Well, I needed to cut foil for the final project in Mrs. Reilly's reading class." Jessica talks like this was only what any reasonable person would have done.

Mama puts one hand over her eyes. "Foil—you cut foil with my embroidery scissors."

"And the box was my rough draft for my diorama."

"Did you ever think to ask, before you used my scissors or ruined perfectly good shoe boxes?"

"They're just stupid boxes and besides, we've got a closet. What do we need shoe boxes for? It's just dumb. You're not making any sense."

I get up and leave them to it. This is going to last awhile, so I go find Daddy in the recliner. We can hear Mama and Jessica clear into the den.

"Daddy, how long is it going to be like this?"

"About as long as the War of the Roses, except more intractable."

"More what?"

"Like your grandmother and Aunt Janet."

"Oh." Daddy's mother and sister have fought for years, so he knows. And they're grownups and all. That means Jesus will return before this conflict is over.

CHAPTER TWENTY-EIGHT

It's after midnight, and I lie in my bed squinting and rubbing my eyes. I feel confused and groggy, because I have just awoken from the weirdest dream. I was so happy when it began. I was barrel racing again, but on a beautiful palomino. Its blond mane was streaming in the wind and I was sitting up, balanced just right, making a snappy turn around the first barrel. It's crazy how you go back and forth in dreams. Sometimes you are doing stuff and sometimes you are watching yourself do stuff. I looked great. I was wearing a shiny red shirt with silver threads all through the material and silver top stitching too. But then I looked down at the saddle; it was old and beat up and a strange shade of blue. I felt so embarrassed. Why did I have to have such ugly tack? Then my horse began acting up. Just as we were heading for the second barrel, it refused to go around. The palomino bucked, I fell off, and the ornery beast jumped up on the barrel and balanced on it like a circus pony, showing off. I jumped awake and it took me a minute to figure out why I woke up.

Jessica has the desk light on her bed and she's looking at her scrap book again. Sometimes she gets it out and looks at the little picture of her birth mother and the pictures Mama and Daddy took when they brought Jessica home.

A Thing of Beauty

The sleet clicks on our window, and I peek outside. Icicles hang down from the roof like long, bony fingers. The street is glassy, slick, and each blade of grass stands up stiff, all coated in ice and shining in the streetlight. The trees across the road look like some crop duster spray-painted them silver.

"Becky, what are you doing up?" Jessica sounds annoyed.

"What are *you* doing up?" I answer.

"Reading. Go on back to sleep."

"I can't." I get up to get some water and see the blue glow of the television shining into the hall from the den. Mama and Daddy are still up and having one of their talks.

"Cliff, I'm at a loss." This time Mama nestles with Daddy in the recliner. I lean on the old upright piano. I can see the top of Daddy's head, but he'd have to turn around to see me. He leans his cheek on the top of Mama's head.

"I think most parents are, Liz."

"We used to have fun together. All four of us, and now I can't say anything right." Mama pauses and takes a big breath. "Clifford, do you ever wonder what it would have been like if the twins lived?"

"I guess you always wonder. I guess I'm just thankful to have what we have."

"It's not that. I just wonder if I would have known more, done better. And I wonder if we rushed things adopting so soon. I don't know what I'm going to say when Jessica *asks* to know more."

"Well, we've always known that day was going to come. All we can do is tell the truth and let her know we love her. If we can wait just a little longer, I think she'll handle it better."

"It's just got to be so confusing to hear. That whole custody thing with her father. How do you tell the truth, and yet keep her from being damaged from a hurt like that? Kids go into a tailspin over so much less." That made my ears prick up. What kind of truth could damage Jessica? She bawls over nearly everything as it is.

Dad sighs. "And how do we prepare Jessie to meet Peggy?"

"What does Jessica need to be prepared for?" That popped out before I could stop it.

Daddy about fell over. "Good Lord, Rebecca! You scared the living daylights out of me. How long have you been standing there?"

I recover fast. "I just wanted to know. Could I have some warm milk? I woke up—crazy dreams."

"Sure, baby. Go heat up a burner. Put it on low. I'll be right there, Becky." Mama leans forward. "Is Jessie awake? See if she wants some."

Daddy's still trying to get over being startled. "She's like a little ghost, slipping up on people. Rebecca Ramey, you could try out for the CIA, you little booger!" Daddy calls out.

I shuffle back to our room to check on Jessie and ask does she want some warm milk. I lean on the doorjamb. Big old tears are running down her face. Did she hear about that damage stuff too? Or is she just moody? It's too big to ask about.

Jessie wipes her face with both hands. "Did you hear some of that?"

I pause. "Yeaahh. A little. What did you hear?"

"I heard that Mama wonders about those other babies."

"Well, that just means there would have been four girls instead of two."

"No, there wouldn't, you dope." She scrubs off another tear. "They would have stopped after the twins. You and I wouldn't have happened."

That sort of makes you think. I just stand there and twirl a long, curly strand of my hair for a moment. "Welll, maybe so. Maybe not. You want some milk or not?"

Jessie heaves a long sigh. "Yeah, I'll be there in a minute."

Mama's in the kitchen rummaging through the cabinet for the double boiler. Soon Mama and I are watching for the tiny bubbles to appear next to the rim, like we're looking for long overdue company.

I feel like I need to set things straight. "We could have had four girls, couldn't we, Mama? Me and Jessie and the other two babies?" Jessie walks into the room and eyes Mama to see what she will say.

Mama's eyebrows pinch up a little—the sad way—not the frown way, and then she smiles a little. "Well, I know I have two precious girls now. Come here you two." She tries to gather us both in for a hug. I snuggle on in, but Jessie is trying to hold out as long as she can. Jessica looks about as stiff as a coat hanger, but I guess she needs a hug too, because she relaxes and snuggles in for just a moment. Daddy walks in, and Jess backs off from that hug like Mama's on fire.

We all feel awkward, so when the milk is ready, we stand and drink it silently. I mutter, "Thanks, Mama."

"Yeah, thanks," Jessica whispers. We all wander off to bed.

The warm milk didn't help much. Jessica thrashed around in her bed, and I stared at the ceiling for the longest. I didn't think I'd ever get back to sleep, but I must have, because a loud metallic crash and crunch makes me sit straight up in bed, the back of my head prickling in panic. Jessica's eyes stare at me, confused and sleepy.

"What was that?"

Jessie and I rush to peer out my window. In the early morning light, we can see Daddy and Mr. Wright easing as quickly as they can over ice to a car that has just slid into a light pole. A lady and a girl about my age sit looking dazed and frightened in the car with a smashed fender.

Jessica and I grab our robes and rush into the kitchen. "Mama, there's a wreck outside."

"There's a lady and a young girl." Jessica adds.

"I know girls. I'm calling the police."

We rush and open the front door. Daddy and Mr. Wright are guiding the lady and the dark-haired girl over the ice to our house. Daddy skids sideways a little but catches himself.

"Come in, come in." Mama welcomes. "Are you all right?"

"I'm so sorry. I would have never even tried, but my daughter's ear . . ." The lady is really rattled.

Jessica peers at the girl. "Hey, your ear's bleeding."

"Did you hit your head, sweetie?" Mama gently tilts the dazed child's head.

"No, she was already bleeding. Marcie has had a horrible earache all night long, but she woke up and there was blood. I thought I should take her to the emergency room. That's the only reason I'd ever be out on roads like this. My husband's out of town—airport delay at a time like this." This lady's about to cry.

"Bless your heart." Mama leads her to a chair. "Let me call an ambulance."

"I think I'm okay—I don't think I'm hurt. I wasn't going fast at all."

Mama and the lady examine her daughter carefully. Only a little bruise on her knee. The daughter grins and shrugs. "Mothers."

"I'm sorry to be any inconvenience—what a rude awakening for you all. Really, I have family just across the way."

"Don't you worry—I'm Liz Ramey and these are my daughters, Jessica and Rebecca."

Jessica announces, "I'm adopted."

We all look a little confused. What does that have to do with anything?

The lady blinks and recovers. "What a lovely family. I'm Carrie Waldman, and this is Marcie."

Marcie brightens. "You're the new quiet kid, Becky Ramey."

"That's right. I didn't even recognize you in your jammies and ear and all. Mama, we're in the same class at school."

"How nice. Why don't you girls go make Marcie comfortable? Change your sheets, Becky and she can lie down and rest on your bed until we can reach a doctor."

As we show her the way, Marcie whispers, "Forget the sheets. I feel pretty good since my ear popped. The blood made my mom freak out." Marcie chatters nonstop. "Your room's cool. Did your mother decorate this?" We can hardly wedge in any answers. "Where did you guys move from?"

"A little Podunk town in East Texas." Jessica tries to look bored and sophisticated. "Finally, we can do some real shopping. Do you go to the North Park Mall?"

"Not if I can help it. Oh, look, a horse."

Jessica rolls her eyes. I left out the Breyer paint horse. My sister looks at me like I just threw my entire social life into a pile of manure.

"Yeah, it's from when I was little." I admit. "My mom says they're collectible."

Marcie smiles, delighted. "You have a collection? Can I see them?"

I pull out the U-Haul box and Marcie digs in, pulling out horse after horse. "These are so cool. Why don't you have them out? I have a dog collection, but they're breakable. Someday I'm going to have lots of real dogs. Do you have a real horse?"

"No, but I ride them."

"Luckeee."

We hear Mom call from the kitchen. "Girls, we have waffles in here."

Marcie brings the Appaloosa with her. "Look Mom, how cool."

Mrs. Waldman nods as she hangs up the phone. "The doctor says it's nothing to worry about, just to come in on Tuesday. The eardrum bursting was the best thing—completely natural. It ought to heal on its own. So, it was all for nothing."

"I would have done the same thing."

"All the same, we've got to have you all over. And about the school bus." Mrs. Waldman and Mom look at each other knowingly. "If there's any trouble—if they get tired of the rowdiness and noise, the girls can always ride with us."

"Oh, we won't need to," Jessica declares. "My friends are on the bus."

CHAPTER TWENTY-NINE

It is one week later, but it's a whole different Saturday. It's sunny and sixty degrees outside. That's Texas weather too—ice one week, balmy temperatures the next.

Daddy and I are jogging at the high school track. Early morning runners are stretching or puffing around the track in their Christmas gift jogging suits. We'll see how long those New Year's Day resolutions last. Daddy has slowed, cooling down, but I need to run a little more. We were cooped up awhile after that ice storm. I round the last curve and I see Rusty sitting by my dad, leaned back talking.

"Hey, Becky," he says

I only wave and smile, still into my run.

I hear Daddy say, "There goes Atalanta."

"That's a—stupid—story," I call back. I start slowing my pace, then walking. I cool myself down just like I would a horse. I head back, walking along the track while runners breeze by me.

Dad and Rusty are grinning at me. "So why is the Atalanta story stupid?" Dad asks.

"Well, they've got it backward for one thing. The girl would throw the apples *at* the boys. And you can't catch a girl with food. Now boys..."

"Discrimination," Daddy says.

"That's what I say," Rusty adds. "What if the boys cheered the girl?" he calls as I walk past.

"Well, that might be nice," I say

I turn back ready to stretch and my Dad is frowning a little at my friend. On the way home Daddy says, "Remember—no dating until you're sixteen."

I wrinkle my nose. "Who wants to date?"

Today's a big day. After we get our room clean and some laundry done, we're going shopping. Then I go to my very first sleepover at Marcie's—and Sunny's coming too!

"We're back," I call out.

"Good." Mama's getting all dolled up, because we're going to North Park Mall. She's doing her makeup with the door open. "I've got to let the steam out of the bathroom, before I tackle this hair. Humidity frizzes us curly heads up worse than anything, doesn't it, sugar?" Mama stops looking at the mirror and looks at me. "I'm going to balance the checkbook while you girls clean. And let's do a load or two of laundry."

I hear Daddy say, "Liz, this little guy, Rusty? His dad died in Vietnam . . . they lost their house . . . some so-called army buddy did the mother out of a lot of money . . ."

I hurry off to our room. I go inside my half (the clean half) of the closet to write in my diary, before I start my chores. It's hot, but it's private. I kick out Jessica's shoes on the way in. Jessica gives me plenty of material to write about.

My plan is working. Jessica thinks I still journal in the old blue diary, but it's only my pretend diary. All I put in the decoy diary is boring stuff like what I wore or if we had hotdog day in the cafeteria, because I know she'll look. Sometimes I put in some phony rumors or gossip, so Jessica thinks it's real.

I hear angry voices, so I peek out. My mother and sister are at war again. Mama's standing at the door fooling with a hot roller. It takes a lot of work for a curly-headed woman to fix big hair. She looks like she'd like to throw that roller somewhere.

Daddy is right. He said Mama and Jessie are in a cold war

like the Russians and the Americans. That means they don't hit and say mean things outright, but they want to, and they think of other sneaky ways to annoy each other. Right now, they are annoying each other over our room. Mama wants things organized and spotless; Jessie wants to redecorate a junkyard—without clearing out the junk.

Jessica fumes, "Good gravy! Cleaning's not going to do any good. What's the point? Pink-and-blue bedspreads! This is the most baby room ever! I can't believe I have to live in this nursery."

"What do you mean 'baby'?" Mama wants to know.

"Well for one thing, these stupid posters with those pale, sad-eyed kids. They look like they're saying, "I looove God," Jess moans in this mournful voice.

Mama says, "Jessica, don't be irreverent."

Jessie smiles a little. "I wasn't being irreverent. I'm just saying that's what they look like."

Mama looks unhappy, but she doesn't say anything. She just got her third china sad-eyed kid statue. Jessie told me she just wants to rip them sad-eyed kid posters right off the wall.

"The whole room's just not in style. Anybody can see that." Jessica says this like not another living soul could possibly disagree with her.

Mama calls to dad down the hall. "Clifford, I just want to know how I suddenly got to be so ignorant."

I lean out of the closet. "Don't worry, Mama, you can do my half," I throw in. "I like your decorating."

"Butt out, Becky! You're just trying to butter up Mama."

"Becky, not now, baby," Mama sighs.

"It's my room too! And I'm not a baby." Nobody's listening to me. I retreat into the closet and I write furiously in a little old red spiral notebook—my real diary. Today's topic: Why Jessica Ramey is the Stinkiest Sister Ever.

Number one. She is a slob. I'm so tired of stepping over her dirty underwear, I can't stand it. When she changes clothes, she just drops the dirty ones wherever she is standing.

"This room's just pitiful!" Jess raves.

I poke my head out and holler, "Because you don't ever clean it. *I'm* getting flat sick and tired of our room, because I can't walk through it anymore."

"Amen!" Mama declares. "No point in redecorating when you won't keep your room clean." She teases out her hair like she's mad at it. That hair spray looks like steam coming out her ears. I just know she's as put out as I am with Jessie's bellyaching. "We've got to go. Girls, just get your room clean," says Mama and stomps out.

Which means "Becky, get up and do it, because nobody else will"—as usual. To Jessica, putting up her shoes means kicking them under her bed or in *my* side of the closet. Usually, Daddy tells me to take care of my part of the cleaning and to leave Jessica's mess alone. When he's not looking, I pick up all I can, just so I don't have to listen to Mama and Jessie fight.

"Well, I may as well get started so something gets done around here." I say this through my teeth. I don't expect anybody to pay attention. Jessica looks in the closet door and glares at me. I hug my notebook to my chest and glare right back. I go back to writing when she steps away. My lead breaks and I throw the pencil down and pick up my spare. *Number two: Jessica is the biggest butt-in-ski of them all. She butts in when Marcie and Sunny and I are having important talks and tries to tell us what to do. Or she teases us. OR she gripes about us taking up too much time on the phone, so she can't talk for hours with her friends. I don't get to ride with Marcie in her car, just because Jessica insists on riding the bus with her friends. Mama makes me go with her.*

I write one more diary entry: *Reason number three. Jessica Ramey thinks she's hot snot because she sings, and I'm cold boogers because I don't. It isn't fair. Mama and Daddy listen to her with their eyes closed like she's an angel or something.* I peek outside the door to be sure no one is watching and then slip my real diary in my top-secret hiding place—my Kotex box. Mama gave it to me after one of "The Talks." I don't need it yet, so the top isn't even opened. I open the bottom of the box and slide my diary in through there. Nobody will touch that. The blue diary goes on my desk for Miss Nosy Britches.

Daddy walks in. "Okay, ladies. Let's gather up some laundry here and separate it into piles." I get up and toss my nightie on the wash-and-wear load.

Jessie was fooling with my tape player that *I* got for Christmas, and suddenly she gets her little self into gear and starts gathering up clothes real fast. I think I know why. I clear my throat. "Daddy, I think there might be quite a bit in our hamper."

Jessica looks panicked. "Uh, no, I think Mama got that batch already." She doesn't want Daddy to check.

Now Daddy's suspicious. "Well, let's just see."

Jessica throws herself over the hamper. "No, Daddy, no, no, no." she moans. "I'll take care of it."

"Jessica Ramey, move. Now."

Jessica slides herself back slowly and kneels. She can't bear to look.

He lifts the lid and begins sorting through. "Socks, blouse, jeans, more socks . . . and a stack of *clean, folded laundry*! Jessica, it's not bad enough that you leave dirty clothes all over your room—you won't even take the time to put up *clean clothes*!" Dad stops and closes his eyes.

"Thanks a lot, Becky," Jessica hisses.

Daddy is ready to ground her right then and there, but Mama says Jessica simply must have new bras.

"You're too developed to go without a bra, and furthermore, no daughter of mine is going to go around looking like some wacky feminist," Mama declares.

"Well, something's got to change. I can hardly breathe, and these old things are digging into me and leaving red marks all around my middle." Jessie eases one finger in the elastic around her chest and pulls it out, just to get a little relief.

"What size is that one you have on now?" Mama tries to check Jessie's label and my sister about has a cow.

"Mother, would you stop? This is so embarrassing."

"We've got to figure out the right size *some*time."

Mama has me make my bed and says the rest can wait, because Jessica's going to do it. "I'm putting drawer liner on my shopping list, because we are cleaning out all your drawers." I get to shop too. Mama says we are going for a new pretty nightie and new underwear since this is my very first sleepover at Marcie's.

After we drop pick up drawer liner at Kmart, we head to the mall. Mama doesn't want to make it a fun trip since Jessie's grounded, but it's a shame to go to North Park Mall and not look at the fancy displays at Neiman Marcus. Marcie's mom calls it "Needless Markup." We don't ever shop there, because Daddy's says it's higher than a cat's back, but we always enter the mall through its door, if he's not along, so we can look on the way to Dillard's. Mama's in a big hurry, because she must drop off Avon to her customers, and she's had an extra big order this month. Jessie's dragging her feet, because she's not in any hurry to go back to our room. I'm so excited to go to Marcie's that I can't hurry them enough.

"Nooo, only a few seconds at the purses and no shoe looking, Mama. Jessie, come on. You may be grounded, but I have places to go."

"Oh, do you now." Jessica hisses at me while Mama looks at a navy clutch purse. "We'll just see about that."

We get to the underwear section in Dillard's and Mama just embarrasses Jessica to death. She gets the attention of a round little sales clerk in blue. "Ma'am, we need to buy a bra for my daughter."

"Mother, Shhh!" Jessica hisses. "I can't believe you just said 'bra' in the middle of Dillard's."

"Well, to achieve the appropriate fit, we'll have to..." begins the plump little sales lady.

"You are *not* going to check my bra label." Jessica backs up against a mirror.

"No, hon, you're right. That wouldn't do any good. We have to measure you to get the right fit."

"No way. This is so humiliating."

The sales lady hands Mama a yellow measuring tape.

"Jessica, you're the one creating a scene. Come on now. We still must find Becky's nightgown. Come on in here so we can get your measurements for your bras." Mama looks determined, but so does Jessica.

I can't stand it. I grit my teeth and look at Mama and say, "Give me that measuring tape, please." Mama's mouth just drops open. I think I shock myself, but Miss Jessica is not going to do me out of my sleepover. I take her into the dressing room and I measure her. "She's eighty-seven inches around the fat part and seventy-six around her ribs," I bark.

The plump little sales lady chuckles. "Sugar, I don't think that's possible. Oh, honey, you've got the tape twisted." She leaves the tape in my hands, but she gently straightens it around Jessica's body. "You're a lovely young lady, darlin', but you just can't be that developed."

"Well, if she's so lovely, you can keep her," I growl and stick my tongue out at Jessie. Jessie makes a face back at me.

Mama's eyebrows rise, alarmed. "What a horrible thing to say to your sister."

"What high school are you attending, hon?"

Jessie turns bright red and mutters, "I'm in junior high."

"Oh." The lady's eyes get big and her eyebrows go clear up into her bangs. Jessica does look awful mature for her age.

Jessica takes forever to get dressed adjusting her new bra straps until they are just perfect, with me just begging her to get a move on.

We head to the girl's section. I'm trying to hurry, but I look behind me and see Jessica walking slowly. Two pimply boys in the sportswear section call out, "Hey, hey, pretty mama, you are built!" The boldest guy steps over to my sister, but Jessica is mortified and runs back to the dressing room in tears.

Mama's icy stare freezes them in their tracks. I grind the heel of my Western boot into the bold boy's toe, and I kick the other boy's shin. Goat-roper wear has its points. Mama tells me to cut it out and sends me after Jessica. Then our mother heads straight for the store manager to report those rude boys.

I drag Jessica back to our mother, but then Mama looks at her watch and gasps. "We have to leave this very minute! I've got to meet my first customer at 1:30."

I am silent all the way home. Nobody remembered my nightie. I go and sit on my bed. Mama sticks her head in the door on her way out. "Don't forget to pack your overnight bag, sugar." I don't answer. I hear the back door close behind her.

Jess says, "Aren't you going to Marcie's?" Her voice is muffled because she is reading a *Seventeen* magazine.

"No, I can't go—and I'm not talking about it."

"What's your problem? You are so temperamental sometimes. They're going to be here soon."

I just shrug. I make those tears obey. I'm good at it. I pick up one of the rolls of drawer liner. Mama bought a pretty pattern to line Jessica's chest of drawers, but I don't think there's enough for my dresser. Somehow, that makes me feel even sadder.

The doorbell rings. It's probably Marcie and her mom. Jessica looks at me over the top of her magazine. "Well?"

"I'm not answering the door. I'm not going."

"You are so weird. You're never going to have any friends."

Marcie Waldman is at my door. "Becky, what's wrong? Why aren't you packed?"

"I'm not coming. I can't." I look at the stitching on my bedspread.

"What do you mean you're not coming? Becky, you've got to come."

I don't look up. A big old tear plops down from my eyelashes and onto my hand.

Marcie insists. "No. Now you tell me. What's wrong?"

I look up. "I don't have anything to wear. Jessica took too long at Dillard's and we had to leave."

"Is that all? Why didn't you say anything? Becky, you are such a baby." Jessica rolls her eyes and goes back to her magazine.

"Shut up, Jessica," I rasp.

Suddenly, Marcie's mom is bending down. "Come on, sweetie. Nothing's going to stop this soiree. We're gonna go pick up whatever you need, and then we're going to have a party!"

As I finish packing my bag, Jessica shakes her head. "You make such big deal over nothing—just like Mama."

"Well, it's all your fault, Jessica. You acted like an absolute fool in Dillard's and wasted everybody's time—on purpose."

"Well, ex-cu-use me."

"That is not an apology. It goes like this. 'I'm sorry.'"

"I'm sorry already."

Marcie and I both stare her down.

Mrs. Waldman frowns, "I'll get the car started, girls."

"I said I was sorry."

"Sorry doesn't cut it. I'm telling Mama."

"Let's go, Becky." Marcie grabs my arm, pulls me to the doorway.

"I'm going to get my new nightgown and go on my sleepover, because today I'm the *good* kid. Enjoy the peace and quiet, Jessica."

I duck as Jessica throws my pillow with a blue *R* at the door.

CHAPTER THIRTY

"Rebecca Ramey, you better get happy," Marcie scolds. "You've got brand new silky jammies and matching slippers. You are *not* going to spoil this sleepover by sitting around and being mad at Jessie. Enough already!" Marcie is little, but she sure is bossy. "Get over it, and let's fix the chips and dip. The table needs to be all set up before Sunny and Amy get here."

"I'll mix up the dip, while you get the chips ready."

"That's more like it."

Before long we've got all the nail polish and hair stuff arranged and the Twister game set up.

The other girls arrive, and Amy gets us off track for a little while over the TV. She and Marcie are having words over *Saturday Night Live*.

"I'm not allowed to watch it—you'll get us in trouble," Marcie says, gesturing at the television like it's a scandal.

"I know. Let's not watch TV at all. Let's play cassettes and do our nails and hair," offers Sunny.

Amy has a real steady hand, and we all want her to paint our nails. At first, I want to have "Peach n' Pretty," but then I decide it would be cool to match the other girls, so we all use "Madly Mauve." Amy does her own left hand and Sunny, Marcie, and I take turns painting her right hand.

"Stop bouncing to the music, Marcie. The whole side of

my thumb is madly mauve," Amy fusses. "Let's have secret-telling time now."

"No, games come next," Marcie reminds us.

"We can't play Twister while our polish is wet." Sunny is right.

"We can each tell a secret while we shake our nails dry, and then tell more later," Marcie says. "Sunny, you go first."

Sunny looks uneasy. None of us want to say anything that Amy can spread around school, because she will do just that.

"Ummm. Mrs. Cortez's babies might not be her husband's. They have short legs, long bodies, and floppy ears."

Amy looks confused.

"Mrs. Cortez is a Chihuahua," Marcie says.

"Oh, I was starting to feel sorry for Mrs. Cortez's kids," Amy says. "My secret is my mom buys cheap cold cream and puts it in an Estée Lauder jar."

No wonder Amy likes gossip. She doesn't have any interesting secrets.

"What about you, Becky?"

I jump a little.

"Becky wants to have her very own horse like her cousins," Marcie butts in. "They all do bucket riding."

I giggle. "It's *barrel* racing, Marcie."

"Is that why you have all those horse toys in your room, Becky?" Amy sounds suspicious.

Marcie looks superior. "Those are collectibles. They're called Breyer horses. She could sell them for lots of money when she's grown up." Good old Marcie. She continues, "Let's see. My secret is that I almost wore my swimsuit inside out at the pool —dark locker room—caught it just in time." Marcie's slick. She managed to tell my secret for me, make it sound cool, and do it without anybody noticing.

Amy squints at her nails. "My nails are still wet. Let's tell just one more secret—about boys."

Gross. I don't have any boy secrets. Who wants boy secrets?

"Okay, Amy. You first," Marcie directs.

Amy holds her head back, eyes closed. She opens her eyes, looks at us, and raises her eyebrows. "I heard Audrey Baxter's carrying twins. Somebody said if they're not identical, one could be from Billy and the other from Theresa's brother, Grant."

"That's not a secret." Marcie draws herself up like a disapproving queen. "That's gossip and it's about my cousin and I don't appreciate it."

"Audrey's your cousin?" I ask. "She's my neighbor."

"That's right! They live just down the street!" Amy's looking from Marcie to me, dying for more tidbits.

Marcie and I both say, "We're not talking about it!"

"Okay!" Amy says.

"What's your boy secret, Becky?" Sunny's trying hard to change the subject.

"My boy cousins dip snuff and stink."

"That's not a secret," says Amy.

"Neither is nasty gossip," said Marcie. "My nails are done. Let's play Twister."

"Just one more thing—everybody say who they think is cute," Amy suggests.

Marcie looks up at the ceiling. "Alan Parkman—he's smart *and* cute. Amy?"

"Gary, little Gary. He's short, but he's got nice eyes. Daddy says he'll get taller. Your turn, Sunny."

Sunny doesn't hesitate. "Coach Parks."

"Everybody thinks he's cute," Marcie says.

"I think he likes Miss Powers," Sunny says.

"Well, just as long as she gets him," I say. I'd be jealous of anyone else.

"You're next, Becky. Who do you like?" says Amy.

I'm not telling her. "Coach Park's dog. He's cute. Boys are so immature. If they did anything besides laugh at passing gas and belching, a person might could stand to be around them." I'm done. I go and stand by the Twister mat. "Are we going to play or not?"

That's when the fun really begins. We laugh until our sides hurt—especially when my toe goes up Amy's nose. Sunny's double-jointed, so she wins nearly every time.

The later it gets, the sillier we become. I even read from my real diary. "*Jessie listens to her music all the time and sings along with it like she's an opera star or something and never lets me listen to mine.*" I stand on Marcie's bed and imitate Jessica. "OO-OOOOOh!" I warble. "I sing like an opera-a-a star-r-r . . ."

Marcie joins in, "Because I have big booosoms."

"If I get as big as Dolly Parton, I'll sing even better-r-r." We collapse into giggles.

Amy finally gets her way. She sneaks over to the television and turns on that show. Two men are wearing these loud shirts and silly hats. "Two wild and crazy guys!" they say.

Mrs. Waldman calls out, "That show had better not be on!" Marcie shuts it right off.

I say, "That's why Kenny and Chad keep doing that!" They do this crazy shimmy down the bus aisle and call out that same stupid line, every single day. This explains it all.

We finally lie down. While Amy's in the bathroom, Marcie and I steal a moment to catch up on the news about Audrey. We know Sunny will never tell. She listens, while she watches for Amy.

"Audrey's stepmother is a brat. She's pregnant now and she wants all the attention. Audrey's coming back home."

"Good," I whisper.

"Becky? Do you think the baby could be Grant's?" Marcie asks.

"No way!"

Amy comes back and settles in to share more secrets.

"My dad was married before," she whispers. "But it didn't last. They were too young."

My eyes start to pull shut even though I want to hear all the details. I drift off to sleep before I can hear any more.

I'm the first to hear the doorbell ring and stagger into the kitchen. Mrs. Waldman is pouring coffee for Mama and juice for Jessica. "What pretty jammies!" Mama hugs me and whispers in my ear, "I'm so sorry, sugar. I wouldn't have forgotten on purpose for all the world."

"It's okay, Mama."

"Your pj's are real cute, Beck," Jessie murmurs.

"Thanks." I look at my juice, but not at her.

Mrs. Waldman and Mama go off to look at the living room, so Mama can make decorating suggestions. Sunny, Amy, and Marcie trail in looking groggy. Amy looks at me and then at Jessica and her jaw drops. "*This* is the Jessica that's your sister?"

"Yeah."

Sunny shakes her head. "Everybody knows Jessica and Becky are sisters."

Marcie looks at Jessie and explains patiently, "Amy doesn't get out much."

"Jessica Ramey is Becky Ramey's sister. Jessica, you sing great! Why don't you sing, Becky?" Amy blurts.

I sigh and look off.

"Wow, you two don't look anything alike. You have great hair, Jessica. Nobody would ever think you two are sisters."

Thanks a lot, Amy.

Jessica sighs. "That's because I'm adopted."

"Really? I've always thought that being adopted would be so romantic. Do you know anything about your real parents?"

Jessie sort of frowns like she thinks Amy's an airhead too, but then she sees how much attention she's getting from Marcie and Sunny. Count on Jessica to never pass up a performance. "Well, my mother was from Oklahoma and real young. She couldn't keep me, so I was placed with my adoptive family." She glances to see if Mama is listening. "My parents lost twin babies. I guess I'm the replacement."

"Maybe your parents were really in love and wanted to get married, but her parents didn't approve. I bet your mother could sing too. What was your dad like?"

"I don't know. I think he joined the army."

"Maybe he joined out of heartbreak. Maybe he was in Vietnam." Amy gasps. "Maybe he's missing in action! It would be so cool, if he came back and started looking for you."

Amy's been watching way too many soap operas. Jessica frowns a little and gets real quiet. I'm ready to shut down this performance, when Mama comes in and tells me to get my things together, so we can still make it to Sunday school. I sigh. Can't miss one week.

I go to get my bag, when I hear Amy declare, "Jessica, I don't think your singing sounds like opera at all, and you're way smaller than Dolly Parton." I step away a little bit faster, before Jessica can ask me any questions.

I hug Mrs. Waldman and tell her thanks for the nice time and make plans with Marcie and Sunny to talk later.

"I can't imagine what else they could have to say." Mrs. Waldman chuckles.

"They'll find something." Mama laughs.

I hurry out to our old gold Impala and put my things in the trunk and climb into the back seat nonchalantly. Jessica turns around in the front seat and squints at me. "Now *what* was this about opera and Dolly Parton?"

"You figure it out, Jessica." And I squint back at her.

CHAPTER THIRTY-ONE

Basketball practice is rougher today, because we haven't been doing so hot. We lost the last game 14-2, and Daniesha was so upset she threw the ball against a locker and dented it.

Our coach says, "You got thrown off the horse this last game. It's time to get back into the saddle." She says it's time we revisit the fundamentals—like we are just sorry beginners. So, it's back and forth doing passing drills, then lay-up drills, guarding drills, free-throw drills, and run, run, run. I'm not loving this. After that loss, who feels like trying? I can't even look at the empty bleachers, even though they are empty of disappointed parents or friends. Sweat is soaking my hair and it drops from Freckles's nose, her red cheeks shining. Daniesha attacks every drill, fierce and determined, like it's personal and it's war. She doesn't call out encouragement or clap for anybody. Just silent, hard, punishing practice. Pee Wee and Freckles notice and share glances, eyebrows raised.

Then it's like the team finds our rhythm. Passes are swift and accurate. Pee Wee makes a three-point shot and I make four lay-ups in a row.

"Go Eastwood, go Eastwood!" Freckles and Pee Wee chant. I grin because my nickname feels like an honor now. Now practice is not punishment. Our bodies remember the magic, we go automatic, and it's good. The metallic, hollow thunk-thunk-thunk of the ball is like music, ending in one glorious s-s-swish after another!

We're joking and having fun now. Even Coach laughs along. Pee Wee and Freckles get silly singing some Michael Jackson song and skipping with their arms linked instead of running. They make the mistake of trying to get Daniesha to join in.

Daniesha just about bites their heads off. Especially Pee Wee's. "We lost a game and all you can do is act like a fool. Get your head in the game, Patricia Walker!"

"We were trying to make you feel better," Freckles yells. "Just because Mrs. Goforth is evil doesn't mean..."

Pee Wee shakes her head at Freckles and grabs Daniesha and hugs her tight, rocking from side to side. Daniesha tries hard to hold herself back, but tears well and run. Cool-calm-never-flinching Daniesha is crying.

Miss Powers goes to the girls. Pee Wee steps back and nods at our coach. Miss Powers whispers, "What is it, Daniesha?" Daniesha just looks away and wipes the angry tears from her cheeks.

Pee Wee explains, "The social studies teacher had some other teachers judge the A+ family projects. The best ones are going into the display case. Mrs. Goforth marked on Daniesha's. Nobody else had marks on their projects."

Miss Powers frowns, her lips pressed together. "May I see your project?" Daniesha stands there expressionless and nods once. Pee Wee goes and gets the folded display leaning against the bleachers, and we all gather around. Pee Wee's long fingers unfold and reveal the spotless A+ presentation of how Daniesha's family lived through something horrible in Longview—the 1919 Longview Race Riot. White people burned homes and a business, but some black people defended themselves. When it was over, four black people were killed, and people of both races were injured. It took Texas Rangers and the National Guard to bring peace. Nobody went to prison, but the black people who fought back had to move far away for their lives. I can't see how they would want to, but Daniesha's great-grandparents stayed in Longview. Her great-aunt became a teacher and a great-uncle became a store owner, and her granddaddy, a preacher. Maps and old family photos told the story, but in the lower right-hand corner a chart labeled "The Red Summer" had angry words in red scrawled across it. "Inflammatory and Irrelevant." I bent over and read the chart, and it listed place after place where the same thing occurred that year: Chicago, Washington, DC., Charleston—twenty-seven towns and cities in all. There was not one completely friendly, safe place Daniesha's family could have found. How's that irrelevant?

We are all mad at Mrs. Goforth, just on principal, but one girl shrugs irritably and says, "This all happened so long ago—why didn't they just leave?"

Freckles elbows her and hisses, "Ssshut up!"

Pee Wee points at one out-of-focus picture of a young boy, a cousin. He died in the worst riot of all in Arkansas; over two hundred people were murdered there, and all they wanted was fair wages. Daniesha clears her throat and touches a group family photo before an old farmhouse labeled "Family Reunion, '77." "That's the home place. That's why they wouldn't leave." Miss Powers nods and squeezes Daniesha's shoulder. We girls glance up at each other and look down or away. The whole huge gymnasium feels the weight of old, old crimes and injustice and the sick understanding that folks could want to just brush it away. Like somebody's suffering is nothing. I was born in Longview; I might even know relatives of people who attacked my friend's family. Maybe even my family . . . I can hardly look at my friend, and I don't know if I can ever feel the same about Longview. Daniesha and Pee Wee are in the gym with us, but, somehow, they are alone with a weight all their own.

Our coach tells us we are done for the day, but she's not done with this problem. I remember I need a ride and I go to Miss Powers to ask for one, but she is talking to Reverend Journey, Daniesha's daddy. Her father says, "I thank you for explaining the situation. I believe I know just the place of honor for my daughter's work at our church."

Miss Powers looks serious and asks, "I wonder, may I and our team attend your service this Sunday. We'd like the privilege of showing our support."

Reverend Journey says, "Of course, Miss Powers. Anyone is always welcome."

I do not want to be stranded, so I touch Miss Powers's elbow and whisper, "Excuse me, Miss Powers, I forgot. I need a ride home today."

"I believe Daniesha and I can give this young lady a lift." And Reverend Journey leads us to their car.

I sit in the back seat and keep my mouth shut, because I can tell Reverend Journey and Daniesha are having serious words. "You did nothing wrong. You did an important thing in your project. You remembered your people and honored their struggles. Never forget that. Do not let anyone cause you to act in an unbecoming way. Remember. You are a Journey girl."

And I mutter, before I can stop it. "Sounds like being a Ramey girl."

Daniesha looks back over the front seat, frowning and with eyes bugged out because I am butting in. Reverend Journey chuckles. "Now what is expected of a Ramey girl?"

I list things: "Do a good job, get good grades. Act like a lady, be athletic, but don't be a snot. Be nice, be respectful, use good grammar. Don't get pregnant." I gasp. "I just said 'pregnant' to a preacher! My mother will kill me. Sorrysorrysorry!"

Daniesha looks at me like I have lost my mind, but Reverend Journey smiles and says. "No offense, Rebecca. I am acquainted with the concept. Good guidelines. Are you successful?"

"Mostly, but my sister gets away with things." I frown as I realize this. "I just wish folks would listen to me sometimes," I whisper to myself. I look up and Daniesha nods and sighs. Reverend Journey looks at me through the rearview mirror, and I look back. "Daniesha is always good. I'm not. I knocked the wind out of a boy over some torn stockings."

"Uh-*huh!* Is that right?"

"And by the way, Mrs. Goforth *is* evil. I know."

Daddy thanks Daniesha's father for the ride. Reverend Journey shakes his hand and tells him, "You have a spirited daughter there, Mr. Ramey."

"That's one way of putting it, Reverend."

The Journeys pull away and I tell my father everything I saw and heard. I look at him silently for a minute and then I ask, "Did anybody we know do that?"

"Not so far as I know, but I think we both know, some white people would have agreed. Some would have thought it was awful and low class, but they would not speak up or do anything about it. If any people did take a stand, they were very brave."

"Why? Why hate black people?"

"I can't fully explain it to myself, but I wonder if they thought about what they would have done if they had been enslaved and are afraid of retaliation. Afraid of competition. Afraid of the men who fought World War I for them and now might fight them. When people have evil thoughts, they expect the same from everyone else."

Sunday, Daddy goes with me to the First A.M.E. church. We were headed for a seat on the back row, but we are escorted to a place of honor in front with Coach and the girls. Freckles and some girls are absent. Freckles's mother insisted she had to go to her own church and the others just did not come. At the end of the service, Pastor Journey calls for the congregation to come forward and lay hands on Daniesha and pray for her. The girls and Coach get up and join everybody at the altar. Reverend Journey has folks at the front place their hands on Daniesha and everyone else join in by placing hands on the people before them. I put my hand on an older lady's elbow. She smiles and puts me in front of her, with her hands on my shoulders. I tell my Daddy, "That was powerful. Our church ought to do that."

My daddy says, "Every church should do that."

A phone in the church office rings and a deacon calls for Daniesha. It's Freckles. She got in trouble, but she doesn't care. She left her church service, and her mother found her in her church parking lot praying for Daniesha.

I don't know if our coming helped her any, but it seemed important to try. And I realize something else: barrel racing is still my favorite, but I can't deny that the girls on my team are real friends.

I catch my Daddy looking off in the distance as we make our way to our car, and I tug on his hand. "Dad?"

"You'd like to think that we've moved beyond this kind of thing, but we have not. Rebecca, H.J. had to pick up Burgess out of jail yesterday. He was at the wrong place at the wrong time, and a white cop arrested him for another kid's crime and gave him a black eye for mouthing off. There were no grounds, Burgess was innocent—a *pastor's* kid, but the cop didn't back down until he remembered H.J. from high school. 'Hey, you played running back my sophomore year,' The guy said. No apology. And no consequences. It's not the way it's supposed to be. Not here. Not there."

CHAPTER THIRTY-TWO

It's Tuesday, and I'm days behind in my writing. I turn one rumpled page in my diary and begin a new fresh page. *More Reasons Why Jessica Ramey is the Stinkiest, most Selfish Sister Ever. Number* . . . I pause and look back. *Four. She slept in my bed when I was at a sleepover, because she was too lazy to change her sheets. And then we both had dirty sheets. I bet she ate bean dip and didn't even take a bath that night.* Yuck, makes me sick. *Five: She thinks she's too good for our family. I bet she regrets she was ever adopted. Her family project told all about adoption, but she did not say one thing about the Rameys.*

I can hear her, Beth Markam, and Sue Lynn Tyler in our room. It won't take them long to find my fake diary. I smile. Sure enough, Sue Lynn comes bolting into the den. I'm in here because I'm not good enough to be in there with Jessica's friends, and because Sue Lynn calls me Brillo Pad because of my hair. I'm not putting up with it. I walk out before she can get past "Br-". Jessica never even tells her to stop.

"Becky, what did Kyle Roberts say about me?" The suspense is killing Sue Lynn.

I try to look shocked and hurt. "You are *reading* my diary? Give it here."

"Not until you tell me what Kyle said." Sue Lynn is boy

crazy and she's nuts over Kyle Roberts. She stares at him the entire bus ride. Kyle doesn't know that anybody under fourteen exists, but Sue Lynn doesn't know that. So, I wrote *I heard Kyle talking and he said that Sue* . . . and then I just stopped writing. It's driving her crazy.

"What are you talking about? Give me my diary." I hold out my hand.

"You *know* what I'm talking about. This!" she points at the entry.

"Oh, *that*. I don't know. I got interrupted when you guys came in, and I lost track and forgot."

Jessica and Beth are at the door. Beth's smiling, because she gets the joke. Jessica would like to tell on me, but she'd have to own up to snooping in my diary. Sue Lynn throws the fake diary down, and I return to the real thing.

Number six: She only hangs out with her snooty friends, and she won't even let me stand by her at the bus stop—especially if I'm wearing anything Western.

Jessica's in our room cutting up and cussing. I can hear it plain as anything. I'm going to tell Mama that Jessica cusses. Even the S-word. Marcie says I should tell Jessie "My ears are not your toilet." And that's just what I'm going to do.

I can hear Beth. "You'll have to come to my house. My dad just had cable installed for us kids. My mom was hacked off! 'Where's the child support?' No wonder he left. When he gets settled, I'll go live with him."

Why doesn't he pay to have the lawn mowed, or for new clothes for his kids?

Beth says, "You and I will be popular. With your figure, you could have a high school boyfriend right now—especially if you got the right haircut. Billy likes pretty hair." Beth looks determined. "You can be Lucy and I'll be Ethel." No brag, just fact—that's the way Beth says this.

Jessica says, "One problem. Mama says no dating until I'm sixteen. It's so stupid."

Beth starts in on Sue Lynn. I don't know why she wants to

be friends with Beth. "Becky will fill out a bra before you will." I almost feel sorry for her, but not much.

My pencil breaks. There's nothing to do but go back to our room and get another one.

"Becky, get out."

"I'm just getting a pencil. Some of us have homework to do. Since you have all this free time, maybe you'd like to read my diary some more."

"Let her stay for a little while, Jessica. She's cool. She doesn't cry or whine and she's quiet." Beth looks sharply at Sue Lynn. "And no 'Brillo Pad,' Sue. Kyle wouldn't approve."

"I didn't say one word." Sue Lynn looks wounded.

There are two kinds of bossy kids. There's the mean, bullying kind and the ones who just like to manage things. Beth is the last kind, but it is still smart to go along with her.

"I think your hair's pretty. I'm going to do it up in braids and wrap it around." Beth starts combing through my hair. "I heard you scored at the game last week."

Sue Lynn says, "Becky mostly sits on the bench."

"At least I do something besides chase Kyle Roberts," I say. I did make a lay-up, and then I made an assist and Freckles scored. Daddy said that was as good as making the points myself. "The high school boys at church think I'm good. We play Horse after church Sunday nights."

"You could be popular too." Beth looks at me like she's put me on her list of possible advantages. Beth parts my hair into two sections and makes two braids. "I have an idea. Jessie, ask your mom for some bobby pins, and if we can have a little red gloss. Sue Lynn, look for a white T-shirt in Jessie's drawer."

Beth is just nervy enough to make everybody do what she asks. In a way, she seems so grown-up. She's the oldest of five. I'm not surprised when even Mama comes in with the red lip gloss and Jessica hands her a bobby pin.

"Wait a sec. Becky put on the T-shirt. Now." Beth begins expertly wrapping and pinning each braid into a bun on each side of my head. "Ta-daa!"

I look in the mirror. "Princess Leia!"

"Not until you get your red lip gloss. Can she Mrs. Ramey?"

"Go ahead."

The T-shirt is not a perfect *Star Wars* Leia outfit, but the rest looks real, and I love that red lip gloss. Even Sue Lynn says I am cute.

"Well, girls, it's a school night. You'll have to come over again here real soon."

"Yes, ma'am, Mrs. Ramey." Beth knows her manners. "Becky, next time we'll do Princess Leia's new hairdo."

Before they leave, Jessica gives Beth a sack full of her blouses. "They don't fit me now—they're my favorites."

Good riddance! Those clothes almost made Jessica unpopular. One second soprano in choir got jealous and called Jessica "Miss Fashion Queen." I refused to keep any of those outfits from the crazy Mary Kay lady, except for the embroidered blouse. I don't even wear it. I just didn't think Jessica should get everything.

I don't think Jessica reads the flash of resentment on Beth's face when she takes the sack. The cursed clothes strike again.

After Sue Lynn and Beth leave, Jessica is grumpy. She says, "Well, aren't you the popular one?"

Mama looks amused. "Jealous, are we? Seems to me, Becky was invited. You two need to get your homework done. Becky, blot off that red lip gloss before you get it on that white T-shirt or your pillow case."

I groan, just not in the mood for homework yet. I rummage around in a drawer. Success! Two pieces of bubble gum. I pop one in my mouth and get to work on it. It's a real art getting gum ready for some good popping. First, I get it good and soft. I chew for a while until it's the proper consistency for folding over and over to create the best air pockets. I've only made two decent pops when Jessica practically screams, "Will you stop that! I can't concentrate."

I try to cover my mouth to muffle the gum pops, but even

A Thing of Beauty

that won't do. "Mother-r-r-r! Becky won't stop popping gum."

"Becky, spit it out." Mama's voice echoes down the hall. "How much math do you have done?"

"I'm working on it now." I spit out the first piece, but I put in my second piece of gum and get to work on it.

"Girls, I'm stepping over to see Susan and Audrey," Mama calls out. "Finish your work while I'm gone."

I go by to visit Audrey too when I can, and she is glad I do. Theresa brought the other cheer leaders to visit once, but only Theresa ever came again. Audrey's face and ankles are puffy, and Mama says she must stay off her feet for a while. Mama understands about baby troubles.

Sometimes, I go over there and do my homework while Audrey does hers. She helps me sometimes, and she's still sweet as ever. But now she's got a tough determination about her. She does her schoolwork like everything depends on getting good grades. She plans on working and going to school, and she intends for her little family to be different. Mama says she has tough time ahead of her. I just hope it works out for her somehow. I don't tell her about Jessica having a crush on Billy. And I don't tell her Jessica believes the gossip about her and Grant.

I work through most of the math, drop the book on our bedroom floor, and start on language arts. "I hate school."

Jessie looks up surprised. "What are you talking about?"

"I've got a stupid oral book report." I admit. "If I just didn't have to talk..."

"What's wrong with talking?"

I just shake my head. "Forget it." How can a quiet person ever explain to a girl like Jessica what it means to just want to be invisible? "I wish I could just write it."

"Do one you really like. That makes it easier. Do something horsey."

"I have to have a visual aid too."

"Do a diorama. Teachers always love dioramas. Just be sure you ask permission to use one of Mother's precious shoe boxes."

"Jessica," I begin. "I wouldn't trust Beth if I were you. She's a user."

"Mind your own business, Becky." My sister doesn't look up, and she doesn't defend Beth.

CHAPTER THIRTY-THREE

"It's the back-home way. Folks help out other folks," Mama says. "It's the only way we make ends meet sometimes." We helped Mama's old friend Sharon move in to her new house and now Sharon's cutting our hair at a discount. Jessica calls off the directions to the Mane Thing shop, while I watch for street signs and Mama drives.

Miz Sharon looks up from her appointment book and squeals when we walk in the door. She clippity-clops over in her turquoise high heels and grabs Mama's hair with both hands. "Honey, I have longed for this day. You are going to be so fabulous when I'm done."

"Help yourself!" Mama giggles and hugs her frosted blond friend. Granny B. says Sharon's streaked hair makes her look fast.

"Look at you, Becky Boo! This isn't any little ol' teensie preemie now. Lizzie, she's past your shoulder and look at those long legs. You ready to lose these curly dog ears, girl?"

"Yes, ma'am. My sister said I looked like a cocker spaniel, this morning."

"Well, you don't listen to her. You're gonna be as cute as a button. Why don't we take you first?" Miz Sharon stands taller, arches her eyebrows, and gestures grandly with her shears. "Ladies, we are entering a new day. Finally, the fashion industry has come up with a decent hairdo for women with natural curl." After she shampoos my hair, she begins combing and snipping. "And best of all, you'll only have to wash your hair and pick it out."

"Mama, look at all the hair on the floor."

"Can you imagine how much would be there if Granny got her haircut?"

"Still dyes her hair shiny black?" Sharon asks.

"And piled a mile high in curls," Mama says.

Jessica is looking through the haircut books and marking all the hairdos she likes. One book must have five little scraps of paper bristling from it.

A lady holding the hand of a little girl with long brown hair walks into the shop and Sharon groans. "Here comes trouble again—worst behaved child I've ever seen in my life! Thought Betty would never finish trimming her hair."

But the kid doesn't have an appointment. It's the mother and that means Wild Child has the run of the entire shop. She helps herself to the candy at the front desk, until the lady there takes the dish away. She reaches for the comb Miss Sharon is about to use on my head, but Sharon grabs it first and gives the kid the evil eye. The kid is up and down off furniture, putting her head up the hair drier, and flipping the knob off and on, off and on, reaching for bottles of hair spray and whatnot. All while her mother says, "Don't do that, precious. Don't bother the nice lady. I'm not going to tell you again." And then she does—again and again.

Sharon clears her throat and tries to focus on the job at hand—my hair. "So, how's the barrel racing coming along, Becky?"

"It's not, right now. I haven't raced since summer."

"And last time she was around a horse, she got hurt," Mama says.

I look at Mama and raise my eyebrows. "It's a sore subject. Right now, I'm playing basketball and helping Daddy train for a marathon."

Sharon looks at Mama. "Well, that's a surprise." Miz Sharon's comb slips out of her hand and I catch it. "See, look at those reflexes. Liz, she's a natural athlete."

"Reflexes come in handy with barrel racing too," I say.

Mama frowns. "Becky almost had a mild concussion because of that horse. Rodeo events can be so dangerous. We knew this young boy—he got gored…"

"…in the forehead, bull riding, I know. I've heard this before Mama. I'm not going to barrel race on a Brahma bull. And I'm not going to get gored in my head, unless somebody comes up with a unicorn for me to ride."

"Don't you get smart with me, young lady."

"I wasn't being smart. That's Jessica's job."

Miz Sharon takes a hold of my hair on one side of my head with those long-nailed fingers. "You look at me—you don't talk to your Mama like that!" Miz Sharon doesn't hurt me, but she means business.

Wild Child's mother draws in her breath. "She grabbed that child's hair. Did you see what she did to that woman's child? That's abuse! That…"

The whole shop—beauticians and customers—say all at once, "Mind your own business!"

"Well, I just don't think she has a right to do that…"

"And that's why your kid's a brat," I say.

"Don't say things like that, Becky," Sharon says. Then she says through her teeth, "Even if they are true."

Mama turns her face, so we can't see her laugh.

The lady starts to object and then she cries, "Precious!" Wild Child has just burnt off the front of her hair with a hot curling iron.

When the lady and Precious leave, the kid has a cute short haircut with a burnt fringe for bangs.

Miz Sharon works some hair goop into my new hairdo and picks, picks, picks, and it's done. She whirls me around and I see my smile and my eyes grow wide. I have a mass of little shiny curls all over my head.

"Now, let's do Mother." Sharon rubs her hands together in delight. "Oh, goody, goody, goody. I thought you'd never make this appointment." Sharon flutters her eyelids like iridescent black-and-turquoise butterflies. "I hope you girls appreciate what a wonderful mother you have. How she suffered to get you girls." Her spikey black lashes frame her blue eyes as she gazes in awe at the ceiling, and Sharon puts a reverent long-nailed hand on her heart. "She spent months in bed waiting for you… and look at you now…thriving, absolutely thriving. You were so eensie. Teeny tiny little fingers and toes. And look at you now. Almost a young woman."

Mama's getting uneasy and I'm embarrassed.

"Sugar, here's some change—go get us all a coke."

When Jessica and I return with the sodas, Miz Sharon is earnestly scrubbing my mother's head and asking, "Liz, are you all right? You don't look like you…"

"Thanks, Becky. Go find yourself a magazine and read now," Mama says.

Soon Mama's sitting beside me with her new curly do and she looks all tired out. I catch Miz Sharon eyeing her.

It's my sister's turn now. Sharon and Jessica find a hairdo in the book that makes my sister smile.

Soon we're looking at a honey blond glory and Sharon says, "Tell Cliff to get his ball bat ready."

CHAPTER THIRTY-FOUR

The inside of my mouth feels like sand, my heart's pounding, but I got through that stupid book report.

"That was a lovely presentation, Becky. I'm surprised you would sacrifice one of your Breyer horses for a diorama," my reading teacher says.

"It was broken anyway. My little second cousin stepped on it and broke its leg." I was proud of my visual aid. I took some craft paint and turned a white horse into a dappled one—Bree."

Chad raises his hand. "Do horses really roll around in pastures?" Mrs. Burton looks to me to answer.

"Sometimes. That's how they scratch their backs. Bree was embarrassed that he did it, because he was afraid of what other talking horses would say." It was cool to be the kid who knows stuff and likes to tell about it.

The bell rings and I head for the bus and climb on in.

Jessica, Beth, and Sue Lynn are in their seat. I walk by Jessie and our eyes meet. She has her new hairdo with the front sides and bangs curled back and it's gorgeous. She looks like an older girl more than ever.

"I got an A on my report. I even had to answer some questions. I'm pooped now though," I announce.

"Oh? Okay." Jessica looks disinterested.

Jessica laughs and tells jokes, and everyone laughs with her. She's finishing up some silly story about the locker room and a wet towel fight. "And then Miss Powers said, 'You girls better use those towels for something besides whacking each other.'" She sounded just like the PE teacher—grumpy voice and all. Beth and Sue Lynn laugh and laugh, and then Jessica does her snort laugh, and they all giggle some more.

I smile, and then Sue Lynn looks back at me. "I don't know how the two of you can be sisters. You are so quiet."

I just shrug and wish Sue Lynn's eyes and her big mouth would go away. I hate it when people say that. What's wrong with being quiet?

Jessie's shiny long hair glows in the sunlight streaming in through the bus windows. Her freckles look like cinnamon sprinkled on her nose. Her blue eyes sparkle, and her nose wrinkles up all cute while she continues her story. "And then Miss Powers checked and made sure all our towels were just damp. She actually touched all those nasty towels."

The bus heads over to the high school and the big kids climb on. Billy hauls himself up the steps. Our bus driver says, "Haven't seen you in a while."

"Once my car is fixed, I won't be back." He stops by Jessica's seat. "Well, hello there. Don't I know you?" Jessica looks at her lap, flustered.

Beth says, "Jessica sang the national anthem at your big ball game, Billy."

"Is that right? Cool. See you around."
Jessica and Beth look back and then grin at each other. Beth glances back at me. "I like your new curly do, Becky. It looks good on you."

Sue Lynn can't leave it alone. "I think she looks even more like a Br-"

Beth and Jess cut her off. "Stop it right now, Sue Lynn."

Sue Lynn slumps back and looks sour. She tries one last dig. "Becky, how come Jessica sings and you can't?"

"Look, Sue Lynn, I'm quiet, but I just might bite off the

head of the next person who asks me why I don't sing. There wasn't a Ramey ever born that could carry a tune. That right there proves Jessica's adopted."

I'm sorry right away that I ever said that, because Jessica looks like someone hit her. "Jess, I didn't mean it like that. You sing better than anybody does—you're the only Ramey that can sing."

She smiles a little and nods. "It's okay."

I look up and Jessie's hand is hanging over the back of the seat. She forgives me. She's handing me some bubble gum.

Suddenly, a wiry, blond high school boy plops down in the seat in front of Jessica. Sue Lynn looks delighted and terrified at the same time. It's Kyle Roberts. He whispers to Jessica, "Hey, give me some gum. Did you do something different to your hair?"

Jessie shrugs, because Sue Lynn has murder in her eyes. Kyle's real cute, and he's wearing a letterman jacket. His eyelashes are real blond so that makes him look a little like a piggy.

"You got better at receiving this fall," I say.

"Well thanks, Curly-top." He puts his hand on the back of his seat. "Come on, gimme some gum."

A boy with a ball cap climbs on the bus and he spots my sister. I don't like the expression on his face. I've seen it before—in the eyes of a stallion put out to stud and I don't appreciate it.

"Did somebody ever tell you it isn't polite to stare," I say.

Ball Cap leans down and gets in my face. "Well, excuse me for looking." He smirks and walks on.

"You told him, Curly-top," Kyle chuckles.

"Her name's Rebecca." Jessie looks scornful, but she is blushing.

He looks back at Jess and down at her chest and grins. Jessica turns redder and looks out the window.

I narrow my eyes. Jessica liked his attention a little bit at first, but it bothers her when people think she's older, and it really bothers her when boys do. They notice her big bosoms, and she hates it. I speak up. "So, who do you think is going to win the Super Bowl?"

He looks at me surprised. "Cowboys, of course. You're not rooting for the Steelers?"

Daddy and I talk football all the time. All the Rameys do. It's a family thing—and we *are* Texan, right? So, I tell Mr. Cowboy fan, "Not necessarily. They could still win."

"I've just got one name for you: Roger Staubach, the man with the arm."

"I've got one name for you: Terry Bradshaw, the man with the *younger* arm."

Sue Lynn and Jessica look from Kyle to me, frowning with their mouths open. Suddenly, it's not about them at all. They don't know football, and they have nothing to say.

"Roger Staubach, MVP."

"Terry Bradshaw who *will* be MVP this year."

"He's from Louisiana. What kind of Texan are you?"

"I've got one more name for you: Mean Joe Green from Temple, Texas—graduated from North Texas State University, The Mean Green. Nobody's getting past the Steel Curtain."

Football player frowns at me and I looked at him with my sassy face. I look him right in the eyes as bold as Tigre, my Ma-maw's cat, when he gets on my grandmother's furniture and stares at us without blinking. I just could be right, and he and I both know it.

"Betcha a pack of gum."

"Done."

I don't know who was the most jealous that I got all Kyle Robert's attention, Sue Lynn or Jessica. When our stop came up, they flounced out ahead of me.

They don't notice that Ball Cap is following, and when he grabs my sister's rear, she yelps, shocked and embarrassed.

Billy says, "Cooper, cut it out!" and follows us off the bus. "Ignore him, he doesn't mean any harm. Are you all right?"

The bus driver says, "Billy, I have to stay on schedule…"

"Okay. Don't I know you?" Billy steps up the first step, still looking at my sister. Then he grins. "I remember you—you gave me back my ring!"

Jessica nods, beaming.

I speak up. "You helped us move in, remember? Audrey introduced us."

Billy steps back, the door closes, but he's still watching my sister as the bus pulls away.

CHAPTER THIRTY-FIVE

"Did the driver see that boy grab you?" our father asks. "Maybe . . ." I shrug. "Maybe other kids noticed."

"Well, I'm still going to report it," Daddy declares.

"Daddy, don't. It's so embarrassing," Jessica says.

"Beside the point."

Jessica draws her breath to protest.

"Forget it. It has to be done," Daddy says flatly.

"You girls put your things away. Jessica, put your stuff in your room—not on the kitchen floor. Let Daddy and me talk a minute." Mama looked like she had something on her mind when we walked in, and now she worries about that boy too.

"Yeah, Becky, go check out your room." Daddy smiles at me. Then he turns to my mother, serious.

I grab an apple, hold it in my mouth, and take up my coat and backpack to see what Daddy's talking about. As I walk off, I hear Mama say, "Clifford, do you know anything about this boy?"

My new room's special, but somehow, I feel had. Mama and Daddy separated us because Jessica and I fought all the time. The last straw came when I hid all the socks. Jessica kept using up all of hers and then the sorry sock thief would help herself to mine. How is it that the slob gets the big room, and the neat kid gets Mama's tiny sewing room?

"Daddy put up my new shelf!" I announce to myself as I walk in. I get out the U-Haul box and unpack and set out my Breyer horses. I space my horses evenly on the rugged wooden plank, and step back to appreciate. My horses look at home in my new room. They go with the rusty horseshoe above my bed. Mama let me frame one of our bluebonnet pictures. Every year we go down to Granny's in Waxahachie, and Mama takes pictures of Jessie and me wearing our Easter dresses and sitting in a field of bluebonnets. My nose runs for days, but it's a tradition.

Suddenly, Daddy's standing in the doorway, looking counselor serious. "Becky, I've got some unhappy news. It's about Tabby."

"Is she okay?"

"Yes, everybody's okay, except Uncle Richie is out of work, and they're having to give up Tabby's horse."

"Patchwork? We could take Patchwork."

"Well, see that's the thing. Richie offered her to us free, but..."

"We're taking her, right?"

"No, Becky, we're not. We don't have anywhere to keep her."

"Couldn't we find somebody?"

"It's not that easy. We'd have to pay for her food and board, vet bills. Until Mama gets a job...well, we might not be able to afford it even then."

"Have you tried to find a place, Daddy?"

"There really isn't any point."

"You said I'd ride again."

"And I said it'd be awhile."

"You're not trying hard enough." I fall over onto my bed and bawl. "You give me hope and you take it away. It's not fair. It's not fair." Daddy sits beside me and strokes my hair.

Mama's at my door. Daddy looks at her and says, "She knows."

I look at my mother and frown. "I guess you're happy."

"How could I be happy? I know you're disappointed." Mama pauses.

And now Jessica's at my door and she has my red notebook. "Becky had this in a Kotex box and it fell out when I moved it. Becky, I just want you to know I read this, and I don't appreciate it one bit!"

"Well, join the club!" I was angry the last time I wrote in there. She had it coming. "She read my diary. She's got a lot of nerve." I try to sound extra indignant, but my parents are not reacting.

Jessica turns and marches back down the hall.

I walk into my old room with my arms crossed. Jessica is sitting quietly, pale, with silent tears streaming down her face. I guess I was looking for sobbing or yelling. She looks up at me with angry red eyes with tears welling like hot lava. Mama's sits on the bed with her. Daddy reads the entry: "'Jessica Ramey is not loyal. She keeps talking about her other family. I don't see why she even thinks about those other people. Our mother and daddy are nice. When Mama asks her to please turn down her music, Jessica says snotty things like, 'My real mother would love my music. My real mother would sing with me.' If those other people were so great, why would they give up a pretty baby like Jessie?'"

I feel a little uneasy, but well, she's a pain and there you are. Finally, it's going to get out in the open. We all just sit there silent, expectant, like we're in a cellar, waiting for a tornado to tear through the neighborhood.

Jessica dabs at her runny nose. "Daddy, I don't mean to be bad."

"I know." He sits down by her and she leans into his hug.

"Daddy, why am I crazy?"

"You're not crazy. You're thirteen. You are just trying to figure out how to be."

"Daddy, do you think you can inherit the way you are?"

Now she's playing on Daddy's tender heart. I'm not buying it.

"Some folks think people inherit part of their personality. I think it's a mix."

Jessica's face twists with pain, and she looks at me with angry tears. "I'm not disloyal. I love you and Mama and Becky. I just get mad sometimes. And I wonder...that's all."

"Nobody said you couldn't wonder. Do you *have* to be so hateful?" I snap.

"Becky..." Mama says and turns back to Jessica. "We know you wonder, sugar. It's okay." Mama strokes her hair.

"Why didn't they keep me?"

"Well, we've told you all along, your mother was young."

"Was she bad? You know, a *bad girl*?"

"No." Daddy's emphatic. "She was a very good girl, an excellent student. She and your mother are distantly related—second cousins, and they knew each other from church camp. She loved your mother. Followed her like a shadow."

I look at Daddy closely. He's not saying anything about Jessica's birth father. How come?

"Honey, her mother died and her life kind of spun out of control." Mom paused searching for words. "She did not feel it was best to marry your birth father. She and her own daddy were not able to do you justice, so they placed you with us."

We've heard most of this before. Jessica's just trying to make them feel sorry for her.

"They put a lot of thought and care into the decision. They are very good people, and they look forward to meeting you—when the time's right."

"Have you told Jessica everything?" I ask looking Daddy in the eyes.

"Anything she wants to know, she can ask, and you know her birth mother has arranged to meet her when Jessica's eighteen."

Jessica leans in toward our father, "What do I really know about me?"

Daddy murmurs, "We know you are creative, musical."

Jessica says, "With a broken-down piano."

"We're looking for something affordable," Mama says.

I just knew she was going to use this to get her way. "Bull-poop!" I holler—except I don't say "poop."

"Rebecca!" Mama and Daddy are floored.

"Well, it is!"

"Rebecca Ramey!"

"No. I can't believe I'm hearing this. If this was me, forget it …and you are falling for it. Why am I the bad girl? I kept my half of the room clean, but I get the little room."

"Becky…"

"No. Jessica will just fill the big room up with dirty underwear. The more room she has, the more mess she'll make. A piano? How about barrel racing? You're looking for a cheap piano, but you pass up a free horse."

"Becky, we don't have to feed a piano," Mama says.

Daddy tries to reach for me, to pull me in for a hug, but I'm not having it.

"No way—not barrel racing. That would be for Rebecca. Man, I just wish I was adopted. Maybe my parents would care about what I want to do."

❋ ❋ ❋

Back to my old journal. They didn't give my other one back. Mom just thinks about Jessica. Unless she thinks I could get hurt or die. She thinks she has me covered so long as I am not on a horse or near a horse. She doesn't know horses. Horses can read you and I can read them. A horse knows when you're sad. And they like it when I help them be calm. They don't expect stuff all the time.

CHAPTER THIRTY-SIX

"If you people ever got it right, I believe I would faint and fall over." If nasty looks could burn a hole in somebody, I figure Mrs. Goforth ought to go up in flames about any time now. I'm not the only one looking at her in this classroom. Even the good smart girls are extra quiet, extra watchful. Marcie is hunched over, her head down low over her paper. If she could get under her desk, she would.

Mrs. Goforth holds up a paper and shakes it. "Ranger? Who is Ranger?"

I raise my hand. "That's me."

"Rebecca, put your correct name on your papers."

"I prefer 'Ranger.'" I pause. "My dad says it's a small thing to ask." I'm bluffing, and Mrs. Goforth doesn't want to mess with the counselor's daughter—yet—so she backs off.

Mrs. Goforth is making us all jumpy. Patrick is rummaging around in his nose for a booger to chew. Rusty says Patrick does that because he's nervous and I can believe it this morning. Bad nerves can drive a person to desperate habits.

A new boy, Julio, has scooted over and is whispering, explaining the directions to Patrick. He's a quiet smart kid who wears the same kind of plain jeans and white T-shirt every day. He doesn't want attention, so he never raises his hand, but he always knows the right answers when Goforth asks. She still put him in the back with us slow, bad kids.

"No copying!" Goforth grabs Julio's chair and scoots the chair and boy back to his desk. Julio's eyes flash, but he says, "Patrick didn't understand. I was explaining, Mrs. Goforth."

"He needs to do his own work. Copying is unacceptable. I'll be calling your mothers. Look at me when I speak to you."

Julio's dark angry eyes were looking straight ahead, but his gaze moves up, outraged. "I don't cheat."

"Well, we'll let Mrs. Buckley decide that. You two go sit in the office and wait for my referral."

Sunny's already done. She's chewing her lip while she checks that her heading is right and that all the punctuation is in place. That makes me mad. That old hornet shouldn't make good kids afraid.

I do my work fast just to get it over with. Goforth's not going to be happy with my paper no matter what I do. I cram the worksheet into my book. She's not going to get a chance to fuss at me. I'm gonna look busy. I get out more paper and do something I want to do, draw.

I feel Goforth before I see her. It's like a big hot ball of meanness just rolled up behind me. She snorts, and I feel her angry breath on my neck.

"I might have known. Drawing horses again." She snatches my paper and holds it up like a TV lawyer holds up exhibit A, proof that Rebecca Ramey is the sorriest language arts student ever. "This is why your grade is going down, down, down—doodling instead of completing your assignments."

I pull out my class work. "I finished my work, Mrs. Goforth—not that it matters."

"What did you say?"

"No matter what we do, we're still bad and we're still stupid."

The bell rings, but I know it's not going to save me.

"This is not over, Rebecca Ramey—you're getting a write-up." Everyone but me rushes out to PE, like they're running from a swarm of yellow jackets. "Well, go on to gym. I'll deal with you later."

A Thing of Beauty

I take my time stomping through the hallway in my Western boots. Every stomp I feel angrier and stronger. I like my boots even more because Jessica and Mama hate them. Mama begs me to wear a dress, but it is jeans and cowboy boots from now on. Mama can't stop Mrs. Goforth from being mean. She can't stop Jessica from being a slob and loving Billy. She can't stop me from wearing boots and jeans. They can make me live in this stupid place and go to this mean stuck-up school, but they can't tell me what to wear.

I stomp into the gym and flop down on the bench.

Miss Powers can tell I'm in a mood.

"So, Ramey. You're late. You're in boots again. You're not suited up."

"I don't feel like it."

"Join the club. Don't stomp over my gym floor—get in the locker room and get your gear on."

I get up slow like I'm only doing it because I decided to. I try to look like I think it's not worth doing.

Today it is basketball and I fight feeling glad about that. I don't want to be glad about anything but barrel racing. Basketball and running are Daddy's ideas.

Feeling even a little glad doesn't last for long, because a good-sized girl, Gracie thinks she'll foul me and get away with it. I'm making a lay-up and Gracie shoves me aside by whamming into me with her meaty hip.

Marcie helps me up. "You okay, Becky?"

"Yeah, I'm fine. At least Gracie's big old rear is good for something."

"What did you say?" Gracie's mad now.

"You heard me. You just try that again." My elbow is going to be ready for her.

We're up at the other goal and all the girls are flocking around the basket going for the rebound. Gracie gets ready to wham me again, so I just accidentally on purpose have my elbow cocked and ready so she can run into it.

"Oooh!" She flops on the floor like I jabbed her with a

spear.

"Watch it, Ramey." Miss Powers is eyeing me. "Don't you throw an elbow."

"I didn't!" That's not fair.

Gracie thinks she can get away with it now. She smirks and coils up to shove me. I won't put up with it. If I'm going to be blamed, I may as well give them something to blame me for. I launch my elbow and it lands right in her boob, and Gracie hollers like I busted it.

I feel Miss Powers's hand on my shoulder. "Rebecca Ramey, what is your problem? Hit the shower. Get dressed and sit on the bench."

I shower, and scary thoughts drill my brain like the water drills my body. *Miss Powers doesn't like me now. Nobody will. I'm a thug and a disgrace to my family.*

I drag myself up and Miss Powers is waiting for me with a referral slip in her hand. "Mrs. Goforth just dropped this by. Man, you're on a roll today. What's with you, Rebecca? Look at me."

I look back, but there's too much to say.

Miss Powers sighs. "Well, head to the office. Mrs. Buckley's waiting for you."

I carry a referral slip to the office and it feels like power in my hand. At least I know the way it is now. I'm Ranger, one of the bad kids, and I stomp extra hard and proud. I enter the office door and look at the secretary's raised eyebrows and disapproving pursed lips, but I stop myself from wilting. I remember I'm not supposed to care and that puts back a little starch in my spine.

Rusty walks in the door of the office—tardy again. His mama was sick again most likely, and he had to take care of his little nephew. He spots the referral slip in my hand. "Ramey, have you lost your mind?" The secretary shoos him off to class, but we lock gazes and I know he'll grill me later until he knows it all.

Mrs. Buckley's office door opens, and she motions for me to come in. Her iron gray hair is trimmed short and matches her gray suit jacket with the big squared-off shoulders. She offers me a seat and then she sits and looks at me—not angry, not accusing—like she's sizing me up. "Rebecca Ramey. What brings you to my office, of all people?" I feel some starch leaving my spine.

"Mrs. Goforth sent me."

"And?"

"She says on the paper that I 'was off task,'" I read off. "'and insubordinate and argumentative.'"

"And what does Rebecca say?"

"What difference does it make? She doesn't like any of us, but the smart kids, and she's not fair."

"How so?"

"Eric Cook—his name got drawn from the perfect attendance bowl and she threw it back in, because she said he shouldn't get anything. When a kid finally gets something right, he ought to be rewarded. She got on to Julio for nothing—for helping another student."

Mrs. Buckley looks at me and then picks up a sheet of notebook paper and clears her throat.

"Back to Rebecca…this is what you produced instead of your sentences. A horse, and tell me about this other object?"

"It's a barrel—for barrel racing—and I did do my work. Mrs. Goforth wouldn't listen. That's okay. I'm not doing any of her work anymore."

"Ah." She looks through a grade book. "Your grades have had some ups and downs. Looks like we've got some low grades here in language arts? How come?"

I shrug.

"You miss your old home—and animals."

I clench my jaw and nod. *No tears. Not for them. No tears*, I tell myself.

"Mrs. Goforth has a right to expect you to stay on task. And Miss Powers has a right to expect you to use your, ahem, talents in a basketball game, not on your teammates."

I look at Mrs. Buckley. I'm not sure what she's saying.

"It is never a good idea to let the opposition run over you." Mrs. Buckley looks me right in the eye. She means what she says. She looks down at some papers on her desk and straightens them. "About this decision to not do Mrs. Goforth's work—not that she owns it. It has been said that living well is the best revenge."

"Ma'am?"

"Make her give you an A, Miss Ramey. Prove her wrong. And now if you'll excuse me, I have a phone call to make to your father. The secretary will write you a pass to your next class."

For just a second, I feel scared, but then I remember. So what? Mama plays favorites and Daddy's too busy.

CHAPTER THIRTY-SEVEN

I climb on the bus and that referral feels like lead in my pocket as I haul myself up each step.

Sue Lynn says, "You're gonna be in *trouble*."

Jessica won't look at me, but she looks at Beth, "It is so humiliating—I don't even want to act like I know her. So redneck."

"Who says I want to know you?" I shove Jessica's shoulder as I pass. If I am a desperado now, I'm going to go all out. I sneer at Sue Ann. "Nobody's gonna do anything."

Beth looks at me and turns away. It's not to her advantage to know me right now.

I go to Chad's seat and make him scoot over. I want to be closer to the front because I'm going to beat Jessica out the bus door if I can. I'm faster than my sister is, but she has a head start sitting in the front of the bus. Kenny made me a cassette tape of Willie Nelson and I mean to get to the tape player first. They say Willie's an outlaw, and I guess I am too.

The bus pauses for the high school kids and I get ready to sneak up to the next seat. If Jessica doesn't notice, I might be able to crash right past her. Theresa climbs on—her ride must have fallen through. Billy and that nasty boy with the ball cap get on.

Ball Cap says to Billy, "You won't do it."

Billy pauses by Jessica's seat.

Ball Cap says, "Go on, ask her."

Billy says, "Go sit down and mind your own business." He smiles, and Jessica lights up, because today he decides to notice her. She just takes whatever Billy dishes out. Some days Billy gets on the bus with a high school girl or his friends, and he acts like he doesn't know Jessica's alive, and Jessica wilts like last week's homecoming mum. I don't know what she's thinking. Mama and Daddy won't let her date until she's sixteen—no way.

But today he says, "Hey, let's talk." His thumb points to the back of the bus.

Jessica hesitates, trying to play just a little hard to get.

"Come on Jessica," Billy laughs. "Don't act so blonde." Jessica looks only half-happy now.

Ball Cap needles Billy. "She won't come."

Jessica frowns and doesn't budge.

Billy croons, "Come on, baby. I was just kidding."

Yeah, right.

He takes her hand, so my sister heads back with the jerk.

Theresa gives Billy and Jessica a dirty look as they pass. "What's next, Billy? First graders?"

"Jealous, Theresa?" Billy laughs and pulls Jessica to a back seat.

She shakes her head, disgusted.

Smelly Frank is awake for once instead of nodding off. He sits up and whispers to me. "Becky, one of those guys is bad. Tell your sister not to drink anything." And then he sits back. What was that about?

Billy starts to put his arm around my sister and she scoots away. He whispers something and Jessica smiles. He pulls her to himself and whispers into Jessie's ear and then Billy puts his hand on her chin and makes her look at him. Jessica's forehead wrinkles, and Billy moves away from her frowning. Jessica looks back at him with big eyes appealing to him to do what? Billy pulls away with a stony face. Whatever he wants—he wants it all his way and Jessica must give in. Jessica's shoulders sag and

Billy grins and pulls her to him.

Jessica sees me watching them, frowns, and says, "What are you looking at, Roper?"

"Not much, Blondie."

Billy laughs and tries to kiss her, and Jessica pulls away.

"Mm-mm-mm-mm, I'm telling Mama," I say.

"You're the one with the referral. You better worry about your own self, Rebecca Ramey."

I slip up two more seats. "I'll tell Daddy too."

Billy frowns like he doesn't want that to happen.

Jessica frowns too, but then she looks all smarty. "I thought you said they won't do anything."

Billy closes in on Jessica again, and Theresa pipes up, "I guess it's okay now for high school students to neck in the back of the bus with little girls."

The bus driver glances in the rearview mirror, "Jessica Ramey, you come right on back up to the front."

Jessica flounces past the cheerleader and hisses, "Some people need to mind their own business."

Ball Cap laughs. "She don't look like no little girl to me."

The bus stops and I rush out the door with Jessica right after me.

We hear a bus window slide up. "Jessica, remember. Tomorrow morning." Billy smiles and reaches out his hand.

She nods and waves, smiling like an idiot at a musclebound wad of trouble. Beth watches, calculating.

I tear through the front door and past the den. Mama's not in the kitchen. She's on the couch, her hand on her side. I don't even say hi. She doesn't even notice I've come in right away. "Oh, hi, sugar."

I hurry down the hallway and to Jessica's room.

Jessica pauses behind me. "Mama, are you okay?"

"Yeah, I'm fine, but my shoulder hurts." Mama's voice sounds strained.

"Just where do you think you're going?" Jessica stands in her doorway as I pull the tape player's cord from the socket.

"Getting my tape player that Ma-maw got me for Christmas."

"She said you had to share."

"I have—you play it all the time, and now I'm going to use it."

Jessica opens her mouth and then she shuts it. "Well, I want to play cassettes later, so I'm coming back after it."

"I'll let you know when I'm done." I step on Jessica's toe on the way out, go to my room, put in the cassette and crank her up loud. Pretty soon I'm bellowing along with Willie. I get up on my bed, and I don't even take off my boots. I sway back and forth singing along to the top of my lungs.

"Motherrrr! Make Becky stop."

Mama calls out, "We listen to your music all the time, Jessica." She sounds weak, tired, like it takes effort to speak up.

I smile and throw back my head and holler Willie's crazy outlaw lyrics louder,

"Okay, Becky, that's enough now." Mama appears at my door. She holds her side and leans against the doorway.

Being a bad kid makes me reckless. I don't even slow down, and I stare my mother in the eye, and I don't stop singing for one second.

Mama's finger pushes the stop button.

"You never stop Jessica's John Travolta music."

"It's the Bee Gees, Becky and they don't sing through their noses." Jessica just thinks she's going to get my cassette player back.

"No, they sing like girls. And they sang for a nasty movie. Jessica watched *Saturday Night Fever* on cable at Beth's house—even after you said no, Mama."

Mama raises her eyebrows and looks at Jessica. "Did she now? And how would you know, Rebecca?"

"You made me go to Beth's with her, but I didn't watch the movie. I sat in the kitchen and read Louis L'Amour. I heard all the dirty words though. It might scar me for life. And that's not all…"

Jessica's desperate to stop me. The next second, I might tell about Billy. "Well, at least I don't throw elbows in gym and get thrown out and sent to the principal's office."

"Well, at least I don't go making dates with high school boys."

"Well, at least my best friends aren't jail bait."

I punch Jessica right in the nose and she sits on the floor with her mouth open. She can't sling me around anymore. I'm ready to fly at her again, but I'm half waiting for Mama to pull us apart. Jessica's looking right past me.

"Mama?" Jessica sounds frightened.

Our mother lies crumpled on the floor. Her skirt is soaked in blood.

CHAPTER THIRTY-EIGHT

We don't wait for Daddy to come home, though we know he'll be here soon. I call the hospital and Daddy pulls into the driveway just as the ambulance pulls away with Mama.

We rush to his car and tell him Mama fainted and about the blood.

Daddy's stunned but he recovers fast. "I'm going to the hospital. You stay here and wait for my call."

"Nuh-uh!" Jessica and I don't even give Daddy a chance to say no. We get in the car and we don't mean to leave.

"No way, we're coming too. What about Granny and Mamaw and everybody?"

"We'll call them from the hospital." Daddy glances and notices a little dried blood on Jessie's upper lip. "What happened to your nose?"

"Nothing, Daddy, really."

"I hit her for calling Rusty 'jail bait' and then Mama fell."

"Have you two lost your minds? What are you thinking?" and then Daddy stops and shakes his head. "We've just got to get through this."

We rush into the emergency room with its heat and medicine smell. There are clusters of frightened patients and waiting families scattered around the room. Daddy goes to the desk and asks about Mama and the desk lady gets all busy asking for information.

"That is spelled *R-a-m-e-y*?"

Daddy tries to be patient. "If I could just talk to someone..."

The lady looks at him. "I know this is hard, but we've got to know some things, so we can help her."

Daddy goes to the pay phone and pats his pockets for change. A nice lady gives him some coins, so he can call our preacher. Daddy sighs and flops down. "Pastor Lewis will call your grandmothers."

A nurse opens a door, "Mr. Ramey?"

Daddy nods and she gestures for him to come quickly.

As the door opens we catch a glance of gurneys and equipment, but no Mama.

Jessica and I follow Daddy, but a big mean nurse with frizzy gray hair shakes her head. Daddy says, "No, girls. You have to wait out here." Jessie and I can only sit and hold hands.

The preacher and his wife come rushing in and make over us because we're all alone. "Why don't you girls come up to the cafeteria with us?" urges Mrs. Lewis.

Preacher Lewis agrees. "We reached your grandparents—they'll be here real soon now. Why don't we get a Coke while we wait?"

We sit in the cafeteria, but the Cokes don't help any. Jessica fidgets and asks, "Can't we just go back? They might know something now."

We're just out of the elevator when a ruckus makes us all turn our heads. Mama's mama, Granny, comes busting through the wrong door with a nurse fussing at her, and she's fussing right back.

"Well, all I can say is, you people need to mark your doors better. I am going to see my daughter and you can just get over it!" Granny shakes her finger at the nurse and her black tower of curls trembles.

"Over here, Granny," Jessica calls. Pastor Lewis guides Granny to our seats and tells her the little we know. Time moves so slow, but every noise makes me jump. I can't say how long we've been here when Ma-maw comes thumping in through the outside door. Her ankle's in a cast and she's holding on to our cousin Dub. Soon Jessica and I are crushed in her hugs and swamped with questions.

"I told her she should get those pains checked out," Granny frets. "And you two have been worrying her to death. She's been weak and completely worn out for weeks."

Jessica starts squalling and chokes out words we can hardly make out. "...so sorry...I told him I couldn't...I didn't mean to..."

Ma-maw pulls her over and smothers the wails and tears against her shoulder. Since Ma-maw's got Jessica, Granny grabs me, and I relax and bawl too.

"I was bad Granny. I gotta tell Mama I'm so-or-ry." I sob.

Granny shushes me, "It's all right now. She knows. You're a good girl."

"No, I punched J-Jessic-ca, and Mama fell down."

Ma-maw and Granny both hug on me. "Here now," Ma-maw whispers. "That didn't make your mother sick."

Preacher Lewis tries to settle us all in chairs, so we can calm down a little. Mrs. Lewis says, "Mrs. Ramey, how did you all get here so soon?"

"My great-nephew here, Dub Ramey, drove me. My husband couldn't leave right away, and I can't drive with this ankle —broke it at potluck—slipped on ice. If we went an inch we went ninety miles per hour over the interstate. It's a small miracle we weren't pulled over."

"Aww, Aunt Eileen, I know where all the troopers are between home and Dallas."

"Uh-huh. I'll just bet you do."

Dub just chuckles all proud. He doesn't act like the brightest penny in the Ramey coin purse, but Granddaddy says Dub's the best linebacker in East Texas.

Daddy comes out of the swinging door, tense and pale, and Reverend Journey is with him, looking grave. I look to see if I can catch sight of Mama, but no luck. We all stand and gather about Daddy. He pulls Jessica and me over to some chairs and sits down with us. "The bleeding has stopped, but things are very serious. Mama has to have some surgery." He swallows and pauses and looks past us to Granny and Ma-maw. "Liz had an ectopic pregnancy. It implanted in her fallopian tube. They won't know until they get in there, but they're pretty sure it ruptured."

"Mama's pregnant?" Jessica's voice sounds quivery.

"No. Yes, but not anymore." Daddy looks down, tears slipping down his cheeks. He runs his hand over his face, trying to get a hold of himself.

Ma-maw puts one arm around Granny and one around Jessica. "Girls, that means the little baby implanted outside your mother's womb."

Granny nods. "And there wasn't room there." Tears and mascara run in black tracks from her eyes.

Dub tries to pinch his tears back with his big old thumb and forefinger like jocks do, but then he just lets them flow and I hug him, and we cry together.

Preacher and Reverend Journey holds out their hands. We all link up and Preacher Lewis leads us all in prayer for Mama, and some folks we don't even know join in. Other folks sit there quiet, looking like they're afraid we might do something else weird and religious.

Daddy says, "Thanks, Brother Bob, Reverend." And he and the preachers give each other guy hugs, pounding each other on the back. Daddy hugs and kisses his mom. "Mom, I'd like you and Dub to take the girls on home," Jessica and I start to protest, but Daddy holds up his hand. "It's going to be awhile, and you need to eat, and Ma-maw needs to get off her foot. Granny and I will call as soon as Mama's out of surgery and we know anything."

"Well, I gotta go to the ladies' room before I do anything else," I declare.

"Hurry, sugar. We don't want Ma-maw's ankle to swell in her cast." Daddy hugs me and kisses me on my head.

I go to the restroom door and look over my shoulder. They're all hugging or talking, and the desk lady is taking information from some guy with a bloody toe. I take my chance and dash through the swinging door. I slip from curtain to curtain looking for my mama. The nurses are busy looking at charts. At the last gurney, I find her.

I whisper in my mother's ear, "I'm sorry Mama. I'm sorry I stood on my bed and sang Willie Nelson. I'm sorry I hit Jessica."

Mama's eyes fly open, frightened. "Jessica?" she whispers. And then her eyes close.

Jessica. Not Becky.

A young nurse grabs my shoulder, "I'm sorry, but you must come with me. It's against regulations…"

The mean frizzy-headed nurse looks around the curtain.

I look her in the eye. "I need to tell my Mama one more thing, before…" My chin trembles.

"Miss Smith," the mean nurse growls, "this young lady can break the regulations long enough to talk to her mama."

I quickly bend down. "Mama," I whisper. "I'll take care of Jessie. I won't let that boy hurt her." It's not much, but it's all I can do.

CHAPTER THIRTY-NINE

I sit up in my parents' bed. "Why am I here?" I squint, feeling all dopey and confused, until I see Ma-maw beside me. Jessica and I crawled into bed with her and Granny last night. Neither one of us felt like being alone in our rooms. We huddled next to our grandmas and cried and crying and worrying just sort of wears a person down.

Granny was worried sick when she came in, but she still wrapped her big hair in toilet paper before she went to bed. She says even in a crisis, a lady's got to keep herself up. Part of the toilet paper came unrolled, and now it's sticking to Jessica's face. Jessie must have drooled on it in her sleep.

I feel like crying again and I'm so groggy, I can't remember why. Then I look at Granny, and it's like the truth scalds my brain. I remember my mama's sick.

When she came in last night, Granny told us Daddy made her go on home, so she could rest up and sit with Mama today. She sat down with us on Jessica's bed and said, "Girls, your mama lost a lot of blood. She made it through surgery, but now they must watch out for infection." She and Ma-maw looked at each other. "Her system could be just filled with poison." Granny never did like to cushion hard news.

Ma-maw wakes and sits up because she feels me move. She

gets up and she and her cast thump into the bathroom and then to the kitchen to get us some breakfast. Ma-maw mouths, "Try to get some more sleep."

No sleeping now—I have a mission. I put my hand on Jessica's shoulder. She doesn't stir. I carefully pick up a corner of the toilet paper stuck to her face and peel it away, and Jessica's eyes slowly open and she frowns. She looks at the toilet paper in my hand, and her eyes follow the length of it to Granny's head. She almost giggles, but then her eyes grow sad, and the giggle dies away. She remembers too.

I point to the door, and Jessica nods. We ease out of bed, and I grab her hand and pull her to my room. Jessica and I are going to have a talk. I must keep my promise to Mama.

"Okay, Jessica. What's the deal with you and Billy Markam? I know he made plans with you."

Tears spring up in Jessica's eyes and slide down her cheeks. "He wanted me to sneak out this morning and go out with him on a date."

"Date? We're not allowed to date yet."

"He wants to take me to the lake." Jessica looks down and sighs like she knows how foolish this sounds.

"What kind of stupid date is that? No movie, no Dairy Queen, no Sonic Drive-In? A lake? What's he gonna do, take you water skiing? I don't think so."

"He said he wanted to go somewhere quiet, where we could just talk," Jessica's voice trails off.

"Yeah, right. I may be just a sixth grader, but even I know what he's after—and it ain't no conversation and it ain't no water sport."

Jessica straightens and looks serious. "Well, I already decided to go meet him and tell him the date's off."

"You better tell him it's all off."

Jessica murmurs, "I know."

"And I better go with you."

"No. I should tell him myself. I owe it to him."

"I don't trust him, Jessica. We should tell Ma-maw."

"No. No way. Ma-maw and Granny will think I'm terrible."

I start to protest, and Jessica shakes her head.

"No, Becky, I mean it. I'm going to call off the date and tell Billy it's over. I don't want Ma-maw to know and that's final. You don't tell either, promise!"

I promise, but I don't like this one bit. My tummy feels funny like it's telling me this could turn out bad. And I feel like I've got another weight on my shoulders, knowing I really should tell Ma-maw.

We straggle into the kitchen and Jessica catches my arm and squeezes it. She doesn't want me to slip up and tell.

Ma-maw's cooking up a storm in Mama's red-checked kitchen. There's a pot with a chicken boiling, and her eyes are streaming, as she whacks away at a smelly onion like it's her sworn enemy.

Granddaddy is at the table sipping coffee and we both go over for hugs. "Don't worry now. Everybody back home's praying. Come eat some of Ma-maw's good waffles. She put in pecans and everything."

Ma-maw wipes her eyes and starts eyeing me. "Now what's this I hear about you hitting your sister over some boy? Rebecca, you do not need to be thinking about boys at this point in your life. Granddaddy and I have seen it again and again—girls get caught up in that mess too early and they absolutely ruin their lives. Jessica could tell you the same thing. And those poor little babies." Ma-maw stops and blushes—she remembers Jessica is one of those poor little babies.

Jessica's got her back to Ma-maw and her face just gets longer and guiltier.

"Well, how old do *you* think a girl should be before she dates, Ma-maw?" I ask real casual.

"You're not getting me into *that* debate—whatever your parents say is right."

Jessica bugs her eyes out at me like she is saying "Will you shut up!" I feel her foot brush past my shin and then Granddaddy jumps.

"Ouch!"

"Oh, sorry, Granddaddy. Are you okay?"

"That's all right." Granddaddy is looking closely at Jessica and me. He knows something's up.

"Granddaddy, I'm going to send you and Becky to Piggly Wiggly for a few things." Ma-maw writes one more item on a scrap of notebook paper and hands it to our granddaddy.

Granddaddy clears his throat. "I believe Miss Jessica needs to help me this time."

Ma-maw looks at Granddaddy a little surprised. "Well, Okay. Jessica run and slip on some clothes and go help your granddaddy."

Jessica glances at me as she heads to her room. Her eyes beg me to keep quiet.

"Miss Rebecca, you're going to help me with dicing onion and bell pepper and then you're going to cube some Velveeta."

"What are we cooking, Ma-maw?"

"Chicken spaghetti for tonight and a couple of pans of meatloaf for the freezer."

I've got to call for help, but first I must get this mess chopped up for Ma-maw. I chop as fast as a person can with tears flooding down her face. Ma-maw sends the bell pepper back for finer chops. It takes a couple of tries before the cheese cubes are small enough to suit her.

"Ma-maw, I need to call some folks who ought to know about Mama."

"Mmmm, okay, sugar." Ma-maw is busy stirring her cheese sauce. I almost get clean away when she says, "Just a couple of short calls. We've got to keep off the phone. Your daddy might call with news from the hospital."

CHAPTER FORTY

I get on the phone in the living room and whisper. My cousin, Dub's asleep—dead to the world—on the couch. Marcie answers the phone. I tell her about Mama and she hollers the news to her mom.

"Marcie!" I hiss. "I don't have much time. You've got to listen. I've got to stop Jessica. Billy Markam wants to take her off to the lake today and I don't trust him."

"Tell your grandparents."

"I can't—Jessica made me promise."

"Well, you better do something. I gotta go—Mama wants to run to the store and get a cake or something for y'all. I'll try to think of something before we get there. Bye."

All I can think of is Jessica being the latest rumor on the bus and in the school hallways with everybody whispering and wondering and snickering, while her heart is breaking.

I call Sunny, but I hardly get out the story, when she hangs up.

Ma-maw calls from the kitchen and I jump. "Becky, you almost done with the phone? Finish and then wake up Dub. He's got to mow the lawn before he heads home."

"Yes, ma'am." Rusty. I've got to call Rusty.

The phone rings seven times and then Rusty's sleepy voice mumbles, "Mmmm. Hello?"

"Rusty," I whisper. "Listen fast. We've got to stop Jessica.

Billy Markam's talked her into sneaking off to the lake with him. She wants to break the date, but I'm scared."

There's a long pause and I can only hear Rusty breathing. "Becky, I didn't want to say anything, because she's your sister. You're a good girl and I guess she is too. But those high school boys talk about her. They say since she's so, um, developed that she must be...um."

"Easy." I finish.

"Yeah. She better not go if she knows what's good for her."

"Oh, Rusty. What are we going to do?"

"Rusty?" Ma-maw has one hand on her hip and one eyebrow is raised a full inch higher than the other. "What are you going to do, indeed? Get off the phone now. Young ladies do not call young men. What are you thinking? We will talk later. Get Dub up—keep at him—don't stop until he's awake and heading to the kitchen."

I turn and look at my cousin. Dub. The linebacker's so big about half of him hangs off the couch. He's big enough to stop even Billy Markam. Jessie said I couldn't tell Ma-maw, but she didn't say anything about Dub.

I shake and pester Dub and then in desperation I lick my finger and stick it in his ear. It's a good thing I back up fast, because he wakes up swinging.

"What are you doing, Becky?" he fumes.

"Listen, Dub. It's an emergency."

I tell him the problem as fast as I can and Dub's eyes narrow and flash like green fire. He looks off like he's passed judgment and ready to hang the guilty. "That ain't right."

"We've got to be on the lookout for a boy in a football jacket."

Dub sits leaning forward with his big hands braced on muscled legs like he's planning some power play. "Okay if I tell your granddaddy?"

I consider for a moment. "Well, I didn't promise about that either. Sure."

Dub's wolfing down the last four waffles as Granddaddy

and Jessica carry in some grocery bags. Jessica still looks uneasy and Granddaddy looks at Ma-maw and shrugs. Ma-maw sends Jessica off to clean the bathroom, but she has me put up the groceries. Ma-maw, carrying a load of damp dishtowels, limps to the laundry room.

Dub clears his throat and says, "Coach, I'm kind of concerned about some of the football talent around here. I think we need to be thinking about defense. Their passing game's pretty good at this school."

Granddaddy looks at Dub like he can't imagine why on earth he's talking football right now. "Son, we've got a good while yet..." Then he notices Dub's raised eyebrows.

"We better give this some serious attention now, sir, if we're going to prevent serious incursions." Dub looks secretive, as Ma-maw walks by with a stack of clean linens.

Granddaddy's starting to get it. "Is that right? What kind of passes are you concerned about, son?" Granddaddy tilts his head in my direction raising his eyebrows.

Dub shakes his head no, and then looks at Jessica as she enters the den. "I'm afraid our less experienced players won't be able to handle a passing game."

Granddaddy leans back and nods like it's all beginning to make sense. "Ma-maw, Dub and I have to run a little errand," my grandfather says.

I feel desperate and helpless. Trouble could come any moment, and Dub and Granddaddy just walked out the door.

Jessica sits in the den hugging herself like she's cold. "Becky, can you help me with something?"

She gets up and I follow her to our old room. "I want you to distract Ma-maw while I sneak out," she whispers. "It's time and I think she's suspicious."

Some promises are just stupid. I don't have to keep a dangerous promise. I cross my arms. "No, I won't do that, but I'll go with you. I either go too, or I tell Ma-maw now."

Jessica agrees. And to tell the truth, I think my sister is relieved.

I feel like I need to be armed, so I pick up the only surefire weapon I've ever used and that's a ball. I grab my basketball off our porch and bounce it as I leave to protect my sister. If I can take out Chad, maybe I can take out a football player if I must.

Jessica and I walk across the grass, like it's a wilderness and only danger lies ahead. I make one last bounce and then hold my ball in one arm and put the other arm around my sister.

We go around the house to the side street and Billy's waiting in his Trans Am, but so is Ball Cap, and another pimple-faced weasel to boot.

Ball Cap and Weasel get out and Ball Cap has that stallion look.

I step in front of my sister and get ready to launch my basketball right into his gut or his evil face.

"Hasn't anybody ever told you, it's impolite to stare?" I say.

"What are you doing here?" Jessica asks, scornful.

"Aren't you glad to see us?" Ball Cap says.

We hear squealing brakes. Mr. Wright has parked his car behind the blue car, and then a truck from Earth Day nursery parks and blocks Billy's way. Sunny's dad and Rusty are in it. Sunny, Marcie and her mom are across the street with Audrey's mother. Rusty leaves the truck and bolts across the lawn and stands, wiry, tan arms crossed, as he glares at Billy.

Granddaddy and Dub step up on opposite sides of the car and Ball Cap's nasty smile disappears. Dub's got fire in his eyes, and nobody's getting past him. Dub grabs Ball Cap, but he wriggles free and jumps into the passenger seat of Billy's car. Only Ball Cap's shirt is left in Dub's big hands and he flings it into some shrubs. In the uproar, Dub's foot crushes the boy's cap, and it lies all squashed on the curb.

The Weasel gets ready to bolt, so I lob my basketball at his side, and he lands on top of Ball Cap. That feels mighty satisfying. "I think she broke a rib! Am I bleeding?" he whines. The other boys don't care. They make him squirm into the back seat.

Rusty retrieves my ball and passes it. "Hit 'em again, Becky!"

Granddaddy grabs the ball, because he can see I'm about to lob it at the car door. "Not the poor car, Ranger. The car is innocent." He returns my ball and pats my shoulder.

We hear our Ma-maw's voice and she says, "Come on Jessica, let's let your grandfather handle this." Jessica looks at Ma-maw and then me and frowns. "Nobody told on you, Jess. Your grandmother isn't totally oblivious."

Jessica hesitates, but then she feels another arm about her shoulders. It's Audrey. "Let's go, Jessica. Nothing for us here." Pregnant belly and all, she guides my sister home without giving Billy Markam one look.

CHAPTER FORTY-ONE

I put my ball at my feet, cross my arms, and watch. What is my grandfather going to do now? Dub stands by the passenger side of the car with his thumbs hooked in the belt loops of his jeans, while Granddaddy casually leans against the left front fender of Billy's car and chews on a toothpick.

"You can't hold us here," Ball Cap says, his arms crossed over his bare chest.

"Oh, yes, we can, son. Suspicious intruders in the neighborhood. Mm-mm-mm!"

"Are you calling the cops on us?" Billy tries to sound tough, but his voice shakes.

Granddaddy takes out his toothpick and examines it. "Oh, I expect they'll show up after a bit. Right now, we're waiting for your football coach, the junior high principal, and your father, Billy."

Billy's head slumps forward onto the steering wheel.

The pimply weasel boy says, "Just let us leave. We'll never bother anybody again."

Granddaddy chuckles. "That's right, son. You won't."

A white Mustang pulls up to our house and Mrs. Buckley gets out. My principal is wearing a sporty red warm-up suit. She pats my shoulder as she walks by.

"Patricia Buckley, the girls' principal. Your wife called."

"A pleasure, Milton Ramey is my name."

Coach Hammond and Mr. Markam pull up in a pickup and the tense men get out and stride over.

The boys in the Trans Am just now roll down their windows. Sweat has soaked their hair. Ball Cap's hat is off, but you can see the ring it left. The boy keeps peering over the door and frowning at his smashed cap.

"Coach Ramey, I believe."

"That's right and you're Coach Hammond. We've seen each other at events, I believe. And you are this young man's father."

"What's this about?" Markam begins.

Hammond puts up his hand to stop Billy's dad. He knows something different is happening here. "What can we do for you, sir?"

"As a professional courtesy, I am letting you know that we have narrowly averted the commission of a crime on the part of these young men. I hate to pull in the authorities, when the adults concerned can handle things."

"Yes," Coach Hammond agrees. "What was the nature of the offense, Coach Ramey?"

"At a time of severe family crisis, they were attempting to take my thirteen-year-old granddaughter on a trip she did not necessarily want to take. All while her mother is gravely ill." Granddaddy turns to Mrs. Buckley. "The arrangements for this event were made on a district school bus."

Mrs. Buckley's eyes narrow. "Is that right?" and she looks at Coach Hammond who rubs the back of his neck.

"And we have witnesses who saw this transpire," Granddaddy continues.

"No doubt," my principal nods.

My grandfather sweeps his arm and points. "As you can see, her family and friends have successfully intervened on her behalf."

"So, they made a date with your granddaughter?" Markam

says.

"Leave it alone, Markam," Hammond warns.

Granddaddy shakes his head. "No. This is how you date a Ramey girl. You wait until she is sixteen. You meet her parents. You take her with a group of nice friends to a safe public place and you bring her back early. These young men have forever disqualified themselves from that privilege." He looks at Markam without blinking. "But let's not get sidetracked. This is the deal." Granddaddy draws closer to the coach and says in a lower voice, "We are reliably informed that there are controlled substances in this car. Retired Police Officer Wright is already in communication with local law enforcement."

Markam goes to the driver's side window. "Give me the keys." Billy hands them out the window without looking at his father. The father and the coach look inside the trunk and Markam cusses under his breath.

Dub's looking in the car, down at the floorboard. "Coach Ramey, they've got stuff in here too."

Hammond goes to Ball Cap's window. "I want all of it." He puts his head down and looks at each boy. "You don't want a cop to find this." He straightens and looks grim at my grandfather.

Granddaddy holds his hands out like they hold a gift. "Now we are all able to win here today. We have already prevented a grave felony. Mr. Markam can fill you in on the gravity of a conviction for abduction—not to speak of other grave crimes." He looks at Markam and squints. "My granddaughter need not be smeared and dragged through the legal system. Am I right, Mr. Markam?"

Markam looks straight ahead and nods.

"The police will be here in—" my grandfather looks at his watch "—five minutes. Mr. Wright here can see to it that these controlled substances are turned over to the proper authorities after everyone leaves."

"Exactly what do you want, Coach Ramey?" Mr. Hammond asks.

"That these young men will not ride the bus or otherwise contact my granddaughters ever—I leave all other consequences to your discretion. I do have just a few final words." Granddaddy goes to the car. "Young men, look around you. These people here love these young girls and they know your faces. You have officially worn out your welcome in this neighborhood." He goes to Billy's side and peers in the window. "Son, let me leave you with one piece of advice." Granddaddy points all about him. "Go west. Go east. Go north." Granddaddy jabs Billy's shoulder with his finger and the kid jumps. "But do not enroll in an institution in the Southwest Conference, if you want a long career in football. I have taught and am friends with numerous young men and coaches on these teams and they are exceedingly loyal."

Granddaddy straightens and smiles. "I believe this concludes everything. Thank you for your time." He walks over to me and pulls me in for hug. "Brave girl. You performed a thing of beauty. Yep. You go check on your sister now."

I turn, and Markam is sliding into the driver's side of the Trans Am. The coach has the other two boys. Billy sits in the passenger seat watching Audrey slowly cross the street. She goes into her home, shuts the door, and never looks back.

I find my sister on the couch in the den. "Should have told them in the first place," I said. Ma-maw tucks a quilt about my sister, while Granny B. stirs a glass of Ovaltine and passes it to her. Jessica is watchful, but our grandmothers are keeping their cool.

"I was in over my head," Jessica murmurs.

"Yes, you were, and it was dangerous. That's why we all need family," says Ma-maw.

"And friends," Granny B. adds.

"I thought you'd be really mad—and disappointed."

"I won't lie. We're hurt and mad and worried," says Granny B. "But I think we both want you to know whatever happens, we're going to stay calm and help you anyway we can."

"You must feel really hurt," Ma-maw says, holding and stroking my sister's hand.

"At first. Now I feel stupid and embarrassed."

Granny B. nods her head, approving. "Well, that's the beginning of some wisdom."

I go to the front door. Sunny, Rusty, and Marcie wait there to say hi and bye. Ma-maw says, "What precious friends, Rebecca. You always want to treasure your friends." And she hugs them all. Rusty reddens, but he hugs her back.

We watch Sunny's dad and Dub mow and edge the lawn. The big man with the vague, sleepy smile has also brought my mother potted pansies.

The phone rings and we all jump. Ma-maw grabs it. "Clifford? Let me let you talk to your daddy."

We sit hushed, so we can hear my grandfather. "Son, you need to come on home. Something has come up. Everything is totally under control now, but the girls need their daddy."

Jessica tugs on my hand. "What about Beth and Sue Lynn? What if they spread gossip?"

"We're going hold our heads up—because we did right," I say. I try to sound bold.

My sister and I look at each other and we both see worry, because we're not one of Beth's advantages anymore.

We hear the front door open and our daddy calls out, "Becky, Jessica?" He rushes and grabs us in his arms. He looks at us and asks over and over are we okay. Granddaddy pulls him into the living room and Dad and our grandparents worry and whisper about boys who brag and talk and take sides with sorry friends. They are not so far away that we don't get it. And Jessica's relief dries up, and dread just floods in.

CHAPTER FORTY-TWO

Jessica and I were right. We are no longer one of Beth's assets. She lets us know that right off. Granny drops us off at school so we "don't have to put up with any nonsense" she says. Our school bus is unloading as we get out of our grandmother's sedan. Beth and Sue Ellen jump off the bus dressed just alike and laughing, arms linked. They look bold, powerful in boots and denim skirts. Sue Ellen looks back and spots us. She whispers in Beth's ear, and they both stride off laughing like only they are in on a joke.

Marcie and Sunny rush up and join us. Jessica tries to smile at us, but it's not much comfort having three sixth graders on your side when you're thirteen and heartbroken and the whole world is watching. We walk as far as we can with Jessica and still be on time to Old Hornet's class.

"I wish we could go with her." Marcie says. We watch Jessie as long as we can.

"It's a weird comfort, but I think Jessica's too worried about Mama to think much about Beth and what she thinks." Marcie and Sunny look at me, their eyes watchful and serious. "Our folks try not to let on, but Mama's so sick, the hospital won't let us see her."

Marcie, Sunny, and I walk into our class and there is Miss

Powers, not in athletic gear, but in a royal blue suit. She is writing her name on the board. She brushes the chalk dust from her hands. "Good morning, Becky, how is your mother?"

"Coming along, I guess. Why are you here?"

"Mrs. Goforth has a new assignment. I am your language arts teacher—for the rest of the spring anyway."

We all settle into our seats in wonder. I turn and Rusty is grinning big. "Magnificent!" he whispers.

We are just opening our books, when Jessica runs past our doorway. I stand up.

Miss Powers sees her too. "Yes, go check on her."

Jessica is in the girls' room washing her face and trying to gulp down sobs.

"What's wrong? What'd they say? What'd they do?"

"I started to sit by a kid, a boy in science lab, and Sue Lynn said, 'Look out, you don't know what you could catch from some people.'" A tear drops off Jessie's chin and she dabs at her nose.

"No tears. I mean it, Jessica." I grab her arm and shake it. "No tears for them. They do not deserve our tears. Now you stop it."

Jessica breathes in deeply and nods. "Go on back to class. I'm okay."

And then Daniesha and Pee Wee walk in. And Freckles. Daniesha takes Jessica's arm. "You are a fool about men, but you did not deserve that," Daniesha declares.

"We have your back," says Freckles.

"Those two aren't right. Two-faced and wearing boots in eighty-five-degree weather," Pee Wee scoffs.

The rest of the day, the whole team of tall basketball friends look out for my sister, and fierce, prissy choir girls protect her reputation because she is one of their own. Rusty is late to a few classes, because he escorts Jessica. Miss Powers calls him a gentleman and a scholar, and I guess that's right. Chad and Kenny tag along and it's hard to tell if they are helping or just cutting class.

Beth watches, recalculating, but I think school opinion is turning on her.

During lunch, I go into the office and I see Beth bringing an attendance slip, I guess. I don't look to the left or the right. "Can I use the phone?" I say to the secretary and she looks a little surprised.

"Well, sure. Go ahead."

"I need to tell my Granny she doesn't need to pick us up. My sister and I are going to ride *our* bus." We're not hiding from anybody. I look over at Beth. Her eyes meet mine and then she looks away. Let her ride the bus if she dares—or find another way home.

Just outside the office Mr. Parks is talking to Mrs. Buckley and I hear the name "Goforth" so I listen.

"Just what was her reassignment?" Parks asks.

Mrs. Buckley smiles and says loud enough for me to hear, "The board office. Mrs. Goforth will edify teachers instead of children."

If edify means torment, that sounds about right.

Mrs. Buckley nods at two smiling women who are laughing and chatting with Miss Powers. Patrick and Julio's mothers will like their boys' new teacher just fine. And there's some tardy justice—Daniesha is installing her project in the place of honor it deserves: the school display case. Over those ugly red words is glued a neatly written strip: "Atrocious and Unjust!" As we pass, she whispers, "My whole church is praying for your mama, y'all."

The bell rings and I meet Jessica by her locker. She looks better, but she's drained and weepy.

"Shoulders back, Jessica," I direct. "We're getting on that bus and facing down those fake friends."

"Quit bossing me, Becky. *You're* the baby."

"No kidding."

"How'd *you* get to be so bossy?"

"Having to take care of everything."

Jessica gets on the bus smiling—but only a little and it

fades. She dreads the trip home. She did not need to worry about those girls. Sue hurries past us, her head down, and Beth is nowhere in sight. The big worry is the high school kids.

The bus pulls up to the high school and Jessica just stares out the window.

Suddenly, Frank leans over us, and he's cleaned up! "I always knew you were too fine for the dumb jock—he's off the bus for good."

Jessica smiles.

"You're looking good, Frank," I say.

"Thanks." He looks at me. "I warned Rusty about Cooper's drugs."

"Thanks." I look at Frank and I get it. "Drugs. That's your problem, isn't it?"

Theresa steps on and stares a second. "I didn't expect to see you two today."

"It's our bus."

"Yes, it is," and she sits with us and I'm glad.

"Sorry to hear about your trouble. I'm sure your mom will get better soon." Theresa puts her arm around me. "Hey, I heard about that basketball! You're an Amazon!"

Chad says, "She has a deadly aim."

I grin a little, but Jessica whispers, "Are they talking about me?"

Theresa pauses. "Well, the two other boys—they're suspended for now and off the football team for good, and none of the guys much care. They weren't any good. Everybody likes your dad and they're sorry about your mom and all but . . . if Billy weren't a senior, and they were counting on him for next season, I won't lie. There would be talk. Word is he's going to some university in Tennessee, and he ought to be grateful he can do that. It's not his first problem and the guys know it. The school should have kicked him out too, but it's not going to happen."

Kyle leans in from across the aisle and says, "It'll be okay, Jessica. But, I would look out for Cooper. He's one to get even.

Just saying. Y'all be careful."

Jessica and I sit in silence. I think we're both worn out. Frank gets up for his stop and nods his head at Jessica and smiles as he leaves. My sister smiles and waves back. This can't be good. Two drowning kids will just wind up drowning each other.

"Hey, Frank," I call to him. "You talk to my daddy because I'm going to."

I can't keep rescuing her. We get off at our stop. I walk in and I holler to anybody that'll listen, "*Something* has to give."

CHAPTER FORTY-THREE

"Somebody better call that lawyer, or I swear I will." I throw my book bag down and stand with my hands on my hips.

Granny's sorting out the mail on the kitchen bar and looks up. "Well, who you gonna sue today, sugar?"

"The world if somebody doesn't have Jessica meet up with her birth mother. We just rescued her from a bunch of nasty football players. Now she's making friends with dope addicts."

Jessica eases her backpack off her shoulders. "I was just being polite."

"Uh-huh. You don't know *how* to be just polite. You gotta go making sorry friends and taking their advice and it's going to get you into trouble. And then you're going to cry some more about how you're pitiful or you're bad, or you're talented and nobody understands, and you must have gotten it all from your mother."

Ma-maw slips into the room cautiously.

"Rebecca wants to call the lawyer," Granny reports.

"I'm sick and tired of the stupid mystery. Let's find out and get it over with." Ma-maw looks confused. I hold my hands out like they're holding the plain truth. "Jessica's birth mom."

Ma-maw looks at Jessica. "So how do you feel about that?"

"Well, I don't want to hurt Mama." Jessica ducks her head and looks up at us.

"She'd rather you talk to your mother than take up with dope fiends." Am I the only person with good sense around here?

"Well, she kind of has a point." Jessica looks up through her hair to check our grandmothers' reactions.

"There's not a thing wrong with your wanting to know." Granny throws down the phone bill like she dares it to disagree.

Ma-maw sits down thoughtfully and motions for us to sit at the table. "Well, I just want to caution you. Meeting long-lost family might not be all you expect. I am adopted."

Jessica and I sit up straighter for a story we've never heard. Adults don't give up the deep, dark stories too easy and you must grab them when you can.

"I guess you two know about the school explosion. My folks were very poor, and my dad came to Rusk County to work the oil fields. For a while it was such a relief, because we had enough to eat and wear for once and, above all, we had the privilege of attending one of the best new schools around. It gave you hope.

It was the day after St. Patrick's Day and the first warm day of spring. I remember Ethel had to break up a squabble over hair ribbons between our sister and me on the way to school. There were four of us: Robert, Ethel, then Edna, and I was the baby. Robert ran on ahead. He was always running. We were all excited because the next day school was dismissed so we could support our classmates at an interscholastic meet at Henderson. And Thursday wouldn't even be a full day. It was a PTA day so school would let out early." Granny B. looks down and shakes her head.

Ma-maw paused and gazed out the window. "One comes to wonder so many times in life how changing or not changing one detail can so alter events. Our superintendent decided we needed a full day of instruction since we were missing Friday. We would stay until 3:30. The explosion occurred at 3:17.

"I remember rubbing my forehead. I had had a headache off and on for days. It was the gas fumes. I was sitting in my classroom, when the wall blew out. Some of our classmates were pinned beneath the chunks of the ceiling. A boy grabbed my hand and we climbed over the debris and to the lawn. We were covered in thick gray dust, coughing and bloody and bruised, but no serious injuries. Dust hung in the air—we could hardly see, but moans and screams came from everywhere. I almost stepped on a little hand and I wanted to say sorry and reach out to help, but that was all that was there—a little hand." Jessica's eyes meet mine and I see the same horror I feel.

"Our sister Edna died in the explosion. We never got to make up that squabble. She was crushed under a concrete slab. Eileen was trapped for hours. A young oil worker found her. He was a good young man and they married, but he died soon after, the last good man in Eileen's life. Accident at an oil derrick. They happened so often. Ma-maw looks at Jessica. "I'm sorry. Young girls shouldn't have to hear this."

"Young girls shouldn't have to *see* things like this. We're okay, Ma-maw." Jessica reaches for and holds her grandmother's hand. "Go on. We're all right."

Ma-maw smiles but closes her eyes and breathes in deeply before she continues. "Our parents died. My mother just wasted away in grief. Our father had always been a hard drinker, and soon he drank himself to death." Tears course down her cheeks. Jessica and I get up and hug her close. Ma-maw gathers herself. "A lot of folks just left the county. No one could talk about it for years. Granddaddy's mother would wake up screaming night after night.

Milton and Shrimp and their father helped haul rubble and looked for their brother, until it was clear to their father that they must look for Buddy at a hospital or among the dead. No children should ever have to look on such carnage. Clayton was never a big boy, but he was determined. He did not stop until he and Milton found what was left of their brother at a makeshift morgue in a garage."

We sit silently.

"I thought your folks were all school teachers, Ma-maw." Jessica leans her cheek on her hand.

"My adoptive parents were—in fact my father was a principal. I owe my love of learning and my life to them. I was very ill when they got me." Ma-maw sighs. "But I never lost my desire to know my other family." She strokes the tabletop with her long, white fingers.

"Your adoptive great-grandparents died when I was in college, but it wasn't until after I married your granddaddy that I felt able to look for my older brother and sister. I never found my brother. He dropped out of school and joined the service and then he dropped out of sight completely. I'm told he could run like the wind—like you and your daddy, Becky." Ma-maw pauses and looks at us. "You know my sister."

"Aunt Ethel."

"When I found her, she was unconscious in a trailer with broken windows and weeds up to the bottom of the mobile home. Her third husband had beaten her senseless. Her son was a very troubled young man. We did what we could for him—camps, school clothes. He ran around with your daddy for a while, but a different life didn't seem to stick. He killed a store clerk during an armed robbery. Ethel's health is going—gone really and she's not caring for herself. Her only child, her son is in the prison in Huntsville. Your granddaddy and I have spent lots of money trying to help. I moved her closer to home, so we can care for her, but she's moved back to her old trailer park, so she can see her son, if he will ever see her. Ethel will call again wanting help or money. Her son will turn down her visits, and I'll offer advice she does not want. Seems like family is bent on frustrating family, sometimes."

I say, "Well, however it is—at least Jessica will know."

"That's easy for you to say. You know how your people are. You know who you're like," Ma-maw says.

Jessica leans back. "Well, I think I'd still like to know. If I don't like what I see, maybe I could be like you, Ma-maw."

* * *

It's taken a couple of weeks of finagling, but today is Jessica's big day. I wondered if it was ever going to happen. Peggy agreed right away to meet Jessie once she found out about Mama being sick. But then my sister's birth mom wanted something weird. The lawyer guy called and said some of Peggy's friends wanted to meet Jessica too. Said they were special friends when Peggy was expecting Jessie. Jessie was ready to call the whole thing off—and then she got this picture in the mail. It was an old black-and-white Polaroid of some kids laughing. There was Peggy with long hair sitting at a table with a lanky boy with wavy bangs over his eyes. He was looking at Peggy like he was sneaking a look at somebody special. Another boy stood to the side with a sort of "I'm-almost-too-smart-to-be-here" look on his face. A skinny little girl laughing with her head thrown back sat on Peggy's left. Her hair was short and wispy, and she looked pale, as though her color wouldn't be a lot different if the photo weren't black-and-white. A note came with it and said, "We loved you from the start—can't wait to meet you." It explained that they lived in the neighborhood when Peggy stayed with her aunt, and that her aunt kept the little girl during the summer while her mother worked. I turned over the picture, and a label was taped on the back with their names: Gary was the guy with the bangs, Allan was the other boy, and Chrissy was the little girl. The label also said, "She had leukemia—that's why her hair is short."

Jessie was curious enough to keep the date. "Okay, I'll go, but Becky has to come too."

"Jessica, are you sure about that?" Daddy said, "Maybe you and Peggy need a little time to yourselves."

Jessica laughed. "You may as well give it up, Daddy. Becky will just smuggle herself into the trunk of the car or something.

Besides, Peggy has those people there. I want somebody there with me too."

Pastor Lewis and his wife are going to take us. Daddy doesn't want to be in the way and our preacher says we all need some relief.

They pick us up early, so we can drop by the hospital on the way. Mama's weak, but she's coming home day after tomorrow. Jessica kind of dreaded what Mama might say, but Mama just hugs her. Mama sits back and looks at her with eyes sunk in and bruised looking and said, "Well, what have you learned?"

"Lots Mama. More than I cared for." They looked long and deep into each other's eyes.

"We'll talk more. You have a good time meeting your birth mom. Peggy's a wonderful woman and she's my friend." Mama reaches out and takes my hand. She shakes her head. "You're no baby anymore. Jessica, I believe we have a strong young woman here. May I have the honor of a hug?" That hug is one for the records.

Denton really isn't all that far away, just a little north of Dallas. Jessica goes back and forth between trying to doze and fidgeting. I am itching to get this over.

"Here, you two navigate," Preacher Lewis directs. Jessica reads off the directions while I look for street signs. We turn off onto a street lined with live oaks and scan the ranchers for the right street number.

"Ranch homes and no ranch," I fuss.

"This is it," Jessica points. "And there's a horse trailer."

We step out and I peek through the trailer and see warm brown hide.

We go to the door and ring the doorbell. The door swings open before the ring even ends. A tall slender lady with graying dark hair says, "Well, hello there. Come right on in. Rebecca, except for those green Ramey eyes, you are all Beauchamp like your mother. Until I went gray, I had those dark Beauchamp curls. Jessica, we have looked forward to this day for fourteen years."

Jessica grabs my hand. "Hi."

"So good to meet you both. I'm your great-aunt Vera."

Pastor Lewis reaches out his hand. "I'm the Ramey's pastor and this is my wife, Evelyn. We're going to go browse in a bookstore and let you all visit. A couple of hours sound right?" Soon the Lewises are pulling away and we're left with total strangers.

We tried to imagine last night what Jessie's mom might look like now. Funny, I keep thinking of her looking like she did in her school picture, but she's a grown-up now. Vera leads us into her kitchen. Three adults are there, and it's hard to say who's staring at whom the hardest—them or us.

A perky-looking lady with short, frosted hair breaks the silence. She's wearing lots of mascara and shiny lip gloss, and she hops up and gives us both big greasy smooches on our cheeks. "Hi, y'all. I'm Christine Morgan." Jessica has a little glossy O on her left cheek and I expect I have one on my right. It doesn't seem polite to check.

"I thought you were dead," pops out of my mouth. Jessica elbows me hard. "Ouch!"

Christine laughs. "Well, you can live a long time real sick, but as it happens I'm in pretty good shape now. This has to be Becky—we hear you're a real firecracker, taking on football players and everything."

A good-looking guy with Han Solo hair stands up and offers his hand to Jessica and then to me. "Ladies, I'm Gary—an old, old friend." He's tall and we can still see the lanky boy with the too-long wavy bangs in his grown-up looks.

Sitting at the table is a lady with a soft dimpled chin, but a practical measuring gaze. Her head tilts as she looks at Jessica, and I wonder what she sees. I have to smile. Peggy's wearing a white nurse uniform and her dark brown hair is pulled back in a banana clip. She stands and moves toward her daughter. Jessica's hands rise slightly from her sides and fall again, and she glances at me.

"Well, hug her already!" I say.

Peggy chuckles and pulls Jessica into an embrace. Jessica's eyes widen, but she doesn't shy away from her mother's hug. All bets would be off if Peggy had a hypodermic in her hands.

"It's good to meet you Jessica." Peggy murmurs. "Real good." She smiles at me. She likes what she sees. "I hear a real tiger's been looking after her big sister." Peggy grows serious. "How's your mother?"

"She's better." I put in.

Jessica takes over. "She had peritonitis after her tube ruptured, but she's coming home day after tomorrow." Jessica's proud she knows the big medical words. She wants to impress Peggy. Show off.

Peggy gets right to business. "Well, where shall we start? What do you want to know?"

Jessica looks flustered. "I don't know where to begin."

"I can't believe you." I hold up two fingers. "Two things. First of all, were you a good girl? And number two, who gives up a pretty baby like Jessica?"

CHAPTER FORTY-FOUR

"Rebecca Jane Ramey!" Jessica looks mortified. Gary looks appalled, but Peggy's impressed.

Christine is delighted. "Kid, you are a trip." She puts her hand under Jessica's chin and makes my sister look her in the eye. "Your mother was the best."

"The absolute best kind of girl," Gary declares.

"At first, I was kind of ticked off having to share Miz Vera with some strange niece," Chrissy says.

"Well, you were wearing me slap out," Aunt Vera points out.

"It's what I do. Your great-aunt Vera was my private plaything and caretaker while my mother was at work paying my medical bills. And then I had to share."

Peggy shakes her head grinning. "You were such a brat. Getting well enough to be a pain."

"Guilty as charged. My mama was a little concerned about the influence."

"Your influence on me or mine on you?" Peggy asks deadpan.

"Hard to say." Then Chrissy gets serious. "I was young, but I knew a pregnant belly on a teenager was not a cool thing. But you just could tell there was something special about her."

Chrissy bites her lip and grabs Peggy's hand. "Whatever happened, she was special."

"Well, that might be stretching it just a little."

"How did you come into the picture?" I ask Gary. I knew Jessica would never ask.

"I just mowed lawns for Miz Vera. And then your mother yanks me in to play spades."

"Well, Chrissy was making us all crazy and we needed another hand."

"I never said so, but it was love at first sight—pregnant belly or not. And I'll have to second what Chrissy said. She was a very fine lady," Gary says.

"Aw, hush," says Peggy.

"Pretty soon, we were a foursome—us three and my brother."

"Where's he? That Allan guy?" I ask.

A stocky blond man steps into the back door. "Right here. It took a little while to dig up these pictures, but I thought you'd like them. I'm Allan Morgan, ladies."

Jessica says formally, "I'm Jessica and this is my sister, Rebecca."

"I could tell who you were." He smiles.

I don't really see how. Her mother has brown hair. Kinda flat and skinny. A nurse. Calm and practical—not like Jessica. Not at all.

"I had my reservations about my baby sister hanging out with a loser pregnant teenager. I was in my first year of college, a know-it-all journalism major. But Peg was so good with Chrissy. And very serious about her studies. Well, here's some pictures of her senior homecoming."

Her homecoming? The photos were all taken here in this kitchen.

"One day she was blue and weepy, and Chrissy decided it was all because Peggy missed her homecoming. So, Chrissy ordered us to make one." Aunt Vera pours us iced tea. I take a gulp and wince. No sugar. West Texas iced tea.

"I took her for a new haircut and while she was in the salon I picked her up a cute blue dress."

Chrissy jumps in, "I made Gary help me make Rice Krispies Treats—why I thought those were a part of a homecoming dance I'll never know."

"Gary and I danced," Peggy smiled. "We had to stretch out our arms to make room for you."

"And I took photos," added Allan.

Jessica and I looked at the eight black-and-white pictures spread out before us. There was one fun shot with Peggy's eyes scrunched up in laughter at a gooey block of rice cereal.

Chrissy smiles, a little sad. "I started fantasizing that we could keep the baby—keep you."

"And it almost seemed possible. If I had been ten years older, I swear I would have tried." Gary looks at Jessica's mother just like he did in the picture—at someone very special.

"Vera was wise enough to redirect things." Allan has a deep voice.

"I suggested the kids make a time capsule for the baby." Aunt Vera smiles at the memory.

"I sacrificed my *Man from U.N.C.L.E.* lunch box. And we all put something in it." Chrissy took a metal box from her lap and pushes it toward Jessica.

Jessica opens it like a treasure chest and takes out each item: newspaper clippings from Allan and one "homecoming" photo, God's eyes ("We made those together—Popsicle sticks and yarn—*Ojos de Dios*," adds Chrissy), a lock of her mother's hair, and a box top from the cereal.

Gary pulls an old barrette from his pocket. "Here's another contribution. I kept it for a keepsake after your mom got her haircut."

"I wondered where that went," Peggy says.

"My wife was getting jealous. I had to give the hair clip to Jessica or give it to my better half," Gary says.

Allan stands up formally and gestures to them all. "Well, we're going to let you all visit now. It was wonderful to meet you both." Chrissy, Allan, and Gary take turns hugging us and then we are alone with Peggy.

I get ready to leave too and then Jessica clamps onto my hand. "Don't go."

Peggy sits back and looks at us for a moment. "You know my mother was very ill. It was cancer. She died the summer before my junior year. I might not have even dated your father at all if things had been different. Dating a cute guy is a lot more fun than grieving.

My daddy was a good man, but he was so lost without my mother. Neither one of us saw things as clearly as we might have.

The young man who was—is—your birth father was not a bad person. He had something in common with his daddy. A drinking problem. I don't think he understood how bad off he was. One night he had too much to drink, and it was too much to handle. I let him talk me into joining in. I was so naive—I didn't see it coming." Peggy swallowed. "I think that's all I want to say about that now."

"That's okay." Jessica whispers.

"I knew pretty soon that you were on the way. I always knew before the doctor did." Peggy smiles just a tiny bit and then the smile fades. "I told David the night he graduated from high school. He took off and joined the army. I didn't know until he was gone.

My grandmother was so hurt. He was a family friend's child. They went to church together. My grandmother tried to take over—to make up for setting us up. She was determined to have my mother's brother raise you. I wasn't going to have it. We argued a lot—didn't speak for the longest. I wasn't going through that mess. Watch other family raise you and lie like I wasn't your mother. Your grandfather and I couldn't do you justice. No, you needed a fresh start.

Daddy and I agreed. Aunt Vera offered for me to come stay with her right then, but I didn't want to be around people I knew. I left Oklahoma and went to a home in Arlington.

There was quite a mixed bunch of young women there —some pretty messed up. I only made friends with one. Kacie was so wild, so funny. Her maternity clothes were sweatpants and this crazy peasant top. One night we were bored and so homesick. Kacie wanted us to sneak out. We slipped out and we walked to this old building that had been a home for unwed mothers. There was a graveyard in the back. In the moonlight, we looked at markers for babies and mothers who didn't make it. Of all things, the girl pulls out a bottle of Southern Comfort. How do you smuggle a bottle of Southern Comfort past a pack of nosy housemothers? Kacie stood there in that cemetery, swigged whiskey, and offered it to me. 'Guess we're in good company,' she said."

"What did you do?" Jessica squeezes my hand.

"I walked to the nearest 7-Eleven, alone in the dead of night, in a neighborhood I did not know, and I called your Aunt Vera."

"But you left your friend."

"That's right. I tried to take her with me, but she stayed. She needed somebody to tell her no and to take over. I wasn't that somebody. I loved you, and all I knew was that this wasn't what I wanted for you, and it wasn't what I wanted for myself. I got myself where we'd be safe. I got you a good home with family I knew I could trust. I got my education at Texas Women's University, I have nursing, and I have my husband and my two little boys, and you have the Rameys."

"You didn't go to North Texas State?"

"What would I go there for?"

"Music, what else?" Jessica holds her hands palms up on the tabletop and then balls them into fists.

"I don't know anything about music." Peggy's forehead creases, frustrated.

"So where does her music come from?" I ask.

"Her father's family, I guess. They sang." Peggy leans forward and puts her hand on Jessica's. "Look, hon, I don't know what you came here expecting. I did what I could for you. Your parents have done most of what they can do for you. We all love you, but your life is up to you. You have got to make the big choices, choose the right friends. You can't keep expecting folks to bail you out, least of all this one." She points at me. "Who's taking care of her? Her big sister ought to be—some at least."

Jessica gazes at her mother's hand on hers and pulls her hand back quietly. "So much for fairy tales." Jessica sighs.

"Tell me about it." Peggy nods slowly. "Your grandmother sent something for you."

"I thought you all weren't speaking." I remind her.

"We are now—some." Peggy reaches into a shopping bag and unfolds a crocheted afghan in delicate pinks. "This was a baby blanket. I told Nana she had better add some to this. You're a good-sized girl now." Peggy sighs and laughs. "You are your nana all over. Big bosoms, drama, everything but the music. I'll just bet you are a handful."

"You got that right, Peggy." I cross my arms and nod my head.

Jessica frowns. "Thanks a lot, Becky."

Peggy reaches in the bag and shakes out a throw with granny squares in about every possible shade of blue. "My nana is always making afghans. We thought this one was right for a true-blue sister." She tosses it to me. "Here you go, Rebecca."

Jessica scowls. "How did this trip get to be about Becky?"

"You'll get over it. Somehow I think it's probably a good switch for you." Peggy chuckles.

A shadow fills the doorway. About the best-looking cowboy, I ever saw stands there. He is long and lean, and his muscular arms are braced against the doorjamb. He's scanning the room and those steely blue eyes are promising trouble for anyone who deserves it.

"Girls, this is my husband, Doug."

Doug's eyes meet Peggy's and a gradual smile curves her lips. He smiles back slow and lazy. I sit there holding my breath watching. Any woman alive would give anything to have a guy smile at her like that.

Peggy breaks the spell. "I think this young lady would love to see what's outside."

Doug leads me to the horse trailer. "You must be Becky. I understand your Uncle Clayton works with horses."

"Uncle Clayton? Not so much lately."

"Well this is Lady May."

I look up at the liquid eyes of the most beautiful quarter horse I have ever seen. I can hardly speak.

"What do you think?"

"She's wonderful."

"I'm on my way to deliver her."

"Lucky owners."

"Yep. I hear you barrel race."

"Used to."

"Ought to get back into it."

"Yes, sir. Someday I'll have my own."

"Quarter horse?"

"Naw. Not like this one. She's a Cadillac. I need a Pinto." We both chuckle. "There's this lady in California. She got this little mixed breed cheap and she's won all kinds of medals with him. She named him Geronimo. I'm going to find one too and name him Endurance. Because see, I don't think it's right to name a horse after a person."

"You've thought a lot about this." Cowboy's almost laughing at me.

"Yes, sir. I'm going to see if I can't keep him at my Uncle Clayton's and let my little cousins ride him—we'll trade out for chores."

Doug nods his head impressed. "Sounds like a plan."

"I'm staying in shape. I run and all. I just have to find a way to stay in practice riding. I'll figure out something."

"I believe you will."

Jessica butts in. "Well, mister... Doug, if you hear anything about somebody needing a girl to ride a horse—let us know. Becky's good and she oughta have her chance."

CHAPTER FORTY-FIVE

I found it before Jessica. Ugly, red, nasty words about my sister. A police car has pulled up to our house because Mr. Wright caught Cooper really and truly red-handed. The spray can paint matches the hateful words on our garage door. Jessica ran off in tears the moment she saw it.

My dad is repainting the door. Somehow Kyle and Frank got word, and they are helping my father. I think they are competing for my sister. My dad makes it clear that Ramey girls do not date until they are sixteen, but they are welcome to come to our church.

I go to 7-Eleven to buy treats for them, and I hear someone say, "Hey, kid."

It's Billy standing by the sunglasses. "Tell Audrey that Cooper, he won't try anything again. I'll see to it. For sure." He doesn't look at me as he says this. "And tell Audrey I'm sorry."

"What about my sister?" I demand.

He glances at me and then away. "I'm sorry—about everything."

I tell Audrey after I deliver the Cokes and chips. She sighs and shakes her head. "Well, I guess that's something."

When I come home, I see that Jessica is painting too. That made me proud.

* * *

    I got my old red journal back and another green notebook with it labeled "Ramey Family Journal." Inside was this note in my dad's handwriting. *"Rebecca, your mother and I read this, and we learned a lot we needed to know. For one thing, you express yourself well. We moved for you girls and because we needed to make our own home away from family problems I could no longer help. In the busyness of the new job, I forgot my main reason for moving—you girls. I took too much for granted. We have let you down and let you especially fend for yourself. I want to ask your forgiveness. Working with horses is important to you, and you are good with them. We get that. We are going to have to look over some numbers together, because we are not a rich family. We don't have much money, but we have family. Missy will help and somehow, we are going to make this work. You are our daughter and we love you. We do care about what matters to you."*
    I write a note by this, *"I'll carry my weight and I'll work hard."*
    Mama added, *"Let's you and I go looking for patterns for Western shirts. Maybe just one skirt?"*
    Jessie added, *"I want in on that. If my sister is going to ride, she is going to look good. By the way, she needs new boots. Her old boots stink and are worn out and her feet look awful. A pedicure alone cannot cure it."*
    Mama adds, *"We'll plan over a cup of hot tea."* I add, *"Coffee for me."* Mama adds, *"Decaf."* And I add, *"Ha ha. Deal.*

CHAPTER FORTY-SIX

"Girls, if we're going to make the first feature, we've gotta go," Daddy calls out. School's out and he wants to celebrate at the drive-in movie.

"Have you fed the bunnies?" Mama says.

"Yes, ma'am. Their hutches are clean too."

"You better name those bunnies before the county fair," says Jessica.

"I'm getting to it. I want them to have the right ones," I say. That's one of the most fun things in 4-H: coming up with cool names for your livestock.

"Make sure the puppy has water," Dad calls.

I check on our sleeping puppy and Dorada is fine.

"It's all done. Let's go," I say.

The phone rings, Daddy sighs, but Mama answers. "Well, hello there. What a nice surprise." Mama covers the phone and mouths, "Peggy's on the phone." She holds up her hand for quiet. "Yes, we'll be home. Jessica? Oh, she's okay."

I dash into the living room and pick up the other phone. "No, she isn't, Peggy. She's crazy. Jessica says she won't sing anymore—because of you know who."

"Is that right?" Peggy says.

"Rebecca Jane, get off the phone. Peggy's going to think we are all crazy. Sorry, Peggy." Mama pauses.

I wait, hoping she thinks I'm gone.

"Becky, get off now."

I sigh and hang up. I slip back into the kitchen and sit by Jessica while she watches Mama talk.

"Okay, sure, that will be fine. We'll be here. Here's Jessica."

"Yes, I'm being good. No. Becky's mean."

"I am not."

Jessica grins. "No, I'm kidding. She is nosy, though. You got that right."

"What?" I demand.

Jessica eyebrows rise. "Okay. Okay. I'll tell her. Bye." Jessica hangs up the phone. We've got to clean. Peggy's coming and she's bringing someone with her." Jessica slaps my arm a little. "She says she's got a surprise for you."

We beg off on the movie for tonight and promise Daddy we'll go tomorrow. "May as well wait," Daddy grouses. "All three of you will just fret over the mess at home and I won't have a moment's peace."

The vacuum cleaner roars late into the night in Jessica's room. Mama didn't have to say one thing. Jessica even asks Mama for a spare shoebox for hair doodads. Mama says, "Well, at least she'll use it for some type of organization."

The doorbell rings and we can see two pickups parked in front of our home. Peggy steps out of her truck and greets a muscular guy with long blond hair. Mama calls it ego hair—she says grown men who wear their hair long are stuck on themselves. Peggy and the blond guy walk up to our door and we're all there before they can knock. Mama and Peggy hug for the longest and I can hear, "You did great, Liz. Jessica is beautiful—both your girls are just beautiful."

Soon we're sitting at the kitchen table and Mama's bringing out the best mugs.

Peggy says thanks to Mama as she pours coffee into her harvest gold mug and then turns to say, "Jessica, I want you to meet your Uncle Travis."

Jessica extends her hand for a handshake and when Travis grips her hand, I notice the thick blond hair on his hand and arm.

I look from his hair to Jessica's long hair. The same color—she gets her hair color from her daddy's side.

"Rebecca, why don't we let these folks visit?" Mama says.

"You don't have to go, ma'am." He points at Jess and me and says, "I already understand these two are a package deal."

"Well, I'm going to go look for some picture albums, so you can look at them if you like. I'll be back."

Travis looks at his coffee mug and clears his throat. "Welp, better get this started. All we Duncans are from Duncan, Oklahoma. Absolutely no relation to the Scottish trader that it's named for." Travis sighs and reaches into the pocket on his blue work shirt and pulls out a small jewelry box and pushes it across the table to Jessica. "My wife thought you ought to have this."

Jessica opens the tiny white box and pulls out a silver pin —a flower with a stickery stem and leaves.
Travis sits back like he doesn't want to have anything to do with the pin. "It's a Scottish thistle—something about invading Vikings stepping on one and hollering so the Scots know they're being attacked. Lee Ann could tell you all about it. More than you want to know. My wife is all into the Scottish heritage thing." Travis smiles a lopsided grin and shakes his head. "We've got plaid pillows and throws in the den." Travis leans forward, "She even got the Duncan coat of arms framed and put that up. I can tell you right now that none of our bunch ever had any coat of arms. We were probably happy to have coats." Jessica's uncle wrinkles up his forehead like he's in pain. "Now this was the last straw. Lee Ann got me a dad-gum kilt for Father's Day last year!" He tries to act like he thinks it's awful, but he smiles a little like he'll put up with it somehow. Travis sweeps the air with his hand like he wants to brush it all away. "I'm just a good old boy from Oklahoma."

"Maybe they ought to make you grass burr pins instead of thistles," I suggest.

"You have a point there, Becky." Travis nods his head agreeing. "A 'goat head' pin would be more fitting."

Jessica laughs, then she and Travis look at each other and their faces grow thoughtful. Do they know how much they look alike? The same lift of the eyebrows, and set of the jaw—Jessica's a soft, feminine version of this man. "Thank you for coming and for my gift, but I want to know about my dad."

Peggy and Travis look at each other. "Jessica, are you sure? Some things can be harder to hear than you might think."

"Mister, we've heard some pretty tough stuff. Whatever it is, I don't think it could get much worse." I look him in straight in the eye.

"Becky's right. We have, and I want to know."

Travis raises his eyebrows and shrugs. "Here goes. Jessica, I want you to know that your grandmother is a fine person. Your grandfather could be a good man in his way, but he was a drinker. We all did sing together. He'd sing with his family on Sunday and drink the rest of the week. I don't do church now. My brother went to church with my mother, and he thought that would keep him straight, but it didn't. He's the kind of person that's a goner the first time he drinks. After things…took place with your mother, he took off and joined the army.

Peggy looks concerned. "Travis, do you think she really…"

"She's asking to know." Travis looks at Jessica. "What your mother is a little reluctant to bring up, is that your father wanted to marry her after you were born. He felt bad about what he'd done, and he thought he'd get himself straight and make things right. He wanted to get you back from the Rameys."

Jessica's face is a study. She smiles a little, then the smile fades and her eyes widen, and her forehead creases. She opens and closes her lips for a moment, struggling. "So, what happened? Why didn't they…you marry?"

"He thought he was better. I wanted to believe he was. His mother knew he wasn't and she was ready to testify to that. You had been a Ramey for months. She insisted they think of you first," Travis says.

"In any case, I told him no straight off. I did not want to

marry him. That was no way to fix things," Peggy says. "In my heart, I knew it was best for you to stay with your parents."

"What did he do?" Jessica says.

"He did what his father would do. He left and went back to drinking," Travis says. "And he never forgave our mother."

"Well, I asked to know." Jessica swallows. Peggy grabs one hand and I take Jessica's other.

I look in Jessica's red eyes. "Tough like Ma-maw."

Jessica nods. "Tough like Ma-maw."

Travis puts his hands behind his head and leans back, looking up. He leans forward and sighs. "Jessica, my brother's ways are not my ways, but I have to give him his due. After a long, dark time, he got help. He's sober now, and he's done his best to make amends with everyone he's hurt—your mom—everyone but his mother."

"What about me?" Jessica says.

"He's doing what he sees as best . . . staying away and letting you have your life." Travis snorts and shakes his head. "Anyway, his wife won't let him do anything else. She figures she got him cheap, and she doesn't want him having anything to do with any child but hers—too insecure. Makes it easy for him because, well, he figures he doesn't deserve you anyway."

My sister sits a moment looking at her fingernails. "I have more siblings?" Jessica asks.

"Two half-sisters. They whine a lot. They look a lot like their daddy, so they're not as cute as we are."

A tiny smile dawns on her face.

"Say, Becky," Travis says. "You all have a cassette player?"

I run to my room and dash back, so I don't miss much.

Travis pops my cassette and reads the label. "Willie Nelson, huh?"

"Yes, sir. That's my tape."

"Good choice."

Jessica squints and wrinkles her nose at me.

"I'm an electrician by trade, but the boys and I play weekends. I sing and do bass. We've been on the same stage as Augie

Myers and Shake Russell." He puts in a tape and looks at Jess. "This isn't me. It's your grandmother. I thought you'd like to hear this."

The recording is scratchy and sounds far away, but the soprano voice is sweet and pure. Jessica gazes at the tablecloth and croons along in alto. "And He tells me I am His own…" She looks up, hushes, and her face flushes pink.

The song ends, and Travis pops out the tape and slides it across the table. "This is yours too."

Jessica takes it and looks at the label. "Maybe your mom and I could sing together sometime."

Travis looks down nodding, and when he looks up his eyes look moist. "That'd be real nice. She'd like that," he murmurs.

Then bold as Tigre, Jessica says, "Maybe you can come hear me sing on some Sunday."

Travis squints and one corner of his mouth turns up. "Maybe so."

Peggy stands up and pulls a slip of paper from her jeans pocket. "By the way, Miss Rebecca. I have something for you, and you better do something about

❈ ❈ ❈

I let Jessica read my journal now. I surprise myself. Sometimes I write things that I did not know I think or feel. And Jessica and I talk about it. Life is not what you expect. I did not know I would make wonderful friends here near Dallas. Peggy is not what we thought she would be, and Jessica's dad is not what she thought he would be. She wonders about her other sisters, but she knows it may be awhile before they meet. She loves her little brothers. Once Peggy figured out the best way to tell them about their sister, it all worked out. Jessica bought them each Hot Wheels cars and they fell in love. Her Uncle Travis and Aunt Lee Ann are crazy about her, and now Lee Ann wants to measure my sister for a kilt. Ha Ha.

CHAPTER FORTY-SEVEN

I feel like life is not so much easier, as it's getting bigger.

I started helping to train a three-year-old horse. She's not nearly ready for barrels. She boogers at them, shies away, afraid. It'll take a while to train her.

We're making a little progress. The little chestnut mare and I stood together by a barrel and I fed her sugar, and she stayed calm the whole time. We'll be doing loops around the barrel before long. If you can ever experience something good in a scary, new place, then it's not so bad. Anyway, I'm Rebecca Ramey. I'm used to high-strung creatures. I have a sister after all.

The stable owners like me, and I ride the trails every day on a bay that just retired from barrel racing. The Powers, folks back home, and Peggy have been helping me keep an eye out for a horse of my own. Pastor Lewis and Reverend Journey even prayed for success, and we found her, a sweet mare named Feisty owned by a couple needing to sell out and retire. Daddy and I will swap out repairs and cleaning for Feisty Endurance's place at the stable. Things will work out some way. Then I'll worship at church and on a horse! First, Endurance and I have some work ahead of us. That's a good part of life getting bigger.

There are some sad parts too. One sad part caused my sister to do a thing of beauty.

A Thing of Beauty

Last spring, Audrey had her baby and it was too soon. They say little girls are stronger, that they do better premature, but baby Theresa didn't. Audrey and Billy's baby died. Audrey worked so hard and loved that little girl so much. I don't understand how a baby that's loved that much could die.

Billy came to the funeral home, but only with Mr. Wright there. Audrey had been through enough. Mr. Wright said Billy wept like a seven-year-old boy who had lost his mother. "She looks like my little sister," he sobbed. People don't know what they've thrown away until it's too late.

Preacher Lewis did a real fine service for the baby. And this is where Jessica's thing of beauty comes in. She said, "That baby ought to have someone sing for her," so my sister did.

Jessica stood calm, her eyes looking far away, in a place where she could sing for a lost baby and not break down and weep. "I need Thee every hour..."

Dad has found a job for Audrey working at a lawyer's office. She fetches coffee and files documents at this office that sometimes helps ladies who have problems for free. The lawyers already like her and are rooting for her to think about studying law somehow. She and my mama still sit and cry together sometimes, and that is a sad thing of beauty. I think that's what folks mean by "bittersweet."

Sometimes there are some fun parts, like when I was in my first wedding. I wore a lacy green prairie dress with my shiny Western boots. I watched the guest book until the music began. Rusty ushered me to my seat with Freckles and Pee Wee and Daniesha on Miss Powers's side and then he joined the boys on Mr. Parks's side of the church. Mr. Parks wore his high heel Western boots and Miss Powers wore white satin flats, so they almost stood eye to eye when Mr. Parks read an E.E. Cummings poem to her. It was peculiar in his West Texas drawl, but sweet.

Rusty looked over at me and grinned. "I told you so," he whispered. He brought me punch with lime sherbet at the reception.

Dad says he hopes evil Mrs. Goforth at the board office doesn't give Mrs. Powers-Parks any trouble at school next year.

Goforth is already raising a stink over novels.

This weekend we are in East Texas, and we are going to a homecoming. Uncle Elliot thinks it's kind of weird, because we have it at a graveyard, but he's not from around here. Daddy says we celebrate the whole family from beginning to end. We clean up the graves, tell stories, and remember.

Before we leave Ma-maw's house, the phone rings. I answer it and Reverend H.J. says in his unmistakable baritone, "Rebecca, may I speak to your father?" I hand the phone over to my dad, but I linger nearby so I can catch what's up.

"Cliff, I thank you for the invitation to your picnic, but I'm going to have to miss it this time. We're still having some issues with Burgess, and right now, we've got to focus on him." There's this big sigh and a pause. "It seems my son is set on becoming a Muslim. It could be a passing thing. It could be the way it is. I'm just trying to ride this out, but some of the elders at the church are less understanding. Burgess has been insisting on changing his name to a Muslim name, and that will not go over at all with the congregation, if you know what I mean."

Dad says, "I'm sorry, Harold. I don't know what to say."

"Burgess's mother is trying to direct him toward an African name. He knows that 'Burgess' is a beloved family name from her people, and he does love his mother. He's looking at a couple of choices. 'Zuberi,' powerful. 'Olufemi,' adored by God. We're trying to ignore the whole process and let him choose. He seems to be leaning toward 'Jabari,' or courageous. He overheard one of the elders scoff at the very idea of an African name. That alone right there might push Burgess into courageous." H.J. chuckled, but it sounded like a sad chuckle to me. "In any case, we may have to head west ourselves to a congregation that's a little more willing to take things in stride."

"I understand, Harold. Maybe another time. I just want you to know what your friendship has meant…"

"I know. Give my greetings to the family. That reminds me. Did you know your father stayed sober the entire month of March? Burgess said he showed up to school every day. I think

A Thing of Beauty

you have your brother-in-law to thank for that. They meet every morning, bright and early, at the café for coffee."

"Well. How about that. Good to know."

We drive on over to the cemetery and Dad goes and joins Uncle Elliot and Uncle Richie as they weed and tidy the plots. While they work, Uncle Elliot and Uncle Richie talk about President Carter again.

"What did you think about that last speech?" asks Elliot. "Somebody calls it his 'malaise' speech."

"Well, if malaise means you're out of work, out of gas, and out of luck, I guess I have a malaise." Uncle Richie says. He pauses from weeding and stands up. "Actually, I am going back to college and finishing my degree. I will have to take some additional coursework because I want to be a physician's assistant. I have that GI Bill. I may as well use it. I plan to work with veterans. Of course, this is going to mean a move for the whole family. I'll stay in touch with your daddy, Clifford." Turns out, Uncle Richie and Granddaddy talk about their long-lost friends—promising young people all, lost to war and disaster. Richie swears he will muster our folks to next year's New London reunion.

People can dazzle you. How they can suffer loss in a horrible, blinding second, but find the heart to struggle on, to heal and live and bless some way.

All the men laugh about the video of our president fending off a wild swamp rabbit, and now I know what I will name my 4-H bunnies: Swamp Rabbit, Rosalynn, and Chief.

"Don't name a rabbit 'Carter.' We put our presidents through enough without naming rabbits after them," says Daddy. "Even Republicans have to know that beast was rabid."

It's Sunday, so we make a stab at a worship service. They turn off the huge fan in the pavilion, so we can hear Jessica's solo, but then they turn it up full blast so the poor little preacher hollers to be heard. Daddy and Uncle Elliot sit forward to hear him over the wind and the vibration. The young preacher with the red mustache throws in something about adoption before his voice completely gives out.

After worship, Jessica and I remember our family's struggles and pay our special respects to graves inscribed "March 18, 1937." We have brought flowers for a grave marked "Walter 'Buddy' Ramey" in particular. Our grandparents and Uncle Shrimp and Aunt Lou all give us girls big hugs, and then our father hugs all of them, especially Granddaddy. My dad and grandfather give each other a big old guy hug, pounding each other on the back.

Then we do what all Baptist families do. We eat. Mama's green Jell-O salad is in the cooler with our grandmother's potato salad. Ma-maw and Aunt Janet will fuss over when to set them out—but maybe not quite so much. Aunt Janet already has a new position teaching home economics near Uncle Richie's university, and she's going to work part-time with a caterer, learning the ropes. For all they fight, our Ma-maw is going to miss her in the worst way.

We eat with our cousins and swear we will write each other right away. "We're real excited for you all, but it's going to be a change," says Jessica, "Let us know how it goes."

"It will be different at first, but if I can make new friends, you can," I tell Tabby.

"You got that right," Tabby says.

"Smile when you say that," I say.

"Jessica, we heard you met your family," says Brittany.

"Yeah, they invited me to a family reunion, but they warned me it could be strange. I told them that's okay, we Rameys are used to that," Jessica said. That made our cousins smile.

Jessica says, "I'm not a thing like my birth mother."

I say, "You have her dimpled chin."

Jessie puts her hand in wonder on her dimple and says, "Why yes, I suppose I do."

When it starts getting dusky, I sit between my mother and father and hold their hands under the picnic pavilion. "Daddy, what was that preacher saying about adoption?"

"Well, it's a theological term." He stops and looks at my

hand. "It means we are all orphans and strangers on this earth. And we all need grace."

ACKNOWLEDGMENTS

I first wish to give my appreciation to my two Seton Hill University mentors, Karen Williams and David Shifren and to my critique partners Krista Russell, Tricia Tighe, Tracy Wilson-Burns, Ginny Walker, Kathleen Davidson, Brooke Linn and the many, many generous writers who have critiqued, advised, and supported my work in the Seton Hill Popular Fiction Writing program.

My deep thanks to the Myers family and to the New London School Disaster Museum for generously providing vital background information about the New London Explosion of 1937.

I must also give enormous credit to Martha Josey for educating me about the brilliant sport of barrel racing. She shared time and her literature with a woman who had only greatly admired horses from a distance.

Other horsewomen shared their time, their resources, their insights. Above all, Peggy Butts, my English Department head, native Texan, rancher's daughter, and rancher's wife advised me and combed through my book and verified each horsey detail. Former students, Alixandra Lake and Allex Benedict shared time, books, information and encouragement. Elizabeth Gotterdam likewise counseled me on horse care and safety.

Many thanks to Tim Butler who shared his broad knowledge of football and sportscasting as I created my thoroughly Texan novel replete with Texan football.

Much gratitude must go to Kelly Johnson who had a vision for my work.

Most of all, my most profound thanks must go to my loving husband who has not flagged in support and encouragement of my writing and my spirit.

Made in the USA
Middletown, DE
10 June 2019